THE WOMAN

Nicole Berthoud

She was the wife of a marquis condemned to die, bound by secret vows to the imprisoned Queen, Marie Antoinette, engaged in an intrigue that might lead her to the guillotine—and in love with a man who could never be hers. . . .

THE MAN

Jean Audubon

He was married to a woman he didn't love, marked for death by men he didn't know, involved in a desperate mission as dangerous as it was impossible—and damned by his passion for a fiery beauty he could never call his own. . . .

THE STORY

A sweeping historical adventure of deceit and daring that spans continents and human emotions with an intensity rarely equaled in fiction!

A FLAME ON THE WIND

Irving A. Greenfield

A DELL BOOK

Published by
Dell Publishing Co., Inc.
1 Dag Hammarskjold Plaza
New York, New York 10017

Dell ® TM 681510, Dell Publishing Co., Inc.
Printed in the United States of America
First printing—November 1975

1

Captain Jean Audubon walked slowly toward the Flying Gull, the only inn on the road between the village of Le Gerbetière, where his wife's farm was, and the larger town of Coureron, just outside of Nantes.

Joue, a black with blue eyes, accompanied Audubon. Joue's mother had been a Mandingo princess. Before the Revolution, Audubon had owned Joue, and though the government had recently abolished slavery, he was still, if not Joue's master, then certainly his captain.

Audubon was almost as big as Joue. Though his face was wind-whipped to the color of good leather, Audubon was only forty. He was a broad-shouldered man. His eyes were gray, though sometimes, when he was particularly happy or with a woman whose company he enjoyed, they would take on a greenish tint.

He was hatless, and his black hair was tied into a queue. His white, long-sleeved shirt was worn open at the neck, and the bottoms of his trousers were tucked into the tops of his sea boots. A sheathed knife, within easy reach of his right hand, hung from his belt.

The inn, a one-story building of fieldstone with a high, slanted slate roof, had two windows. One looked out on the road and was always closed, even on a blistering August day such as the one that was coming to an end. The other window was in the rear and looked out on the sea. It was kept open until the late fall when the storms began to sweep inland off the raging ocean. The inn was surrounded by the sound of the pounding surf.

Audubon entered the inn, pausing to let his eyes become adjusted to the dim interior. The room was very large. Several roughly made, dark-wood tables and chairs were placed about. A large stone hearth was built into one wall. It was empty and looked like a large open mouth. The bar where André, the proprietor, stood was opposite the hearth.

After a few moments Audubon turned and started toward his favorite table near the open window overlooking the sea. But a man already occupied it.

The man was young, tall, and lean. His blond hair practically touched his shoulders. And though it was August and the late afternoon was still very hot, the man wore a black cloak. A bottle of wine and two glasses sat in front of him on the table, but neither glass held any wine. He faced the open window, and from a distance it seemed as though he were dozing.

Annoyed that someone had usurped his table, Audubon looked questioningly toward André, a cadaverous man with dull black eyes and a heavy black beard.

"He's been here for a while," the innkeeper said. "He told me he was waiting for someone."

In normal times strangers at the inn were a rarity. Since the Revolution, however, the times were anything but normal, especially in their district of Vendée, where government troops and those still loyal to the crown often clashed.

Audubon turned toward the man again. His features were strikingly classic. He was almost beautiful.

Quite suddenly he moved and faced Audubon, who, without hesitation, approached him, saying, "Would it be too much, monsieur, to ask you to move?" And gesturing back to Joue, he added, "We come here every evening to—"

"That is why I am here, Captain Audubon," the stranger told him with a smile.

Audubon took a step back and motioned to Joue. Instantly Joue was at his side.

"There was no need for that," the stranger said, no longer smiling.

"You have an advantage, monsieur," Audubon told him, "that tends to put me on my guard. . . . I do not enjoy being known by someone whom I do not know, and I do not know you, monsieur."

The man's green eyes went questioningly to Joue.

"If you know something about me," Audubon said, "and I must assume you do, you also know that Joue is my first officer."

"I do indeed know that, Captain," the stranger said with a nod. "But what I have to say to you will concern—"

"You have nothing to say to me," Audubon interrupted, "unless you first tell me who you are and then say whatever it is you want to in Joue's presence."

The man's brow furrowed, and his color heightened with suppressed anger. After a moment's hesitation he nodded, and gesturing with his right hand, invited Audubon and Joue to join him at the table.

"Take a chair from another table," Audubon told Joue. He remained standing until Joue had returned to the table.

"My name," the stranger said in a whisper, "is Charette."

"General Charette?" Audubon asked, unable to keep the tone of surprise out of his voice. Charette was the leader of all Royalist forces in Vendée. He was sought by the Revolutionary government, and there was a price of a hundred thousand livres on his head. Now Audubon understood the reason for the cloak. Charette no longer had a left hand. A musket ball had carried away everything of his arm below the elbow, and being vain about his person he did all that he could to mask the loss, even to those who knew him intimately.

"Now that I have disposed of all your conditions," Charette said with a nod, "I would like a glass of wine before continuing." He poured wine into the two glasses, and then, remembering there were three at the table, he called to the innkeeper for another glass. Filling it, he pushed it toward Joue and picked up his own glass. "Long live the Queen!" he whispered.

When their glasses were empty Charette leaned low over the table and said, "I have a proposition to put to you, Captain."

Audubon nodded.

"Suppose," Charette told him, "there was a way for you to earn ten thousand English pounds—"

"General," Audubon said, "I do not like it when the wind teases my sails or blows from every point of the compass. I like a steady wind. Tell me straight out what you think I can do for you."

Charette's brow furrowed again as he said, "Go to Paris. There you will be contacted and given further instructions."

Audubon slapped the table so hard that the glasses jumped. He began to laugh. "For that," he told Charette, "I would gladly go to Paris anytime. I would even make such a trip for five thousand English pounds. But surely you do not expect me to believe that anyone would be willing to pay so much for so little."

"You will be told what you must do," the General said, "by your contact."

"And who will be my contact?"

"You will know that when you reach Paris."

"And you came here," Audubon asked, "to offer me this proposition?"

"I was told you would be interested in anything for a price."

Audubon nodded, reached for the bottle, and filling the three glasses again, he asked, "And what else were you told about me?"

"That once you committed yourself to an enterprise, you could be counted upon to see it through."

"At least part of my reputation has some worth," Audubon responded with a smile.

"And the rest of it can be worth an additional ten thousand English pounds when you complete your assignment."

"Tell me, General, what do you want me to do for so much money?"

Charette shook his head. "You will have to say 'yes' or 'no,' Captain, on what little I have told you."

Audubon lifted his glass to drink. There was laughter in Charette's eyes that made Audubon very much aware of the man's youth. He was somewhat like a boy masquerading as a man. But he had the magical ability to command men, and that was no small gift.

"What will it be?" the General asked.

Audubon set his glass down and said, "Nothing, until you tell me more."

"Then I have been wasting my time?"

With a shrug Audubon said, "It was you who came to see me, General. I did not seek you out."

"If you go to Paris," Charette explained, "You will take lodgings at the Inn of the Three Lilies in the rue Hyacinthe and immediately go to the Ministry of Marine to apply for a commission."

"For what ship?" Audubon asked with a nod.

"The *Arguille*. She is a brig in the port of Le Havre. Your reputation is also known at the Ministry of Marine."

"But my application for a commission is not my purpose for being in Paris, is it?"

"You will be contacted at your lodgings and given further instructions," Charette said, ignoring the Captain's question.

Audubon stood up and went to the window. The sun was low over the sea, and the waves were yellowed by its light. Except for some puffs of white clouds to the northwest, the sky was cloudless and very blue.

He took several deep breaths, enjoying the sharp scent of the sea air. For six months he had remained on his wife's farm doing nothing much more than walking to the inn late every afternoon, and on the way home pausing briefly at the spot where he had burned the body of his son John, who had died of fever on the voyage home from Saint Domingue. For six months he had had no desire to become an active participant in anything. He did not really care whether the Revolutionary government remained in control of the country or whether France reverted to a monarchy. His life, as he had begun to view it after John's death, was, for all its exploits, directionless—more like a ship without a helmsman than one whose course was guided by a sure and steady hand.

His marriage to Anne Moynet, some twenty years before, had been a disaster. He had never loved her. She had never given him any pleasure. For that he had sought out other women, though not recently. He could hardly deny that for the past few months he had been more dead than alive. And now Charette was giving him the chance once more to run free before the wind. With that kind of money he could buy his own ship and return to the West Indies. He could surely be his own master. . . .

Audubon glanced at Charette.

The General caught his look and said, "I am offering you a fortune. You will be a very wealthy man."

"Well, Joue?" Audubon asked.

Before Joue could answer, Charette said, "He cannot be involved."

"General," Audubon responded, "he is already involved. He is, or rather was, my first officer. I do nothing without him."

"You have too many conditions," Charette said, making no attempt to hide his anger.

Audubon shrugged.

"All right," Charette agreed. "He goes with you."

Audubon repeated his question to Joue.

"It'll be better than stayin' here," Joue said. "Here there is nothin', Captain. Maybe in Paris you'll find somethin' to make you smile."

"When do we have to be in Paris?" Audubon asked, coming back to the table and sitting down.

"By the middle of September," Charette answered.

"And the necessary papers?"

"They will be delivered to you by one of my men. You will find him here as you found me, at this table. He will know you when you ask him to go to another table."

"When and how will I be paid?" Audubon asked.

"Half when you complete the first part of your mission and the other half when you finish the mission."

"And who is to be in charge of whatever it is I am supposed to do?"

"You are, Captain," Charette told him. "You are in complete command. Your authority is exceeded only by my own."

"Will I be in contact with you?"

"Through those who will be working for you," the General said, and lifting the bottle, emptied it into the three glasses. "Let us drink, then," he toasted, "to a successful enterprise."

They touched glasses and drank. Then Charette stood up. "I do not make it a practice to stay too long in one place," he laughed. "My men are waiting for me."

Audubon stood up, and they shook hands.

Charette looked at Joue, nodded, and with a half dozen long strides, crossed the room. A moment later he was gone.

Even as Audubon sat down again there was suddenly a clatter of horses' hooves on the hard, dry road outside, and then nothing but the roar of the sea. "You can be sure," he said to Joue, "that whatever is worth ten thousand pounds to someone is probably worth much, much more."

"What do you think it is?" Joue asked.

Audubon shrugged and answered, "Perhaps jewels or gold. I imagine there must be a large cache somewhere in Paris."

Joue lifted his glass, drank off all the wine that remained, and then nodded.

2

A week after Audubon had met General Charette he found another man seated at the table near the open window. This one was also young, possibly younger than Charette. He had bright brown eyes and a black moustache that was too large for his face. Audubon went directly up to him and asked if he would move to another table.

"I have something for you, Captain Audubon," the man whispered as he removed a wallet from inside his jacket. "Everything you and your companion will need to move through our lines and those of the enemy is in that packet. The General suggests you leave at once. Make your way to Le Havre and from there to Paris."

Audubon slipped the wallet into his belt.

"The table is yours," the man announced loudly. He stood up, and as he passed Audubon he whispered, "Long live the Queen!" Then he hurried out of the inn.

Audubon motioned to Joue, and when they were seated he said, "The papers have come."

"When will we leave?"

"Very soon. The General suggests we go to Le Havre and then to Paris."

"That'll give us a chance to look at the *Arguille,*" Joue commented.

Audubon nodded and called to André for a bottle of wine.

When they left the inn the long shadows of evening were beginning to drop over the land. But this time Audubon did not stop to look out over the sea. Instead he told Joue, "I cannot grieve anymore. I must give it up and get on with the things I must do."

"I was wonderin' when you'd come to that," Joue commented.

"It has been a long haul, has it not?"

"Yes, Captain, indeed a very long one."

"Once we are finished with this business in Paris," Audubon said, draping his arm around Joue's shoulder, "we will go back to the islands."

Joue responded with a pleased laugh.

When they reached the farmhouse the windows of the dining room were already ablaze with yellow lamplight.

Madame Audubon was already at the table. She was a tall, angular woman with graying hair and bright black eyes that glared fiercely at Audubon and Joue as they entered the room. She looked disdainfully at her husband and began to say, "The very least you could do——"

"We will be leaving tonight," Audubon said, cutting her short as he took his place at the head of the table.

She nodded and said nothing.

"I do not know how long I will be away," Audubon told her, helping himself to a slice of ham and then passing the platter to her.

"Does it matter?" she asked, her voice choked.

Audubon looked across the table at her. He did not want to argue.

"You come and go as you please," Anne told him. "I don't even have a say about who sits at my table," she said, turning to stare bitterly at Joue.

"Silence!" Audubon roared.

"No," she shrieked. "No. There are things that I must say. I was willing to let you bring that little bastard of yours into my house so that you could have a legal heir. I could understand that. But God saw fit to take him from you——"

"Silence!" Audubon shouted, thumping his fist down on the table. "I do not want to hear about your damn God or anything else."

Suddenly Joue stood up.

Audubon looked at him, understood, and nodded.

Joue hurried out of the room.

Trembling with anger, Audubon reached for the pitcher

of wine and filled his glass. He drank until the glass was empty. Then he had another and a third.

"You vex me," he said in a low, angry voice. "You vex me beyond endurance. . . ." Then with a sweeping gesture he added, "This farm vexes me. We are married twenty years—"

"Twenty-one," she corrected.

He glared at her and said, "An eternity, madame, an eternity. This farm after all that time is still known as Moynet's place . . . Moynet's place. . . . But my name is Audubon, Jean Audubon . . . Captain Jean Audubon. Moynet was your dead husband's name."

"I don't think you've been here more than two years in twenty-one," she told him. "The people around here don't even know you."

"And that, madame," he responded icily, "was more time than I should have spent here. And as for the people—"

"Back to sea?" she asked.

He did not answer.

Anne lifted her hands to her face and began to sob.

Audubon turned away. He was defenseless against her weeping. "I will come back," he told her roughly. "I have always come back."

She lowered her hands.

He nodded to indicate that he meant what he had just said.

"When?" she asked.

"I do not know," Audubon answered. He did not understand why she wanted him to come back. They shared nothing except their anger. He had left her bed more than ten years ago.

"I didn't mean to argue," she told him.

Audubon waved her apology aside, and standing, said, "I must go."

3

After a two-day stay in the port of Le Havre, where they took time to look over the brig *Arguille,* Audubon and Joue arrived in Paris by coach on the night of September 10, 1793. They went straight to the Inn of the Three Lilies on the rue Hyacinthe, where they took lodgings.

Their room was on the top floor. It was small and very hot, even with the window open. Tired from the long journey, Audubon dropped down into the big bed while Joue stretched out on a small pallet that was against one wall of the room.

Audubon was just drifting off to sleep when he was aroused by the sound of someone knocking softly at the door.

Joue heard it, too, and was immediately on his feet.

Standing, ready to draw his knife if the situation warranted, Audubon motioned Joue to the door.

The door opened, and a small, gnomelike man entered.

Joue pushed the door closed.

The visitor said, "The day after tomorrow you are to go to the Pont Neuf. Be there just before sundown. You are not to cross the bridge. Someone will contact you."

"And who is this someone?" Audubon asked.

Shaking his enormous head, the man told him, "I am thankful, monsieur, that I know as little as I do." Then with a crooked smile he whispered, "The King is dead, long live the King!" The next moment he opened the door and was out of the room.

Audubon did not attempt to call after him, though he

was taken aback by the man's cryptic comment. The King was surely dead, and the Dauphin was not likely to become Louis XVII.

"Whoever they are," Joue commented, "they aren't wastin' any time, are they?"

Audubon agreed and suggested they go out for dinner.

"Where?"

"Someplace close by," Audubon answered. "I am too tired to go very far."

"I'd just as soon sleep," Joue said. "That coach jounced me around so much that I don't have any feelin' for grub now."

"Suit yourself," Audubon told him, and going to the door, he said, "Better keep it locked." Then he left the room and hurried down the steps.

When he reached the street Audubon looked up. The sky was clear and filled with stars. He took a deep breath. The air in the narrow street stank of decaying garbage. He shrugged and made his way to the beckoning light of a nearby bistro.

The following morning Audubon and Joue made their way to the Place Michel, where they hired a cab to take them to the Ministry of Marine on the other side of the Seine.

The clear sky of the previous night had given way to cinereous clouds that obscured the sun and threatened rain. Though it was still early, the streets were filled with people, most of them on foot, though a few were mounted. And as they came close to their destination they stopped to let pass three tumbrels filled with people being transported from Bicêtre Prison to the Place de la Révolution, where one by one they would be fed to the guillotine. A number of the condemned were young women, and many were old men.

Audubon was hard pressed to think that they could be enemies of the state, but it was Joue who voiced his thoughts: "They don't look guilty of anything to me."

With a shrug Audubon answered, "They are probably no more guilty than we are."

"Then, Captain," Joue said, his lips parting in a grin, "we are surely in the wrong place."

Audubon laughed until Joue, with a nudge of his elbow,

made him realize that the coachman was eyeing him suspiciously. He fell silent at once. Arousing anyone's suspicions in Paris would be at least as hazardous as sailing in shallow waters—more so, since he had no idea of the real reason he had been sent there. Not only were these waters dangerous, they were shark-infested as well. To allay whatever doubts might have sprung to the coachman's mind, Audubon gestured after the tumbrels, as the last one crossed the intersection, and in a loud voice declared, "The traitors deserve to die!"

"That's the truth, citizen," the coachman said, slapping the reins across the nag's back. "If those people weren't tryin' to hurt the government, they wouldn't be goin' to sneeze their heads into the basket."

Audubon agreed with him.

"They're probably all whores and thieves," the coachman observed. "People who don't want to work. And I say, if they don't want to work, get rid of them."

"To be sure!" Audubon responded.

"It's best for those who are willin' to work," the coachman commented, glancing back at his passengers.

Audubon nodded.

The coach bumped along the cobblestone streets for a while longer and then came to a halt on the Place de la Révolution in front of an imposing building festooned with the tricolor bunting. Within sight of where they stopped, the crowd had already gathered to watch the morning's executions.

Audubon paid the fare and gave the coachman a generous tip. "It is because of men like you," he told him, "that other nations of the world are made to wonder."

The man looked very proud. He even pulled his shoulders back, and calling to his horse to move, he drove off.

Joue looked up at the bunting and asked in a low voice, "Are those the colors we'll sail under?"

"Yes," Audubon told him.

Joue accepted the answer without comment. But Audubon realized that his first officer was already beginning to feel the chill of the real wind that had brought them to Paris. "Come," he said impatiently, "or we will be late for our appointment." And without waiting to see if Joue followed, he hurried into the large foyer.

Several minutes later they were ushered into a large office whose windows overlooked the Place de la Révolution and the grisly proceedings that were taking place there.

The man who came out from behind a highly polished *plat de bureau* to greet them introduced himself as Citizen Claude Renne. He was somewhat shorter than Audubon and heavier. His face was round and pink, his eyes blue, and his hair blond.

Audubon gave his name and then introduced Joue, explaining, "Citizen Joue is my first officer."

Renne shook hands with them, and returning to his place behind the ornate desk, he invited them to sit down. "I would appreciate it," he said, tapping a folder that lay on top of his desk, "if you would give me a while to refresh my memory about your petition."

"We are at your disposal," Audubon answered, noting that the man lisped slightly.

For several minutes Renne went through the material in the folder, now and then pausing to read something. Except for the rattling of the papers, the only sound in the room came from the intermittent roar of the mob each time the guillotine claimed another victim. Though Audubon and Joue exchanged glances, neither of them broke the silence.

Finally Renne looked up and with a nod commented, "A most impressive record, Citizen Audubon, most impressive indeed."

"You are too kind," Audubon responded.

"You have been at sea most of your life?"

"From the age of thirteen," Audubon answered with a gesture of his hand. "But that is not unusual for the son of a captain. I daresay many were at sea even before I was."

"I am sure that is so," Renne said, "but there are also some who never went to sea though their fathers were captains. One of these comes to mind. . . . You might know him since he, too, lived in Nantes?"

Audubon shrugged.

"Fouché. Citizen Joseph Fouché?"

"Practically everyone in France knows him," Audubon answered, his blood suddenly racing. Fouché was one of the most feared men in France, and he was becoming more and more powerful. There were even some who claimed that sooner or later he would make a bid to wrest Robespierre's power from him.

"But did you know him in Nantes?" Renne pressed.

"I knew him," Audubon admitted. "He, too, came from a seafaring family."

"Yes," Renne answered with a smile. "I thought you had." And then he said, "You took part in the American Revolution. The record says you were captured by the British?"

"That is correct," Audubon replied, explaining that he had been captured off the coast of South Carolina in 1779 while he was master of the brig *Le Comte d'Artois*.

"And there was no way for you to avoid being taken?" Renne asked.

Had the situation been different, Audubon would have allowed himself the luxury of giving vent to the sudden rush of anger that swept through him. "I was unarmed—" he started to explain.

"You did have several six-pounders," Renne interrupted.

"Four, to be exact," Audubon answered acidly, "and that, citizen, is not sufficient to cope with the firepower of a British frigate."

"You learned to speak English?" Renne questioned, changing the subject.

"Yes."

"Why?"

"Because I thought it would be valuable to me in later years."

"You were freed and then joined the Comte de Grasse off Yorktown?"

"No," Audubon quickly corrected, "after almost two years I escaped."

Renne nodded.

"And then I commanded a corvette, the *Queen Charlotte*," Audubon added. "I was privileged to see the British surrender at Yorktown."

"I am curious, Citizen Audubon," Renne stated, "why a man who would fight for freedom would also engage in the slave trade?" His eyes went to Joue and then back to Audubon.

"I transported whatever cargo came my way," Audubon told him bluntly, "as did most captains."

"Especially those from Nantes," Renne said.

"Our captains have had a long tradition of trading with Africa."

"That seems to be the case," Renne commented, and then, resting his elbows on the top of the desk and looking at Joue but obviously speaking to Audubon, he told him, "You are a man of contradictions, citizen. On one hand you fight for freedom, but on the other you engage in slavery. On one hand you yourself have owned slaves, and on the other your first officer is a former slave."

"Joue and I have been together for a long time," Audubon said. "He has been at sea with me since his eleventh year. I trained him myself, and today he is probably better than most first officers."

"I am not questioning his ability, Citizen Audubon," Renne told him. "Because he is your first officer I accept his ability as a matter of course. I am merely trying to understand you, citizen. Seldom have I seen a man whose life is studded with so many opposites. You're married yet you return home with a natural son. Most men would have been more than willing to keep their two families far apart, and though you had the perfect opportunity to do that, you did in fact bring the fruit of one woman to the house of another."

"My marriage to Madame Moynet—"

Renne waved him silent and said, "I am sure your reasons were justifiable. I mentioned the situation only to point up the contradiction in it. But now I come to the most striking contradiction, in my opinion, of all. Here you are, an obvious sympathizer of the Revolution, whose home happens to be in Vendée where even at this moment Royalists under the command of General Charette are battling the Republican army under the command of General Carrier."

"I see nothing contradictory in that," Audubon answered with perfect ease, since this was one of the questions he had anticipated.

"Perhaps," Renne suggested, "you would be so good as to help me to understand the situation better."

"My experience in America," Audubon told him, "made me see that the monarchy was doomed when the Revolution began."

"And you chose to be on the winning side?"

Audubon flushed and responded in a tight voice, "I chose to act on behalf of my convictions."

"Well put," Renne said with a smile. "Well put indeed,

since it allows me to come to my own conclusions."

Audubon remained silent. From the very beginning of their meeting he had realized that Renne was baiting him, and now that the interview was almost over he had foolishly allowed his resentment to become evident.

"You realize, Citizen Audubon," Renne explained after a pause, "that I do not make the final decision on your application for the commission. I only make certain recommendations that Citizen Prieur, the director of this ministry, may or may not follow. Or if he thinks it necessary, he will take the matter up with the other members of the Committee of Public Safety, of which he is a member. Should he do that, then you might be summoned before that group."

"I understand," Audubon said, knowing that the Committee of Public Safety, which had come to power in July and was dominated by Robespierre, controlled every governmental agency through its various members.

"Should I have to communicate with you," Renne asked, "where would I be able to reach you?"

"For the present," Audubon told him, "I have lodgings at the Three Lilies on the rue Hyacinthe."

Renne wrote that down, and then, standing, he offered his hand. "It will take some time before the final disposition is made."

"How long?" Audubon questioned.

"There is no way of telling," Renne said. And then he asked, "Have you a particular ship in mind, citizen?"

"The *Arguille*," Audubon answered. "She is in Le Havre. I saw her before I came to Paris."

"The *Arguille*," Renne repeated and wrote the name down. "Interesting," he commented.

Audubon looked at him questioningly, but receiving no further explanation he thanked Renne, and with Joue following close behind, he left the office.

By the time they were out of the building the executions in the Place de la Révolution were over and the crowd was beginning to disperse.

"What do you think, Captain?" Joue asked. "Will we get the ship?"

"I do not think so," Audubon answered.

Joue looked at him questioningly; Audubon replied with a shrug.

4

At the time of evening specified by the gnomelike man, Audubon walked slowly along the rue de Thionville near the Pont Neuf, one of the many stone bridges spanning the river to connect the two halves of the city.

Audubon was dressed in the simple black vestments of the Revolution, embellished only by a small tricolor rosette over his heart. His high boots were turned down.

Joue was not far behind him.

Audubon was still some distance from the bridge when he stopped. There was now a checkpoint just off the bridge where none had existed just a few hours before, and soldiers were scrutinizing the identity cards of those who wanted to cross. Audubon had little doubt that he was witnessing another of the Public Prosecutor's efforts to fill the prisons of Paris with enemies of the state. Since Fouquier-Tinville's appointment to the post of Public Prosecutor with the power to arrest, prosecute, and try anyone suspected of conspiracy against the Revolution, hundreds of Parisians, like schools of fish, had been caught each time he cast his invisible net.

There were other people like Audubon who were watching the activity at the checkpoint. A long queue had formed in front of the makeshift barrier. Those whose identity cards failed to pass inspection were rudely pushed off to one side, where a small knot of people was growing larger and larger despite the supplications of all those whom the soldiers had forced there.

"Poor devils," someone close to Audubon whispered,

"they won't see the light of day again."

Audubon glanced at Joue. Should he require Joue's assistance, Audubon wanted him to be ready. Instantly the black pushed closer.

And another man offered, "If they don't have the right identity card, how can anyone know who they are? Maybe they're the wrong sort. These are times when you can't trust anyone, isn't that so, monsieur?"

The man was unshaven and raggedly dressed. His eyes were brown and dull.

"In these times," Audubon answered, wondering if this was his contact, "I suppose you are right."

The man nodded and moved away.

And then from behind Audubon a woman said, "But would it not be better if we could trust one another?"

He turned to look at her. She was probably in her late twenties. The top of her head came up to his chin. Her face was more exotic than beautiful, with interesting sloe eyes, somewhat sensuous lips, and a strong chin. She was dressed in a gown with the bodice cut short in the waist, sleeves that left her forearms bare, a low neck finished with a fichu that did not mask the impudent thrust of her breasts, and a skirt that hung straight from well-formed hips. Over her left breast was a small tricolor decoration of ribbons. She wore a simple cloak to protect her from the cold. Her hair was dark blond, almost the color of rich honey. It was cut short in front, but clusters of curls fell below her "Charlotte Corday" cap, which was also decorated with a tricolor rosette.

She gave him a slight nod.

And Audubon answered, "Indeed, mademoiselle, it would be much better."

A flicker of a smile passed across her lips.

Audubon eased himself closer to her and said, "Perhaps, mademoiselle, we might at some later time exchange views on the subject?"

"I would like that," she responded. "But I am afraid, Captain Audubon, that we have other matters to discuss."

"Are you—" He began to cough.

She nodded and said, "Your reputation does you justice."

"I never expected—"

"A woman?"

"Yes," he answered.

"Monsieur," she said with a disarmingly coquettish look on her pretty face, "I think it would seem more realistic if you took my arm and we left this place, instead of continuing to stand here and stare at each other."

"Your servant, mademoiselle," he replied, immediately offering her his arm.

"I do not think it would be wise to have your black come after us," she told him.

Audubon glared at her but signaled Joue not to follow; then he said, "I am at your disposal, mademoiselle."

She nodded as they moved away from the crowd, and as they walked along the Quai de l'Unité she said, "I have not been a mademoiselle for several years, Captain. . . . Not long after I first saw you, I——"

Audubon came to an abrupt stop. Again there was that almost mocking flicker of a smile on her lips, but before he could ask where she had seen him she said, "Some eight years ago in New Orleans at the home of Monsieur Pierre Philippe de Marigny. We danced together that evening. I was eighteen then."

Audubon shook his head, not so much to deny what she had said as to indicate that he did not remember the meeting, though in truth he had been a guest at the De Marigny house many times.

"You were too busy to pay much attention to me," she told him. "But as I remember, you were very much interested in Madame Gris."

"I do not remember either our dance or my interest in Madame Gris," Audubon responded. Then with a wave of his hand he dismissed the past.

She gave a slight shrug and with a regretful sigh said, "Those days will never come again. Instead we have—— But you, too, know all too well what we have."

Audubon did not answer. He was still trying to recall their meeting at the home of his friend Pierre de Marigny.

"Two years after I met you," she told him, "I was sent to court and became part of the Queen's household. Not long after I arrived I was married to the Marquis de St. Pierre."

The name was vaguely familiar to Audubon. The St. Pierres had often financed slavers who sailed out of Nantes, though he himself had never had any dealings with any member of the family.

"But last year, during the first days of the Revolution," the Marquise continued, her voice becoming suddenly hard, "my husband was captured and shot."

"I am sorry," Audubon offered, not knowing what else to say.

She looked at him and said, "I doubt it, monsieur."

"I am not so insensitive," Audubon responded defensively, "that I cannot understand another's grief."

The Marquise made a gesture with her right hand that encompassed all of Paris and said, "To allow oneself to feel grief is to bleed a little, and this city is so full of grief that one cannot feel anything unless one is willing to bleed all the time."

Audubon said nothing. The Revolution had not only changed the political system of the country but had changed the people, inuring them with a hardness that had once been foreign to their nature. He glanced at the Marquise and found it easy to imagine her in the gracious surroundings of the court.

And as they continued to walk, Audubon noted that the sky in the west had turned purple though some pink still showed around the edges of the darker hue. In the rapidly deepening twilight the city was drenched with that trembling luminescence that belonged to Paris alone and gave everything a soft, shimmering quality that made even the roofs and the chimneys seem beautiful.

"I am now known as Nicole Berthoud," the Marquise said in a low voice, her words intruding on his musings about the beauty of the evening.

"I have not had to change my name," he told her.

"What you choose to call yourself," she commented, "is your own affair."

"True enough," he replied. "I am known to the authorities, and as far as they are concerned I am here in Paris to seek a commission from the Ministry of Marine for a ship that lies at Le Havre. Even the fact that Joue, the black, is with me is known."

"Can he be trusted?" Madame Berthoud asked.

"He has been my first officer for several years," Audubon replied. His chagrin was obvious in his tone.

"Monsieur, brother has betrayed brother, and children, parents—even husbands and wives have betrayed each other."

"Yes," he said, "I believe you."

"Then why would the black hesitate—"

"Because," Audubon said, "like all men who sail, we are bound by the sea, and that bond is stronger by far than blood or marriage."

"I did not think such loyalty existed anymore."

With a nod Audubon accepted her comment and then said, "And I did not think that my contact would be a woman."

"My instructions were only to contact you and arrange for another meeting."

"Or to put it more bluntly," he said, "to look me over."

"I do what I am told to do."

Audubon frowned. He did not in the least appreciate the situation in which he found himself.

"Have we been followed?" Madame Berthoud suddenly inquired.

Audubon glanced over his shoulder. "There is no one who looks in the least bit interested in us," he told her.

"All the same," she responded, "it would be wiser to take precautions."

He was about to ask her what they could possibly do when she gestured to the other side of the street.

Moments later they were against the stone wall. Below them in the darkness, the river made a lapping sound as it brushed against the stones on its way to the sea. And on the opposite bank the windows of the Château de Vieux Louvre were yellow with candlelight.

Audubon, standing very close to Madame Berthoud, became aware of her scent and the contours of her body. Had the circumstances been different he might have kissed her, and if her response had been warm, he might have. . . .

"There is a man," she whispered, "on the other side of the street. He is staying well within the shadows of the buildings."

Audubon's hand went to his knife, and wheeling around, he freed the blade from the sheath.

Madame Berthoud gasped and pressed herself against the stone wall.

Audubon started across the street.

Suddenly someone began to run.

Sheathing his knife, Audubon returned to Madame Berthoud and said, "Whoever it was, he was not willing to risk a fight."

"Thank God!" Madame Berthoud exclaimed as they began to walk again.

Audubon did not answer.

She asked, "Is anything wrong, Captain?"

He stopped and said, "Your meeting me, madame, was wrong."

Her eyes widened with surprise.

"I do not conduct my business with women," he said. "Women have their place and their value, but when it comes to something such as what happened back there, a woman is best left out of it. You tell whoever sent you," he added, "that I will not meet you again."

"What?"

"Tell him," he said sharply, "that I did not come to Paris to be met by a woman."

"You came to Paris," she told him angrily, "because it was I who sent your name to General Charette."

Audubon stopped.

"I had heard about the death of your son," she explained. "It is not important how I heard," she said, anticipating his question. "But even in these times news manages to travel. I even know that he was your natural son born in Aux Cayes."

"But what has his death to do with you?" he asked.

"This time," Madame Berthoud offered, "it is I who am sorry. Do you believe that?"

He nodded but realized that her apology, though sincere, was meant to evade his question. He was sure that she had made a mistake by mentioning John's death and was trying to correct it by avoiding any further conversation on the subject. For now he would not press the matter.

She suggested they walk again.

After a few moments Audubon told her, "I meant what I said before. I will not meet you again."

"But I thought—"

Audubon shook his head.

"You are an insufferably stubborn man!"

With a shrug Audubon said, "I have been told that before." And he added, "I will be on the rue de Thionville at sundown the day after tomorrow. If I am not contacted by your superior, I will return to Le Gerbetière. Is that clear?"

She nodded.

When they reached the bridge, the checkpoint was abandoned.

5

When Audubon was no longer able to distinguish Madame Berthoud in the darkness from the other people crossing the Pont Neuf, he walked to a small café on the rue de Thionville, a short distance from the bridge.

The café was dimly lit, with more light near the bar than anywhere else in the room. Audubon chose a table off to one side near the hearth. In the deep shadows at the rear of the café were two more tables, one of them occupied by a man and a woman. Now and then the woman's high-pitched titters or the man's deeper, more lascivious-sounding laughter came from that part of the room. All the other customers were at the bar, and from what Audubon could overhear, most of them were talking about what had taken place on the Pont Neuf earlier in the evening.

Audubon filled his pipe. A column of light-gray smoke rose to the low, blackened ceiling. As he reflected on his meeting with Madame Berthoud, the café owner, a bald, heavyset man with frog eyes, approached and asked what he wanted.

"Red wine and cheese," he told him, looking up.

"A glass or a bottle?"

"A glass will do."

The proprietor returned with the wine and cheese.

Audubon paid him, and as he lifted the wine to his mouth, he saw the door open. Another man entered the café. The new customer went to the bar, eased himself into a space between two other men, and ordered a drink.

A few moments later, glass in hand, he left the bar and walked to the hearth, where he turned around to warm his back.

Audubon cut himself a small piece of cheese from the portion on the pewter plate and savored its taste. Then he sipped a bit more wine. He was still thinking about Madame Berthoud and was annoyed at how much she knew about him. From experience he knew that the more mysterious a man was to a woman the more likely she would be to—

"Cold for this time of year," the man at the hearth said.

"The wind," Audubon explained, "always makes it seem colder than it really is."

"That may be," the man commented, approaching the table, "but no matter what the cause, when it is cold this old body feels it."

Audubon found himself looking up at a tall, thin man with a long face and eyes that could have been black or dark brown; his narrow lips turned down at the corners.

He was dressed in the simple clothes of the Revolution and wore a tricolor cockade on the crown of his hat.

"My name," the man said with a lean smile, "is Freneau—Citizen Charles Freneau. May I share this table with you?"

"Of course," Audubon answered, though he would have preferred to be alone.

Freneau settled down at the table, and hearing a sudden shriek of merriment from the rear of the café, cocked his head in its direction and said with a laugh, "Even better than a fire on a cold night is the soft warmth of a woman's body."

Audubon nodded. He did not want to speak with Citizen Freneau. There was something unwholesome about the man.

"But there are enough women," Freneau went on, "to comfort every man. The Revolution has made love and freedom synonymous. To love and freedom," he said, raising his glass.

Audubon drank and then quickly said, "They are quite different, Citizen Freneau."

Freneau smiled and commented, "There are many who would argue that point with you."

"I have no wish to argue with anyone," Audubon replied. "If anything, my desire is quite the opposite. All I wish to do is—"

"Be left alone?"

"In a word," Audubon responded, "yes."

"But there are certain things, citizen," Freneau said, "that cannot be done alone."

Instantly Audubon reached across the table, and grabbing Freneau by the front of his coat, he practically pulled him across the table.

"Let me go," Freneau said in a shaky voice, "before someone sees—"

"Who are you?" Audubon asked, releasing him.

"That was very foolish," Freneau chided. "Very foolish!"

"I have no doubt that it was," Audubon said angrily, "but if you do not tell me who you are, I will be even more foolish and beat it out of you. Did you follow me this evening?" Audubon asked, wondering if he had been the man in the shadows.

Freneau nodded and then in a whisper said, "But I was not the only one."

Audubon looked questioningly at him.

"There are two sides in every contention, but in this one, no doubt," Freneau said, "there are many more."

"I do not know what you are talking about."

"We have the same interest," Freneau answered with a thin smile. "The woman—Madame Berthoud."

Before Audubon could stop him Freneau was on his feet. He moved away from the table, and in a matter of moments he had left the café.

As soon as he was gone Audubon summoned the proprietor and asked, "Do you know who that tall gentleman was?"

The man gave him a peculiar look.

"The one who sat at my table. . . . He just left."

"You don't know him?" the man asked.

"If I did, would I ask you who he is?"

"That, citizen, is one of Samson's executioners," he said, and to give emphasis to his words he drove the side of his right hand into the palm of his left. "You can watch him work every morning at the Place de la Révolution."

Though Audubon tried to stem it, he shuddered.

Shortly after Audubon left the café he realized he was being followed. But he continued to walk as though he were unaware of it. From the sound of the footfalls he was practically certain there was only one man behind him.

Then, suddenly, a man stepped out of the shadows not more than fifteen or twenty paces in front of him. Audubon stopped, and with his heart pounding he glanced over his shoulder. The man behind him had stopped, too.

"Now!" the one in front of him exclaimed.

The two of them rushed at Audubon.

He stayed in the middle of the street and braced himself for the shock. His assailants smashed into him, driving their fists into his body.

For a few moments Audubon could do no more than try to protect his head from the blows, but then he managed to slam his knee into the groin of one of the attackers. The man howled with pain and moved away a bit to recover.

Audubon caught the other man with a blow across the bridge of his nose. Immediately a stream of blood gushed from it.

He came at Audubon with a vicious lunge, and Audubon drove his fist into the man's stomach, doubling him up.

The second man came back but without much enthusiasm. When Audubon knocked him down with a solid blow to his jaw, he scrambled to his feet and ran.

The other was bent over, vomiting. Audubon came toward him, but he, too, ran.

Breathing hard, Audubon rubbed his grazed knuckles. His chest and back ached from the initial blows he had received.

He took no consolation from his victory, and with a shrug he continued to walk toward the Pont de la Raison. Sometime later, when he was close to his lodgings, Audubon found himself wondering if Citizen Freneau had had something to do with what had happened. It was possible. Perhaps too possible to be probable. But a jealous man could usually be counted on to do the improbable.

6

Citizen Renne occupied a table in the rear of the White Horse Café on the rue du Bois. There was sawdust on the wooden floor and the smell of sour wine in the air. It was late, and he was the only one in the establishment. The owner, a big, ugly-looking man with a wart on the left side of his nose, was busy cleaning up behind the bar.

Renne was tired and would have much preferred to be at home with his wife Fleur instead of waiting in a wretched café to hear what his hirelings had found out about Captain Jean Audubon. With a sigh he told himself that a man's duty came before his pleasure.

Lifting his glass of wine, Renne assured himself that he would be settled down next to Fleur by midnight at the very latest. And as he sipped the wine he wondered if she would still be angry when he returned: They had had words about his going out. She had even accused him of having another woman somewhere else in the city.

Renne took another sip of wine and then looked at his watch. It was almost eleven. He snapped the cover shut and replaced the timepiece in his pocket.

He hoped Fleur would be dozing when he came home. That way he would avoid having to answer her questions, and she might, as she sometimes did when half asleep, become amorous. It was something pleasant to think about while he waited for the two men to make their reports.

Ordinarily Renne would have submitted Audubon's request for a commission for the minister's approval as a matter of course, since Audubon's experience eminently qualified him to command a ship. But his suspicions about the Captain's relationship, however tenuous, to Fouché prevented him from doing that. And as soon as his work at the ministry was finished for the day, Renne had gone directly to a bookstore on the rue du Bac, just off the Quai d'Orsay, where he had discussed the situation with the owner, a man named Michel Gide, to whom he reported anything he considered suspicious and from whom he took certain instructions.

Gide was one of Citizen Robespierre's special agents who employed men like Renne to gather information and do other things that were helpful to the government.

Gide, complimenting him for bringing Captain Audubon to his attention, had given him the names of two men who could be trusted to find out more about Audubon. Then he had said, "Come by tomorrow and tell me what you have learned."

Renne poured more wine. Someday soon he hoped to leave the Ministry of Marine and become a full-time member of Robespierre's secret police. When that happened he would be in a position to take advantage of all the opportunities the Revolution offered to anyone who was in the least bit enterprising.

Eleven o'clock was struck on all the clocks in Paris, and the bells throughout the city began to sound the hour. Before the tolling stopped, the two men entered the café.

As soon as Renne saw them he knew that something had gone wrong. They were badly battered.

The two of them sat down at the table, and Renne pushed the half-empty wine bottle toward them. François, the taller of the two, drank first, and then, wiping his lips with the back of his hand, passed the bottle to André.

"What happened?" Renne asked, hoping that his estimation of the situation was wrong.

André stopped drinking and said, "We followed him from his lodgings. The black was with him, so we didn't try then. Besides, it was too light. The two of them went for a stroll on the rue de Thionville, near the Pont Neuf." He paused for another drink of wine, and wiping his mouth with the back of his hand, he continued, "There he picked up a woman. . . ."

"A woman?" Renne questioned.

"A whore," François said.

"The two of them walked along the river," André continued.

François laughed and said, "Her price must have been too high."

"And how do you know that?" Renne asked.

"They did a lot of arguing," François answered. "He even walked away from her."

"We could have jumped him then," André said, "but two other men were watching them."

Renne's heart suddenly began to race, and he rubbed his hands with excitement.

"Yes," François said. "They stopped us from gettin' him then."

"Did you see who they were?"

"No, but later," André told him, "Audubon and Freneau, the executioner, shared the same table in a café."

"Go on," Renne said, impatient to hear something more that might be of interest to Gide.

"We waited until Audubon came out of the café," André said. "We followed him to the rue de Racine before we jumped him."

"What else?" Renne questioned. He had told them that he wanted whatever papers Audubon was carrying. From those he had hoped that Gide would be able to establish whether or not the Captain's connection to Fouché could be considered a source of potential danger to Citizen Robespierre.

François grumbled, "He's a strong son of a whore."

André readily agreed.

Renne looked at one and then the other. And in a voice choked with anger he asked, "And what am I supposed to do now?"

"He ain't easy to take," André said.

"Next time we'll get him," François added.

"Next time," Renne told them, "I will find men who will do what must be done without its having to be done again by someone else."

"Pay us what you owe," François said, "and we'll be on our way."

"Pay you for what?" Renne responded as he stood up. He was not about to pay for nothing.

"Don't think we took a beating for nothing," André commented ruefully.

"You were supposed to give one," Renne shot back, "not take one. You were supposed to—"

"Pay us!" François demanded, leaping to his feet.

"The devil I will," Renne answered angrily.

"The devil you'll join," François shouted, plunging a stiletto into Renne's chest.

Renne's eyes opened wide. With trembling hands he tried to pull the knife out. Then, with a wordless cry on his lips and blood pouring from his mouth, he fell forward across the table.

7

Audubon spent a restless night in his lodgings on the rue Hyacinthe. The room was small, and though the weather had turned appreciably cooler, it was still too warm for his liking. But Joue, even on a hard pallet, slept the sleep of the just, and if his snoring was any indication, he was enjoying every moment of it.

Though the night air was reputed to be unhealthy, Audubon opened the window and looked out. A full moon was up, and the roofs and chimneys of Paris were delicately silvered, transformed into a sight worthy of a poet's eloquence or an artist's skill. But to him it could not equal the beauty of a moon-drenched sea, the crest of every wave crowned with silver. . . . The sea was only thirty leagues or so to the east, but Audubon wondered if he would ever see it again.

He shook his head. Nothing that had happened so far had been the least bit reassuring. . . .

Audubon did not appreciate the fact that Madame Berthoud had been sent to look him over or, as he was beginning to think of it, her intrusion into his life, since by her own admission she had given his name to General Charette. And he did not appreciate having to fraternize with a man like Charles Freneau, whose jealousy was unfounded.

He sighed wearily and returned to bed. For some time before drifting off to sleep he stared at the bottom of the yellow canopy and tried to remember his meeting with

Madame Berthoud at the De Marigny house, but somnolence came before the memory did, so that when he awoke the following morning he had the peculiar feeling that there was something he should have done. . . .

8

As soon as her work was done the following evening, Madame Berthoud hurried to the rue de la Réunion, purposely taking a circuitous route. The sky was darker than it had been all day, and the threat of rain seemed more immediate. Many of the windows in the houses along the way were already aglow with candles or lamps, though night was still several hours away.

A few minutes later she entered a modest-sized house and was led by an elderly woman into a room where a tall man stood facing a hearth, his long hands clasped behind his back.

Neither the man nor Madame Berthoud spoke until the old woman had left; then the man turned, and gesturing with his hand toward the door, he said, "See that it is locked."

Madame Berthoud went to the door and turned the key. "Have you been waiting long?" she asked, facing him. He was a handsome man with classic features, black hair, and coal-black eyes that often glowed with an inner fire, especially when he spoke of his mission.

For several months they had passed themselves off as lovers, frequently meeting in the room where they now were or in other places throughout Paris. And though he knew her name—indeed, he was the one who had contacted her—she remained ignorant of his identity.

Once they parted and went their separate ways, he seemed to vanish. Irked that he never gave any indication he was aware of her as anything more than another agent (and she was sure he had contact with many others, possibly a number of whom were women), Madame Berthoud sometimes dreamed that they had actually become lovers.

He shook his head and told her, "I arrived just minutes before you. . . . Even as the old woman opened this door for me I heard you knocking on the one in front."

Madame Berthoud slipped the cloak off her shoulders, and draping it over the back of a chair, she said, "I met him last night."

The man nodded.

"On the rue de Thionville, as planned," she said.

He moved away from the hearth but not toward her. He went to the window and looked out at the yard. "And what are your impressions of the man?"

Madame Berthoud took a deep breath and slowly exhaled.

"You have doubts?" he questioned, still looking out the window.

"I am not sure."

He faced her.

"I am just not sure," she told him again.

"About his loyalty, his ability, or both?" he asked.

"He is not the way I thought he would be," she said.

"I do not understand," the man admitted, looking at her.

"Nor I," she told him with a shrug. "I have spent a sleepless night and much of today thinking about him."

"Just what is there to think about?"

"He refused to meet with me again!" she said.

"Audubon said that?" he asked, lighting a candle.

"Yes."

The man half-smiled.

She complained, "I did not appreciate it and told him so."

"He was not chosen for his attitude toward you or any other woman," the man said, moving back to the hearth and resting his arm on the mantel above it. "He has certain other peculiar qualifications."

"I am fully aware—"

"I hardly think you are, Madame Berthoud," he told her, his voice suddenly flashing out at her with rapierlike swiftness. "There are a great many other men who can do what he must do. But most lack his experience. He is a man who, through most of his life, has been intimately connected to dangerous enterprises and—"

"Remember, monsieur, it was I who suggested his name to you," she said sharply, not willing to let him treat her as if she were some foolish woman. Madame Berthoud prided herself on being able to discuss all manner of things with men on an equal footing. Before the Revolution had swept her former life from her like so much rubble, her salon in Paris had been famous not only for the many savants who frequented it but because of her own reputation as a woman of wit and intelligence.

The man nodded.

"I am past glorying in the exploits of those who wrest from others by brute force the things they want. I have seen enough brute force in this Revolution to serve me several lifetimes."

"We all have," he said softly. "But Monsieur Audubon not only has certain attributes that make him ideal for the task, he also has the means of masking the identity of the child once he succeeds in getting him out of Paris."

She raised her eyebrows.

"The birth certificate of his son," the man said. "And to make it even more foolproof he will adopt him once he reaches his native village of Le Gerbetière at Coureron."

"But that is in Vendée!" she exclaimed, aware as was everyone else in France that a civil war was raging in that province.

"Nonetheless," the man said, "he must return there."

"If that is the way it is to be," she answered after a pause, "then I can hardly expect to change it."

He agreed and said, "If you do not want to go—"

"I gave my promise to the Queen that I would do everything I could to look after the Dauphin."

"Then the matter is settled," he replied.

"Audubon will have some objections," she said.

"I will meet with him and explain the situation. I am sure he will understand. But if he does not, it will be up to you," he told her, "regardless of the means you must use, to see that he does not object to your presence. Do you understand me?"

"All too well," she answered, her cheeks flushed. "As usual, you have made yourself more than clear."

He turned away from her, and looking at the flames in

the hearth, he asked, "Is there anything else I should know?"

She hesitated for a moment.

"Well, is there?" he pressed impatiently.

"I think I was followed," she told him in a low voice, almost afraid of his reaction.

He seemed not to have heard.

She repeated what she had said, making her voice somewhat louder.

"I heard you the first time," he told her.

"Oh, my God," she exclaimed, "it was you!"

He nodded. "Someone else was there, too," he said, facing her.

"Who?" she questioned in a low, frightened voice.

"I could not get a good look at him," the man said. "He was in the deep shadows."

"Does anyone else know about Audubon?"

"No," the man assured her. "So far we are the only two in Paris who know his real reason for being here. But the old man who told him where to meet you might have guessed."

Madame Berthoud went to the window and looked out. A mizzling rain was falling.

"You have no idea who might be interested in you?" he asked.

"No one is interested in me," she answered, and in a much lower voice she added, "Not even you, monsieur."

Her comment did not pass unnoticed. "I knew your husband, madame—"

She whirled away from the window and faced him. "You never said so," she told him accusingly.

"There was no need to," he answered. "We shared the same cell. . . . I was lucky enough to make my escape. . . . He—"

"All these months you could have said something."

He silenced her with a wave of his hand and said, "Someone is interested in you or what you are doing. . . . You must have some idea who it is?"

"I cannot imagine who it could be," she told him with a shake of her head.

"Perhaps," he offered after a few moments of silence, "it was a voyeur who can derive his pleasure only from watching others copulate."

"That is hideous!" she exclaimed.

"I would rather he were that," the man told her, "than someone from the Bureau of Police, or from—"

"Where?" she questioned.

"From Fouché," he answered.

"But he is not even in Paris," she commented.

"His men are," he told her. "He has organized his own network of spies. Probably in an effort to counteract Robespierre. If he could get wind of what we are up to, you know what he would do."

"All too well," she responded. "All too well."

"Are you sure that you have not become the object of some man's attentions within the past few days?"

Madame Berthoud pursed her lips. She started to reiterate what she had previously told him and then stopped.

"You remember something?"

She nodded and said, "Three or four days ago I was leaving the Temple and Simon was outside talking to a thin, gaunt-looking man. I remember it very clearly because I heard Simon say something about my breasts."

"Oh?"

"That day he had stood by the window and watched me wash a tubful of clothes. The top buttons of my blouse came undone and—"

"Do you think it was Simon?" the man asked.

"No," she said. "He is with the Dauphin at night, at least until the boy falls asleep. Then he usually drinks himself into a stupor. . . ."

"Then you think it could be the other man?"

"Possibly," she replied. "Simon might have said things about me that would excite his interest."

"It is possible," the man agreed, then suggested, "If you can, try to find out something about him. I would like to know who he is and where he might be found. . . ."

Madame Berthoud nodded and then asked, "How long did you know my husband?"

"Not more than a few days," he answered.

"Did he say anything about me?" she asked hesitatingly, afraid that her husband might have told a stranger the truth about their marriage, which had existed only as a legal entity, leaving both of them free to engage in discreet liaisons. For her part, she would have been content to remain a faithful wife, despite the many temptations at court to abandon her marriage vows. But she could not remain indifferent to his affairs. And by calling him to account for them, she had won for herself an equal degree of freedom, though she seldom took advantage of it.

"Only that you were an exceptional woman," the man told her.

"A bland enough way of describing one's wife," she commented, unable to keep the bitterness out of her voice.

"I have heard less," he told her.

"No doubt," she replied tiredly. "No doubt."

9

Even after taking a soporific, Madame Berthoud did not find it easy to sleep, and when she finally did, nightmares forced her into troubled wakefulness.

Her dreams were spectacles of horror in which she again witnessed the death and mutilation of old acquaintances or saw the tumbrels filled with their hapless victims as they rolled through the streets on their way to the Place de la Révolution. In her dreams, one terrifying apparition seemed to spawn another.

Awake, troubled thoughts about Audubon and the nameless man swirled through her tired brain. Audubon angered her. He was absolutely insufferable! But what could she possibly expect from a man who was, for all his posturing, nothing more than a common sea captain? But her mysterious contact—now there was a man whose gallantry was obvious in his speech as well as in his actions. Even the way he spoke about her late husband was evidence of his high regard for her feelings and his respect for the dead man's honor. She was certain that he was perspicacious enough to detect her interest in him.

The aura of mystery with which he surrounded himself had been from the very beginning of their relationship a source of excitement for her. She did not know whether her feelings were the result of the imminence of danger when they met or whether she was titillated by the idea that they were posing as lovers.

That he had chosen to mention his brief acquaintance with Paul, her late husband, when he had, seemed to her a sure sign that he could read the evidence of her growing interest in him. And though she realized that he had rebuffed even the barest suggestion on her part that the relationship between them might become more intimate, she was not as disturbed by that as she was by Audubon's contempt.

Captain Audubon's response made her feel very much the fool, while the other man responded with a gentle grace that had all the elegance of an individual familiar with courtly manners.

Madame Berthoud soon began to wonder how much Paul had told her contact while they had occupied the same cell. For him to have said that she was "an exceptional woman" was just the kind of colorless compliment she might have expected. Paul was never enthusiastic about anyone or anything unless it was about a woman with whom he was practicing some new perversion.

Madame Berthoud bit her lower lip, and the memory of her marriage brought tears streaming down her cheeks and sobs that she stifled by jamming the back of her hand into her mouth.

She wept not for Paul but for herself, for the years she had lived without love, for the times she had lain with a man in order to experience the pleasure of love without loving, or to spite Paul when he was between one woman and another and he would turn to her for the solace she could not give.

The tears ceased, and Madame Berthoud slipped into a restive sleep peopled with phantoms on their way to the guillotine. She moaned and tossed from side to side, but the long lines of the condemned would not stop. And as she fought her way out of this dream of death, Madame Berthoud suddenly found herself once again in the large ballroom at the De Marignys' in New Orleans.

A small orchestra was playing a lovely dance as a man came toward her from across the room where a large rectangular mirror on the wall allowed her to be both observer and participant. The man was compactly built and deeply tanned. Even before he introduced himself she knew he was Captain Jean Audubon, whose exploits at sea against British and Spanish shipping were said to be surpassed only by his exploits in the various bedrooms of

New Orleans, Saint Domingue, and Fort-de-France on the island of Martinique.

He bowed to her, introduced himself, and asked, "May I have the pleasure of this dance?"

Before she could accept he had her in his arms and they had joined the other dancers in the center of the room. His bold glance made her feel that the lovely silk gown she wore hid nothing of her body from his piercing eyes.

"I have not seen you here before," he told her as they moved across the floor in time to the music.

"Nor I you," she responded playfully.

He tossed his head and, laughing, said, "Obviously, we have not visited the De Marignys at the same time. . . . Your name, mademoiselle, for if we are to become lovers, surely I should address you by name."

"And are you so sure that we will be lovers, Captain Audubon?"

Again his flashing green eyes surveyed her breasts, and he said, "It would be a pity for us not to."

She laughed uneasily.

"I am a man who believes in enjoying all that God has put before me," Audubon told her.

"And you think God has put me before you?"

"I would say, mademoiselle," he answered with an almost impish smile, "that He in His infinite wisdom has given me a glimpse of an earthly paradise."

"And you, no doubt, would like to sample the rest of it?" she laughed.

"Naturally," he said. "I would be a poor man indeed if I did not seek true value."

"Then I am afraid," she told him, "you will remain a poor man."

"The fortunes of war," he answered with a nonchalant shrug.

The dance came to an end, he thanked her, bowed, and spent the rest of the evening dancing with a Creole beauty named Yvette Gris.

Even as Madame Berthoud opened her eyes, the dream and all recollection of it vanished. She was confronted by the meanness of her small room, with its battered chest of drawers against one wall, its chair and small hearth where the embers of the previous night's fire were coated white with ash. She shook her head and with reluctance left the bed to begin her toilette. Though it was still early in the morning, she could hear the cries of the vendors on the street, the movement of carts as they bumped over the cobbles, and the sounds of the other lodgers as they prepared for the day.

10

When evening came, the sky over Paris was a yellow opalescence. Here and there along the streets of the city the very poor were already congregating around the small open fires a journalist had dubbed "the hearths of the people," while in the cafés that lined the more fashionable streets noisy crowds gathered, their frantic gaiety an effort to dispel the guillotine's river of blood in wine and revelry. They lived each night as though it were their last—and for many unfortunates it was.

In every café prostitutes moved from table to table, offering themselves for a few sous or even a glass of wine. Seated in the Café Laurent on the rue de Thionville, Audubon was very much aware of the activity around him. Some of the interplay between the men and the women amused him, especially the haggling over price.

But for the most part Audubon was repelled by the blatant, frenetic pursuit of pleasure. It reeked of the unholy alliance between death and sex. The nearness of one always tended to increase dramatically the abuse of the other. Men used sex as an anodyne against death or as an affirmation of their lives. And women were in that way not much different, though they seemed to find a peculiar pleasure in the knowledge that the men they took as lovers had killed.

Audubon preferred his pleasure without the trappings of danger. He did not require any stimulus but the presence of a lovely woman to enjoy himself. Fortunately, most of the women he desired also desired him. There was a wonderful mystery about the alchemy that took place between him and the women whose beds he shared that did not depend on the proximity of danger.

He glanced at the couples who were seated close by. Much of what he saw was hardly more than a form of barter between men and women; a drink and a few coins were sufficient payment for a woman. With a shrug he finished his glass of wine and signaled a nearby waiter to bring him another.

Audubon drank his second glass as slowly as the first.

Bawling something about a murder, a newsboy came into the café to hawk *L'Amie du Peuple,* one of the many evening newspapers.

At first Audubon did not pay much attention to the newsboy's shouts, but then he heard him yell, "Last night it was Citizen Renne, tonight it could be you. . . . Read what Citizen Desmoulins has to say about murder in the streets. . . . Citizen Renne—"

"Here, boy," Audubon called. "I will take one here."

The boy delivered the paper to the table.

The lead story on the front page was about Citizen Renne's murder. He had been found on the Quai du Mail, stabbed in the chest with a stiletto.

According to the writer, Desmoulins, the dead man had been involved in clandestine activities that could loosely be tied to a very prominent member of the Committee of Public Safety. And then the writer made use of the remaining space to denigrate the actions of Citizen Robespierre and his followers.

Audubon folded the paper. He found it hard to believe that a man like Renne could be involved in anything clandestine, even a love affair. With a shrug he finished his wine, dropped several coins on the table, and left the café to keep his appointment, wondering who his contact would be.

The street was crowded and noisy. It was cold enough to make Audubon pull up his collar and thrust his hands into the pockets of his coat. He walked slowly toward the Pont Neuf. He was almost at the bridge when a tall, well-dressed man who had been walking almost beside him for several moments said, "I understand, citizen, that you wanted to meet me?"

Audubon was so surprised he almost lost his footing.

"My name," the man said, grabbing hold of Audubon to stop him from falling, "is Remy Bigot."

"Your servant," Audubon responded, taking a good look at Bigot, who was his height and strikingly handsome, with dark eyes that hid more than they revealed.

They shook hands.

"I wondered if you would come," Audubon admitted as they started across the bridge.

"From the way you expressed yourself to Madame Berthoud," Bigot told him with a laugh, "I could hardly not come, could I?"

With a shrug Audubon nodded and said, "Each of us, monsieur, must do what he must do."

Bigot accepted his response without comment.

"And how is Madame Berthoud?" Audubon questioned as they left the Pont Neuf and began to walk along the Quai de la Magisserie, across from the Palais de Justice, where the Queen languished in the Conciergerie.

"Aflutter, as usual," Bigot answered. "But she is lovely, is she not?" he asked lightly.

Audubon glanced at him.

"I only meant," Bigot explained, "that one tends to forgive a beautiful woman much more readily than—"

"I did not ask to meet you in order to discuss Madame Berthoud," Audubon said in perfect English instead of French.

Bigot chuckled and answered, "You have played me well, citizen, very well indeed."

"I've spent too much time in English prison hulks," Audubon told him, his voice going hard, "not to be able to detect an Englishman masquerading as a Frenchman."

"It is fortunate for me that so few of your countrymen have had your unhappy experience."

Audubon did not reply. He did not like Citizen Bigot, and he detested the British.

Once again speaking in French, Bigot said, "We know many of the same people."

"No doubt," Audubon responded testily, his brain still filled with memories of the time he had spent aboard a British prison hulk in New York Harbor. The rats, the filth, the brutality, and the death! He had fought against the English once, and he would gladly fight them again.

"I do not mean General Charette and other members of his staff," Bigot told him.

"Who, then?" Audubon asked, looking at him.

"Washington, Franklin, and more recently, even Gouverneur Morris, who is Washington's private agent in France."

"But how——"

"My dear Citizen Audubon," Bigot said, "in my particular calling, one finds oneself in the company of many different people."

"That is hardly an answer."

Bigot gestured with his long hands and with a chuckle said, "I was at Yorktown in the service of His Royal Majesty, King George the Third. I was a captain in the Continental Army."

"A spy!" Audubon hissed.

"As you yourself said a short while ago," Bigot commented, "each of us must do what we must do."

Audubon's expression made his disdain clear.

"But, citizen," Bigot chuckled, "consider what you yourself are now."

"It is not the same thing," Audubon shot back, though he instantly realized that indeed it was the same.

"It is entirely the same thing," Bigot told him, unperturbed by Audubon's response. "We are both interested in money, and we become engaged in those affairs that pay well. I have my special skills, and you have yours. But each of us employs his abilities toward the same end."

Audubon could not take issue with that.

"Circumstance," Bigot said almost playfully, "has managed to cast us together. I think that we will work well together—even, citizen, if each of us would prefer the other to be someone else."

"We will work well together," Audubon answered, respecting Bigot's frankness, "but I am not at all sure that I will be able to hold a similar relationship with Madame Berthoud."

"There is nothing I can do about that," Bigot commented. "She is to go with you when you take the boy."

"What boy?" Audubon asked.

"The Dauphin," Bigot said easily.

Audubon came to an abrupt stop and looked skeptically

at his companion. He knew, as everyone in Europe did, that the Dauphin was a threat to the Revolutionary government. As long as the boy lived, he was heir to the throne.

Bigot nodded, and motioning to Audubon to continue walking, he said, "That is why you are here, Captain. You will take him out of the Temple, out of Paris, and back to Le Gerbetière, where you will legally adopt him."

"So that was the connection between my son's death and Madame Berthoud!" he exclaimed. Suddenly he understood the words of the gnomelike man who had visited him the night he arrived in Paris. "The King is dead," Audubon whispered, "long live the King!"

"Just so!" Bigot responded.

"It is insane," Audubon told him. "The Dauphin is held in the Temple!"

"With patience," Bigot told him, "he can be rescued. A way can be found to breach the walls."

Audubon rubbed his chin and asked, "What has Madame Berthoud to do with this?"

"She works in the Temple," Bigot answered. "She is a laundress there and sees the Dauphin practically every day, and she was chosen by General Charette to accompany the boy once he is free."

"Are you telling me that I have no choice but to accept her?"

"None that I can see," Bigot agreed. Then he said, "I would appreciate it if you did not discuss either my identity or, for that matter, anything else about our meeting with Madame Berthoud."

"You doubt—"

"No, no," Bigot hastened to assure him. "She is above suspicion. But she is a woman, and there is always the possibility that she might be taken by one of the police organizations. The less she knows the safer she will be. In truth, citizen, the less each of us knows about the other, the safer we will all be."

They had left the Quai de la Magisserie and were on the far end of the rue de Franciade when Bigot commented that they were within a few streets of the Temple, once the stronghold of the Knights Templars, and before the Revolution, the residence of the Comte d'Artois, the King's brother. But now it was the prison for the Dauphin. "Perhaps," he suggested, "we might have a look at it?"

Audubon nodded.

Neither of them spoke again until they were on the far side of the Abbaye Martin des Champs, and then Audubon asked, "Just exactly what is your role in this adventure, Bigot?"

Bigot laughed. "Not too many men would look upon it as adventure."

"An answer, citizen, is what I want, not flattery."

"I am afraid," Bigot told him, "the very best I can do is to assure you that my role will become increasingly evident as—"

"It is not good enough," Audubon interrupted.

"You do indeed force an issue, citizen."

"It is not usually by choice," Audubon answered fiercely, "that I choose to sail into a fog when I can avoid it."

"There is no simple explanation," Bigot told him. "I have my orders."

"They at least must be lucid?"

"They are indeed lucid and mercifully brief. I am instructed to render assistance and protection to you."

"I can damn well take care of myself," Audubon said sharply, and thrusting his grazed knuckles practically in Bigot's face, he told him, "I got these the other night doing it."

Bigot looked troubled.

"Let's walk," Audubon said, and without waiting for Bigot, he strode rapidly up the street.

"Have you any idea who attacked you?" Bigot asked when he was beside the Captain again.

"There were two of them, but how in God's name would I know them?"

Bigot said nothing.

"They might have been hired by a man named Charles Freneau," Audubon told him gruffly. "At least, that is what I think."

"And you know Citizen Freneau?"

Audubon explained how he had happened to meet Freneau. "The man seemed to think that I was interested in Madame Berthoud. He even admitted to having followed us."

"I saw him," Bigot said.

Audubon halted, and grabbing hold of Bigot's arm,

brought him to a complete stop. "I do not want to be followed," he said in a low but very definite voice. "If I am and I discover the man, I will kill him. Have I made myself clear, Bigot?"

"Quite clear."

Audubon let go of Bigot's arm.

"As I started to say," Bigot told him, "seeing the Temple at night is very different from looking at it during the day. And since what you will do will probably be done at night, I think you should begin to familiarize yourself with the place at night."

"We will go," Audubon said, still furious that Bigot had spied on him.

"It is my responsibility, citizen," Bigot commented in a low voice, "to protect the important members of—"

"And just how do you propose to do that?"

"I have, Captain, as you by now obviously realize," Bigot said, "peculiar talents."

Audubon shook his head, but he knew that to press Bigot for further explanation would be futile. The man would not divulge one jot more than he already had. "Should I have any reason to complain about your talents, I most assuredly will," Audubon told him.

"I was sure you would," Bigot responded.

In a few minutes they came in view of the Temple. In a deluge of moonlight the tower and the outer walls of the structure looked unreal, like something that comes in a dream and vanishes as soon as the dreamer's eyes open. But the closer they came to the walls the less dreamlike it appeared and the more forbidding it became.

"Did you know," Bigot questioned, "that the Queen asked the Comte d'Artois to have the place destroyed when they were lovers, and he refused?"

Audubon shook his head.

"It is just one of those bits of information that I come by," Bigot said. "In itself it is meaningless. But when it is added to other bits and pieces, one almost begins to suspect she must have had some prescience about the place."

"I once commanded a ship named after the Comte," Audubon remarked.

"Yes, I know. You surrendered her to Captain Ridder."

"And spent the next two years in a prison hulk," Audubon said angrily.

"Please, Captain," Bigot suggested, "we must put the past behind us if we are to succeed in our mission. That was another time, and we had different interests. Now our interest is locked up in that tower."

"Old wounds," Audubon grumbled, "pain, when they are rubbed raw."

"My apologies, Captain."

To end the conversation before it took them into dangerous shoals, Audubon said, "We are certainly strange bedfellows."

Bigot agreed.

They walked around the walls of the Temple, taking note of how well it was guarded, not only at the entrance but for its entire length. There were National Guardsmen posted on platforms at intervals along the walls. There were lights in all four windows of the tower and in some of the other buildings visible through the one entrance to the grounds on the rue de Temple.

"Every time I see it," Bigot said, "I am struck by how formidable it is."

"Unless there is a tunnel under those walls," Audubon responded, "I do not know how we will be able to get in or out without being discovered."

"Suppose," Bigot offered, "just suppose we were able to walk in, take the boy, and walk out again?"

"Impossible!" Audubon exclaimed.

"But suppose it could be done that way?"

"I do not see how," Audubon admitted.

"Think about it," Bigot counseled, "and so will I. . . . Perhaps the sum of our thinking will suggest a way?"

Audubon glanced at him. He had the uncomfortable feeling that Bigot was not only laughing at him but had somehow already figured out how to accomplish the impossible.

11

Before Bigot left Audubon he agreed to meet with the Captain at least once every few days. Finally they shook hands, and Bigot made his way circuitously to the bookstore on the rue du Bac.

Bigot was even less enthusiastic about Audubon than Madame Berthoud, though his reasons were substantially different from hers. He did not in the least mind the fact that Audubon was an adventurer or even that he had refused to meet with Madame Berthoud. But he was greatly disturbed by the man's attitude toward the British. He would have thought that Audubon, during the intervening years, would have come to the realization that there was nothing personal about his incarceration by the British Navy, that it was nothing more than a circumstance of war, though Bigot admitted that many British officers still held bitter feelings against the Americans and French, especially those who had been forced to surrender at Yorktown. Luckily for the governments of the world, there were men like himself who could disassociate themselves from past contentions and function in whatever environment they were needed.

By the time Bigot reached the rue du Bac the bells were tolling ten o'clock. To be certain that no one had followed him he stepped into the deep shadows and waited a full ten minutes before turning into the street. The bookstore occupied the ground floor of a narrow two-story gabled structure.

Bigot pulled the bell cord several times and heard the

muffled response inside. He looked through the large window at the right of the door. The interior of the shop was quite dark. But at the far end a thin line of yellow light marked a door left ajar.

After a few moments the line of light widened sufficiently to allow someone to pass between the back room and the front of the shop. A figure holding a turned-down lamp padded through the band of light and into the store.

"Who is it?" a woman called out when she reached the door.

"I want to buy some books," Bigot answered.

"At this hour?" she questioned.

"Better late than never, Louise," Bigot replied.

A moment later the bolt was slipped, and the door opened.

Bigot entered the shop, and Louise, a lovely blond with milk-white skin and no more than twenty years old, who kept Gide's bed warm, said, "He's upstairs."

"I know my way," Bigot said, playfully squeezing her rump.

Laughing, Louise pushed his hand away and accused him of promising more than he ever gave.

"If I gave you anything," he told her, "it would spoil it for Gide."

"You boast, citizen." She laughed even louder than before.

Bigot waved his finger at her in warning, "I shall tell Gide how you provoke me."

"Do, do," she hooted. "Maybe that will make him pay more attention to me."

"If I were Gide, I would not let you out of my sight," Bigot told her, looking at the tops of her pale white breasts that swelled out of the dressing gown.

"Your sight now," Louise teased, baring even more of her ample breasts, "is already filled with—"

"Careful," he told her, "or I will bite them off."

"It would take more than one bite to finish them," she responded, making a shameless offer of her breasts to him.

"Maybe next time," Bigot told her.

"And here I expected you to take advantage of my good nature—"

"Stop being so damn good-natured," Gide called down

from the upper landing, "and let my visitor come visit me."

Feigning innocence, Louise said, "Good night, citizen." She left him at the steps in the rear of the shop that led to the upper story.

Bigot stood for a moment and admired the provocative swing of her hips before he went upstairs and joined Gide in his sitting room.

Bigot settled in a red-cushioned armchair.

Gide offered him a glass of wine.

"I have just come from a meeting with Captain Audubon," Bigot explained after they had taken the time to sip the wine and comment favorably on its bouquet and taste.

Gide eased his bulk down on a sofa and asked, "And how did you find him?"

"Adequate." Bigot answered guardedly.

"That is hardly a recommendation," Gide said, frowning.

"He is going to be difficult to handle," Bigot admitted.

"How difficult?"

"You must remember that he is used to commanding," Bigot told him.

Gide nodded.

"In time," Bigot said, "I do not doubt that he will be able to put some of the pieces together."

"I hope," Gide responded, "that by then the Dauphin will be in the proper hands."

"I will drink to that," Bigot said, raising his glass.

"Citizen Robespierre is very anxious to see this venture brought to its conclusion," Gide informed his visitor. "So much so that he has asked me for very specific assurances that once the Dauphin is removed from the tower the child will be handed into my custody."

"That is our agreement," Bigot replied, finishing the rest of the wine and placing the empty glass on the floor to the side of his chair. "But even Citizen Robespierre must be patient for the necessary arrangements to be made."

"With the boy in his keeping," Gide said, "he might even be able to negotiate with your government—"

"I am not a political man like yourself," Bigot interrupted. "I am here under orders."

"I can appreciate that," Gide responded, "for you this is just another assignment."

"Exactly," Bigot answered. "Which brings me to the reason for my visit."

"Oh, and I thought," Gide commented with a laugh, "that it was to tempt Louise to your bed?"

Bigot waited until his host stopped laughing, and then he asked, "Do you know all the executioners?"

"Some better than others."

"What about Citizen Charles Freneau?"

"No more than a nodding acquaintance. Why do you ask?"

"He may have hired two men to assault Captain Audubon," Bigot said.

Gide shook his head. "It was not Freneau who hired them."

"I am not sure I understand," Bigot admitted.

"It was an internal matter," Gide told him.

Bigot stood up and crossed the room to the hearth, where several good-sized faggots were burning; without looking at Gide he said, "I should think you would consider that anything that concerns Captain Audubon in the least bit would interest me."

"It really was nothing—"

"Kindly let me be the judge of that," Bigot snapped, whirling around.

Gide shook his head.

"Am I to understand that you refuse to tell me?"

"No," Gide said, "since my operative is dead it does not matter any longer that you know who he was."

Bigot returned to the armchair, and Gide explained his relationship to Renne, concluding, "My guess is that he was killed by ruffians."

"I doubt that," Bigot said. "But before we examine the question of who might have killed Renne, I would like to know who gave the information to that writer, Desmoulins, about Renne's connection with Robespierre?"

"That was an unexpected dividend," Gide admitted. "Desmoulins will yet sneeze his head into the basket. . . . Robespierre would have him do it soon, but as you said a while ago, even he must be patient and wait for things to come to pass."

Bigot said nothing.

"And now tell me," Gide asked, "who you think put that stiletto in Renne's chest?"

"Audubon beat his attackers off," Bigot said.

"Are you telling me what I think you are telling me?"

"Only, citizen, if you have come to the conclusion that the two men whose names you gave to your late operator were probably responsible for his death."

Gide heaved himself off the sofa and padded across the room to fill his glass with more wine. "I should hate to have to turn their names over to the police," he said, facing his visitor.

"What you do with them," Bigot responded, "is your affair. I only gave you my suspicion. I may be wrong. But since they did not get what they were after, I would think that some sort of argument arose between them and Renne that resulted in his death."

Gide nodded and returned to the couch. "I will have to decide what to do about them," he said.

Bigot leaned forward and asked, "Is there anything I should know about Citizen Freneau?"

"I can get his dossier," Gide offered.

"Do that."

"Anything else?"

"I want to know if there is anything more behind his interest in Madame Berthoud other than sex."

"I do remember having heard that his taste for pleasure usually takes him into the worst sections of the city."

Bigot nodded and asked, "Did you know he was a friend of Simon, the Dauphin's warder?"

Gide's bushy eyebrows went up.

"Yes," Bigot answered. "I was somewhat surprised to learn that, too."

"Do you think he might be one of Fouché's men?"

"I would not even risk a guess," Bigot answered.

Again Gide heaved himself up to a standing position. He walked to the window, where he looked out at the street and said, "These days it is impossible to know the difference between friend and foe." He shook his head, and facing Bigot, he told him, "I wish I possessed your detachment, citizen. Then maybe I would be able to sleep at night."

Bigot stood up and answered, "The difference between us, citizen, is that you do what you do for a cause, while I do what I do because it is what I do best."

"And you are never troubled by conscience?"

"Never," Bigot replied, shaking his head. "Win, lose, or draw, I strive to be professional."

"And if you should be caught?"

"I do not think about it."

"But if it should happen?" Gide pressed.

"I can hardly give you an honest answer until it does, now can I?"

Gide nodded.

12

For almost a fortnight Audubon and Joue roamed the streets around the Temple, though they seldom were together.

Sometimes Audubon would hire a cab and pretend to be looking for a house in a street nearby; or he would go on foot, dressed as a sansculotte, even wearing a *carmagnole* and a red cap.

On all of these expeditions he took notes on how often the guard was changed on the walls and at the main gate, and which tradesmen were allowed to enter the precincts of the Temple without being searched. While he was busy taking notes, Joue made sketches of the tower, the walls, and the gate.

From his own observations and those made by Joue, Audubon was rapidly coming to the conclusion that the Temple was indeed an impregnable fortress, at least from the outside.

During this time, Audubon, like everyone else who lived in Paris, could not escape from the reality of what was happening as Robespierre tightened his hold on the Committee of Public Safety and those who opposed him were taken into custody, tried, and sentenced to the guillotine.

Each morning the tumbrels made their way to the Place de la Révolution, where huge crowds gathered to watch the spectacle. By the end of the month the Girondists, a political faction recently expelled from the National Convention, were being rounded up for trial, which would inevitably lead all of them to the Place de la Révolution.

To avoid suspicion Audubon and Joue visited the Ministry of Marine again. And Audubon was assured by a Citizen Duffy, Renne's successor, that his application for a commission was being processed.

Audubon accepted what he was told with a nod, shook hands with the man, and left the office. But when Audubon and Joue were out on the street again and far enough away from the Place de la Révolution so they could not hear the shouts of approbation each time another head rolled into the basket, he commented, "I do not think he has the slightest idea where my papers are." Then he laughed and said, "The less he knows about us the better off we are."

"But why would he say your application is being considered?" Joue asked.

"To appear to know what he is doing," Audubon answered.

"Sometimes," Joue said, "I think your people are crazy."

"Sometimes they are," Audubon agreed.

"You know," Joue commented as they turned onto the rue Honoré, "you haven't said much about the man you met a few nights ago."

Audubon shrugged.

"You don't care for him much, do you?"

Audubon laughed and said, "So now you can see inside my head, eh?"

"I can see your face," Joue told him.

"You will meet him soon enough," Audubon said, "and then you can make up your own mind."

"And the woman, what about her?"

"She is to go with us——"

"I mean, do you like her any better?" Joue asked with a smile.

"As much as a good Catholic likes the Devil," Audubon replied.

"Ah, but Captain," Joue laughed, "enough of them do to keep him around."

"And sometimes I think you're one of his own," Audubon said.

With a movement of his hand, Joue brushed Audubon's words aside, and pointing in front of them to where a crowd was gathered, he suggested they change their direction.

"That might draw attention to us," Audubon said. "Besides, I am curious—"

"You know what that did to the cat," Joue commented.

"We can hardly be mistaken for cats," Audubon responded.

They stood at the edges of the crowd, and from snatches of conversation they quickly realized that the people were waiting to see Robespierre, who lived in the small house directly in front of them.

"Not really in that house," a man in front of Audubon explained to his companion, "But the one in back of it. I heard you have to go through a narrow, dirty alley to get to it."

And a woman nearby commented to her friend, "I'll never understand why he chooses to live with the Duplays. . . . Why, Citizen Duplay is only a carpenter. I mean, Citizen Robespierre is the most important man in France."

Still someone else said, "They say he's a saint, won't have anythin' to do with women of any sort."

That evoked the whispered comment, "They also say that he's beginning to think he's God."

Suddenly the door to the small house opened, and almost immediately everyone began to shout, "Robespierre, Robespierre, Robespierre . . ."

"Now there's someone with a catlike face," Joue whispered.

To silence him Audubon crossed his lips with a finger; but Joue was quite right. Robespierre looked like a cat, with his narrow, sloping skull, slightly slanting green eyes, small nose, and prim, simpering lips that greatly enhanced the impression that there was indeed something more feline than human about him. To increase his physical stature he wore high-heeled shoes with silver buckles, and though he was the most important leader of the Revolutionary movement, he affected a powdered wig, a frock coat, and even the knee breeches and hose of the deposed regime.

He took a moment to wave to the crowd, and then in the company of his bodyguards he made his way to a coach waiting at the curbside.

Still whispering, Joue commented, "He looks kind of bilious to me, almost green."

Audubon silenced him with a look and suggested they continue on their way.

"I didn't know we were goin' anywhere," Joue commented as he fell into step beside the Captain, who looked at him and shook his head.

"You are going to get us arrested," Audubon cautioned in a low voice.

Joue glanced back over his shoulder and announced that no one was following them. Then he said, "I don't think much of that Robespierre. He wouldn't be much good on a quarterdeck, or on any other part of the ship, except maybe the cook house."

"He did not impress me much either," Audubon admitted.

"Then why are the people following him?"

"I wish I knew," Audubon answered with a sigh. "I wish I knew, but somehow, Joue, he has taken hold of the helm, and the wind is with him. I do not understand everything that is happening, but somehow something seems to have gotten out of control. . . ."

"And if we get that boy out of the tower," Joue asked after a while, "will that put it in control again?"

Audubon shrugged. There was no answer to that question, at least not then, and perhaps there would never be if they failed to rescue the Dauphin.

Sometime later they came to the Temple, and keeping on the far side of the various streets that formed its perimeter, they made another slow inspection of its walls and entrance.

"I have at least two things worked out," Audubon told his first officer as they approached their starting point.

"How we can get in and out of there?"

"No . . . What we will do once we have the boy, and how we will do it," Audubon answered.

"Isn't that like tryin' to sail without wind?"

"Maybe," Audubon admitted. "But it does give us something for all the time we have spent here."

"I suppose so," Joue replied without enthusiasm.

They had started to walk toward the river when Audubon said, "I want you to see if there is a barge for sale."

"Is that how——"

"Once we have him and his absence is discovered," Audubon said, "every road in or out of the city will be closed. But not the river. The river is the last place they will look. We will stay on the barge and slowly work it downstream. Someplace between here and the coast we'll beach it and burn it."

Joue nodded approvingly.

"And I have chosen the route from the Temple to the river," Audubon told him.

"But how are we goin' to get the boy out?" Joue asked.

"Since it cannot be done from the outside," Audubon said, "it must be done from the inside."

"I don't know what you're talkin' about," Joue told him.

"If one of us could get in," Audubon suggested, "then maybe we would have a chance. What we do must not only be foolproof but it must also assure the boy's safety."

"Maybe, Captain, I'll go back to Saint Domingue and bring some strong voodoo back here?" Joue suggested.

"If I thought it would have even half a chance of working," Audubon said, "then I would send you for it tomorrow. But it would not help us one bit, Joue, not one bit."

"Perhaps it cannot be done?"

"I am almost beginning to think that is so," Audubon answered with a sigh. "That is really what I am beginning to think. . . ."

13

After the brief cold spell, the weather turned unseasonably warm, and though it was the beginning of October the sun beat down with the ferocity of July. The heat brought with it the stench of death that emanated from the Place de la Révolution, where the blood of so many hapless victims covered the cobbles with a sticky carmine stain that was host to flies, maggots, and other loathsome creatures.

Each day the heat continued, the fear of pestilence took deeper root. But the unseasonable weather brought with it another malaise—one that made people restive and angry. Many found life not worth living and put an end to their earthly sojourn, while others fell into a lassitude that made it almost impossible for them to leave their beds.

During this period of eccentric weather Madame Berthoud, like so many others in Paris, found sleep practically unattainable. Each night and even at times during the day she was beset by confused and disconcerting thoughts. If she was not involved in a silent diatribe against Audubon, then she thought about her contact quite fancifully. Though she strove fiercely against succumbing to the emotions he evoked in her, she could not stop herself imagining how his long, slender hands would feel on her body . . . how he might caress her. . . .

Such musings made her tremble with desire and forced her to seek some measure of gratification, as she had done when she was a girl who had not yet been schooled in the ways of love. Nevertheless, she lay awake most of the night, her mind plagued with images of the deliciously shameless pleasures that could be hers if only he would take her into his arms. . . .

But even these thoughts were less disturbing to her than the dread apprehension that clung to her the way the scent of smoke often clings to clothing. And no matter whether she was thinking about Audubon's contempt or imagining her contact's slender body coupled with hers, the presentiment of impending disaster was always hovering over her like some dark cloud. She became more and more certain with each passing day that a terrible scourge would soon afflict her, that perhaps the only embrace she would ever know would be in the skeletal arms of death. This melancholy prospect brought forth tears of anguish, regret, and self-pity.

Then, one day as she was preparing to leave the Temple grounds, Marie-Jeance, Simon's wife, hailed her. She stopped. Her presentiment of disaster became so strong that her hands began to tremble.

"You know," the warder's wife said, "I've been watching you, Madame Berthoud."

Instantly Nicole's heart began to race, and though it was oppressively hot she suddenly felt so cold that prickles broke out on her bare forearms and the nipples of her breasts became taut.

Marie-Jeance nudged her with her elbow and said, "And so has someone else, or haven't you noticed? Like they say," Marie-Jeance continued with a shrug that moved her pendulous breasts under her white fichu, "still waters run deep." And digging her chubby hand into the pocket of her apron, she took out an envelope. "This is for you."

Madame Berthoud looked at the envelope.

"Go ahead," Marie-Jeance urged, "take it. . . . It's from a gentleman who wishes to be of service."

"Who?" she asked in a voice choked with fear.

Marie-Jeance wagged her finger at her employee and said, "Someone who has taken a fancy to you. And from what my husband has told him, he's eager to see things for himself, if you know what I mean. . . . Speaking woman to woman, did you really show Simon your tits?"

Madame Berthoud shrank back and shook her head.

"No matter," Marie-Jeance said, "he's seen them, and he's interested in seein' more. Now you take this note and some advice: Don't be shy with Citizen Freneau. . . . He can be a very generous man." And she thrust the envelope at her. "Ain't you goin' to open it?" she asked.

Madame Berthoud shook her head.

"Give it here," Marie-Jeance demanded, and snatching the envelope from Madame Berthoud, she tore it open and pulled out a sheet of paper. "Now it's open, and he wants to meet you at the Café Godet on the Boulevard du Temple at seven o'clock tonight."

"No," she whispered, "oh no!"

Marie-Jeance nodded and said, "If I know him, he'll be there long before seven."

Madame Berthoud took a step and faltered.

Marie-Jeance caught hold of her and asked, "Is anything wrong?"

"No," she lied, "nothing is wrong." But the heavy cloud that had hovered over her heart for so many days was fast becoming a dark, swirling fear. "Thank you," she said, "but I must go." And she walked unsteadily out of the Temple grounds.

14

With her heart thumping loudly, Nicole Berthoud entered the Café Godet and hesitated. The big room reverberated with laughter, shouting, and even singing. Every table was occupied, and the bar was crowded. The stench of sour wine was in the air, and tobacco smoke hung like a heavy mist between the floor and the dark reaches of the high ceiling. Toward the rear, in a small alcove, she saw Freneau, who was already on his feet waiting to greet her.

"A pleasure, Madame Berthoud!" he exclaimed when she reached the table and invited her to sit down. "I am so pleased that you came."

"I came only to——"

He held up his hand and with a thin smile said, "Let us have some wine before we talk." And he summoned the waiter.

Madame Berthoud wanted to flee. The way he devoured her with his ferretlike eyes made her skin crawl. To add to her nervousness, many of the customers were looking at them.

"The wine here," Freneau commented, pouring some from the bottle into her glass, "is better than is served in most places." Then he filled his glass, and lifting it, toasted, "To a very lovely woman."

She flushed and accepted his toast with a silent nod.

"Did you know that this place is owned by a captain in the National Guard?" he asked, setting his glass down on the table.

"I do not know about such things," she responded, sipping her wine.

His lips parted in a narrow smile. "What *do* you know about?"

Her heart skipped a beat and began to race furiously.

He broke into a soft, cackling laugh and said, "Come, come. . . . If we are to be friends, we must be open with each other. If you tell me what you know, I will tell you what I know."

"What can I possibly know?" she stammered. "I am just a laundress."

"But you do know what I am, don't you?"

She nodded.

Freneau reached across the table, and taking hold of her hands, he said in a low voice, "There's no reason for you to be afraid of me, Marquise."

"Oh, no!" she exclaimed, wrenching her hands free. Abruptly, she pushed her chair back and began to rise.

"Sit down!" he commanded.

She sat down and said tightly, "I disavowed my connections with—"

"No one doubts that you are loyal," he told her, "least of all me. Simon, the Dauphin's warder, says you're a good worker and honest."

"Then what do you want?" she asked, trembling inwardly.

"You know what I want," he answered, reaching for her hand again. "I have watched you for a while and—"

She struggled to be free of his hold on her hand.

"Listen," he said, "I am prepared to offer you—"

She shook her head and began to whimper softly.

He let go of her hand and said, "I have your husband—"

"No," she whispered. "No . . . He is dead. . . . He is dead. . . ."

"He soon will be," Freneau told her, "if you do nothing to save him."

"But my husband is dead," she affirmed, remembering what her contact had said. "He is dead."

Freneau shook his head and showed her a small gold locket with her picture inside. "Once I saw this," he explained, "I recognized you the very next time I was at the Temple."

"He gave it to you?" she asked.

"In return for better treatment," Freneau told her.

She nodded and commented in a low voice, "It would be like Paul to seek better treatment. Did he also suggest that you offer me his life in exchange for my favors?"

"Ah, so that was the way it was between the two of you?"

"Did he suggest—"

"No," Freneau told her, "that idea was entirely my own."

She laughed disdainfully.

"Am I to understand that you're not interested in saving his life?" Freneau asked, his ferret eyes wide with surprise.

"I must have time to think," she responded.

"How much time?"

"A few days," she said. "A few days at the very least."

Freneau shook his head.

"When—"

"Tonight," Freneau said. "He's scheduled to die tomorrow morning."

"But I cannot—"

"You will if you must—and you must if you are going to save him."

She squeezed her eyes closed. Though she did not love Paul she did not hate him enough to see him dead.

"Should you prove satisfactory," Freneau told her smugly, "I might even come to some sort of an arrangement with you."

She opened her eyes and looked at him. The very thought of having to endure his hands on her body made her skin crawl. "And if I tell you," she said, "that you will not have any pleasure with me?"

"I will be at your lodgings before midnight," he said with a thin smile. "I hope you come to the right conclusion."

"And should I agree," she asked, realizing that no matter what she told him, he was determined to have her, "what proof would I have that you will uphold your end of the agreement?"

"Only my word," he answered with a smirk.

"Under the circumstances," she started to say, "that is hardly proof—"

"It is what I offer," he responded sharply.

"How will you manage to free him?"

He wagged his long finger at her, and shaking his head, he told her that if she proved herself in bed he would answer her question.

"No," she told him, angered by Freneau's arrogance. "Either you tell me now, or you need not bother coming to my lodgings later."

"Are you threatening me?"

"Either you tell me," she pressed, "or you will never——"

"A substitute," Freneau grumbled. "I have a substitute for your husband. A drunk who could be his twin brother." Then with a wave of his hand he said, "And even if I didn't have one, for a price I could always get one."

"Then someone else will have to die for him!" she exclaimed, aghast at the idea. What she had agreed to give for Paul's freedom should be more than enough. . . .

"Someone must die," Freneau said.

She shook her head. "Neither one dies. . . . Neither one dies, and my husband never knows about me. On those conditions only, citizen, will I open my thighs for you, do you understand that?"

Taken by surprise, he blinked.

"Neither one dies," she said, aware that she was no longer frightened and that in some strange, inexplicable way she had wrested control from him.

"But someone——"

Determined to press her advantage, she reached down, and taking hold of his hand, pressed it to her breast.

"No one dies, Madame Berthoud," he said in a choked voice. "Neither one dies."

15

Audubon and Bigot met at the corner of the Perron Passage, across from the Café Caveau, where milling crowds provided them with perfect anonymity.

"What are they all doing here?" Audubon asked, gesturing toward the throng with a sweep of his hand.

"Most come to see and be seen," Bigot told him as they stepped off to one side. "To some it is a divertissement. Perhaps the only one they have. And I daresay there are others, like ourselves, Captain, who come here with a purpose equal to our own."

Audubon had had that same thought a few minutes before when he had first seen the crowds.

Bigot chuckled and said, "All the cafés in Paris are breeding places for plots and counterplots. But let us hope that our purpose, unlike most of theirs, comes not only to fruition but also to a successful conclusion."

A few minutes later they were inside the Café Caveau and seated at a small table off to one side where almost above their heads a flambeau jutted out from the wall.

Between the time Bigot ordered the wine and the time the waiter returned with it, he commented on several different women who came within his view.

When the wine was brought, Bigot sampled it before he allowed the waiter to leave the bottle. "To all that we seek," Bigot toasted, lifting his glass.

"To that," Audubon responded.

"Suppose I were to tell you," Bigot said, looking over

his glass, "that in a short time I will be employed by the Prefecture of Police?"

Audubon raised his eyebrows.

And with a nod Bigot continued, "It will come to pass, and then it will be useful."

"Will it be soon?"

"Even if it were to happen tomorrow," Bigot explained, "it would not help us, at least not for many months. . . . But it will put me in contact with several important people."

Audubon scowled and said, "May I remind you that this is hardly a social matter?"

Bigot flushed and took a few moments to pour more wine into his glass before he trusted himself to speak again. "I have already gained the confidence of several people in high places," he said with satisfaction, "which will allow me to learn something about what is taking place behind the scenes in the Queen's trial."

"That may interest you," Audubon told him, "but it does not interest me. There is no hope for her. There is some hope for the Dauphin if we manage to get him out of the Temple."

"Captain," Bigot said acidly, "though I know you have difficulty believing it, take my word that in what we are about every connection is important. You yourself said the boy cannot be taken by force of arms."

"And that is still my opinion," Audubon responded. "I have made a very careful survey of the Temple since our last meeting. It cannot be done."

"I agree, but——" Bigot stopped abruptly and stood up.

An instant later Audubon saw Madame Berthoud. She was coming straight toward them and from the wild look on her face was about to raise a storm.

Audubon got to his feet.

"So at last I have found you!" she exclaimed when she was almost at the table. "You told me," Madame Berthoud all but hissed, looking at Bigot, "that he was dead. You told me Paul was dead."

"It was unwise," Bigot told her, striving to keep his voice calm, "to search me out."

"You lied to me!" she exclaimed, her voice going from a hiss to a shout that made several heads turn in their direction.

Bigot was about to say something, but Audubon spoke first and ordered her to sit down. "All right, Madame Berthoud," he said when all of them were seated, "who did he tell you was dead?"

"My husband," she answered in a cracked voice. "My husband. And he is very much alive," she said, glaring at Bigot. "But he—whoever he is—wanted me to believe—"

"Only that which you yourself wanted to believe," Bigot responded shortly.

Though Audubon understood the implication in Bigot's response, he found himself resenting the man for having done it. Perhaps it was because Bigot was an Englishman and the eventual prize was to have been a Frenchwoman?

"Now that we know your husband is alive," Bigot questioned, "what would you have us do, madame?"

"First," Audubon said, "because I think it is time to stop being mysterious, at least toward each other, Madame Berthoud, allow me to present Remy Bigot."

"That was foolish!" Bigot exclaimed with a sigh of disgust.

"Then consider me a foolish man," Audubon told him with a shrug, and turning his attention to Madame Berthoud, he asked how she had discovered that her husband was alive.

"From Citizen Freneau," she answered tightly, and though her voice became raspy with emotion several times, she managed to relate the essence of what had taken place between herself and Freneau.

"And you actually believe that man?" Bigot asked incredulously.

"I do not see that I have any choice," she said. "Besides, he did have a locket with my picture in it."

"He could have gotten hold of it through other hands than those of your husband."

"But did you ever know Paul?" Madame Berthoud suddenly asked, reaching across the table for Bigot's hands. "Did you ever know him?"

"No, madame," he answered after a few moments, "I never had the pleasure of meeting him."

She let go of his hands, and shaking her head, she whispered, "I could not let him die . . . I could not do that to Paul." Her eyes went from Bigot to Audubon, and she said, "I could not live with his death on my conscience."

Audubon nodded. He admired her stand; it revealed more character than he had given her credit for.

"You were wrong to lie to me," she said to Bigot, looking straight at him.

"We will discuss it another time, Nicole," he responded, using her given name for the first time.

She shook her head.

"Another time," Bigot repeated and then asked, "Did he tell you how he would be able to spare your husband?"

"Someone else was to take Paul's place," she answered.

"Someone else?" Audubon questioned.

She nodded and said, "Someone who resembles Paul. . . . But—" She hesitated and then haltingly told them, "I would not consent to let Freneau have his way with me unless he freed both of them . . . my husband and the man who was to die in his place."

"An excellent bargain!" Bigot exclaimed, rapping the table with his right hand.

"And hardly one that you can expect her to keep, Bigot," Audubon said, filled with an even greater admiration for Madame Berthoud than before.

"Which was exactly why, my dear Audubon," Bigot told him, "she sought us out. She never planned on keeping her side of the bargain. But frankly I do not see how she can afford not to, since the lives of two men are at stake, do you?"

"You are heartless!" Madame Berthoud exclaimed, starting to her feet.

"Sit down!" Audubon told her. "Running off is not going to accomplish anything, madame."

She sat down, and glaring resentfully at Bigot, she accused him of being perfidious.

"No, Nicole," he answered, "I am not. But neither will I risk the success of my mission by involving either myself or Captain Audubon in any way with Citizen Freneau. I am afraid you must attend your meeting with the gentleman and handle him to the best of your ability. . . . Have I made myself clear?"

"You want me to—"

"I am ordering you to handle Citizen Freneau," Bigot told her, "in whatever way suits your purpose. I cannot allow the question of your husband's freedom to jeopardize my mission."

"Perhaps," Audubon said in a perfectly normal voice, "I misunderstood what your purpose was, Bigot. . . . I was under the impression that you were to render me assistance."

"Exactly."

"But from what you told Madame Berthoud," Audubon told him, "I could easily come by the impression that we have switched roles. . . . That is to say, I came here to render you assistance, and you to—"

"Absolutely not."

"And you would agree that Madame Berthoud is part of our small group?"

"Of course."

"Then we must protect her, Bigot," Audubon said.

"But . . ."

Audubon shook his head.

"And what would you have us do, Captain?" Bigot questioned hotly.

"We must ensure that Citizen Freneau lives up to his part of the agreement without requiring Madame Berthoud to honor hers."

Bigot was silent. He finished his wine and poured another glass. Before he drank again he said, "The simplest and most direct way is to be there when he arrives."

"That is just to cross his bow," Audubon commented.

"And what more would you like?"

"Something that would put ropes on our friend Freneau," Audubon answered, "and allow us to use him—"

Bigot suddenly snapped his fingers. "Simon," he said in a low voice. "He knows Simon."

"Yes," Madame Berthoud answered.

"I think it would be a good idea," Bigot said, "if one of us got to know Simon, too."

"Is there anything else?" Audubon asked with a thin smile passing swiftly over his face.

"I will have to have a discussion with Freneau before I can answer that," Bigot responded.

"Are you sure he will free my husband and the other man?" Madame Berthoud asked.

Audubon nodded, and pointing to Bigot, said, "He will be at the prison when they are released. And I will be beside him."

"And once we free them," Bigot questioned after a

silence of several moments, "what will we do with them?"

"I do not want my husband to know——"

"No mention will be made of you, madame," Audubon told her, and looking at Bigot, he said, "They will be sent on their way to England."

Bigot looked as if he were about to object but kept silent and nodded.

"You had better leave now," Audubon said to her. "We will be along shortly."

"A remarkable woman," Bigot commented after Madame Berthoud was gone.

Audubon shrugged, and filling his pipe, began to smoke it. That he would soon meet her husband, the Marquis de St. Pierre, was putting him in a black mood, and he did not know why.

"There are still several things I would like to discuss with you," Bigot said as he and Audubon left the café.

"All right," Audubon answered, "but just let me tell you that what you do or do not do with Madame Berthoud in the future should not have any bearing on our other situation."

"Which was why," Bigot answered as they walked along the rue de Mail, "I did not think we should intervene."

"Would you have preferred that she submit to Freneau?" Audubon asked, unable to keep the quarrelsomeness out of his voice.

"We are men of the world, Captain," Bigot replied after a pause of a few moments. "She would have lost nothing that she had not lost several years ago, and we would not have been involved."

Audubon puffed on his pipe. He did not fully understand Bigot. The man obviously wanted Madame Berthoud for his own pleasure, and yet he was willing to let another use her for the same purpose.

"I think I know what is troubling you," Bigot told him.

"Oh?"

"Suppose I tell you," Bigot said, "of my passion for her?"

"You hardly need tell me that."

"But it is a passion, Captain," he said, "nothing more. I cannot afford the price of anything else, at least for the time that I follow my particular calling."

"Have you never truly loved a woman?" Audubon asked, removing the pipe from his mouth and clearing the bowl by knocking it against the palm of his hand.

"Have you?" Bigot responded swiftly.

"I have tried to," Audubon said with a shrug.

"Then that, Captain, is the real difference between us in this matter," Bigot commented. "I have never thought it worth my while even to try. I have enjoyed women—I daresay many of them—for the pleasure they gave me and some even for their wit. But I have loved none. . . . Perhaps in truth I am too fascinated by their infinite variety to think of ever being satisfied with one. . . . Come, come, Captain, you are a man of the same persuasion, or else your reputation plays you false?"

"I have had my experiences," Audubon said with a chuckle. "But I do not think I ever told a woman that her husband was dead to—"

"It was what she wanted to believe."

"So you said."

"Truly it was," Bigot told him. "And it did give me the instrument to use—"

"More like a double-edged sword," Audubon laughed.

"I will yet turn it to my purpose," Bigot commented.

"I do not doubt that you will try," Audubon said.

"I will indeed," Bigot assured him. "I will indeed."

16

Long before the two men reached the rue Saintonge, where Madame Berthoud lived, their conversation had taken several turns. Bigot had accepted the idea of using a barge to take the Dauphin away from Paris, once they had the boy out of the tower. Then, he had suggested that Audubon introduce him to Gouverneur Morris, the special agent from the American president to the government of France, explaining that, "Morris is rumored to be involved in aiding émigrés, and he has certain friends who might be of value to us."

"You mean to you," Audubon corrected.

"After you and the others are gone," Bigot said, "I will remain behind."

"Meaning, of course, that you will continue to serve your government."

"Delicately put, Captain," Bigot laughed. "Delicately put indeed. But present yourself to Morris within the next few days. You will find him at Meot's, a restaurant he seems to favor for dinner."

Audubon acceded to Bigot's request with a simple nod and without further comment.

"Shall we wait for Freneau outside?" Bigot asked as they approached the building where Madame Berthoud lived.

"I think it would be better," Audubon answered, "if we took him in her room. That way he could not deny his intent and we would have even more of a bludgeon than we would if we were to take him in the street."

Bigot agreed, and without any further conversation they entered the building and went quickly up the steps to Madame Berthoud's room.

Audubon was taken aback at the small size and meanness of the room. Madame Berthoud was nervous and paced back and forth from the window to the opposite blank wall. Bigot remained silent, though his eyes never left Nicole Berthoud, following her movement from one side of the room to the other.

The city bells tolled eleven, and just as they finished, there was the sound of footfalls on the steps. Audubon motioned to Bigot to remain flat against the wall while he himself would stand on the other side of the door, shielded by it, when Madame Berthoud opened it. And to her he whispered, "Do nothing that might arouse his suspicions."

"I will do my best," she replied in a low voice.

"I ask nothing more," he said, reaching back under his coat to draw a dirk.

Nicole looked at him uncertainly.

"It is a friend," he whispered with a smile and took his position. Almost immediately there was a soft rap at the door.

"It's Freneau," the voice announced.

Madame Berthoud glanced at Audubon.

He nodded.

There was another rap at the door, this one louder than the first.

"I am coming," Madame Berthoud answered.

Freneau laughed as the door was opened. Madame Berthoud took several steps back into the room. Freneau followed her and was about to say something when suddenly the door slammed shut. He turned just in time to see Audubon leap from his place.

In an instant the point of Audubon's dirk was at the side of Freneau's neck, and he said with cold dispassion, "Should you attempt to flee, citizen, your throat will be cut from ear to ear."

Trembling, Madame Berthoud moved away and stood by the window.

Bigot came forward. "Citizen Freneau, my friend and I understand you have a business arrangement with Madame Berthoud."

"We—I—" he stammered.

"You now have an arrangement with us," Audubon said.

"I have seen you before," Freneau questioned, looking at Bigot, "haven't I?"

"Perhaps," Bigot replied. "But whether you have seen me or not is of no consequence at this moment. We want the Marquis de St. Pierre and the man who was to die in his place."

"But how—"

"That, citizen, is your problem," Audubon answered, releasing his hold on Freneau's neck and lowering the dirk.

"You have the right to sign for certain prisoners," Bigot said. "You will sign for these two under the pretext of having them transferred from La Force to some other prison."

"And should I refuse?" Freneau questioned.

"You will die," Audubon said. "Slowly, very slowly."

Freneau nodded, and again looking at Bigot, he said, "You're. . . . You're the—"

Before the man could finish speaking, Bigot leaped in front of him, and smashing his hand against Freneau's face, silenced him. Then to Audubon he said, "I suggest that we take care of our business arrangement with Citizen Freneau."

Audubon put the knife to Freneau's back and told him to walk very slowly. "Should you decide to run, citizen," he said, "keep in mind that a well-thrown knife can outdistance you, and I happen to throw a knife very well indeed."

"God be with you," Madame Berthoud whispered as the trio left her room and started down the steps.

Less than an hour later they were outside the walls of La Force Prison on the rue des Droits de l'Homme.

"I will go inside with him," Bigot volunteered.

"I will be close behind you," Audubon said, "and as for our friend here, Citizen Freneau, do not do anything that might cost you your life."

"I am not foolish enough to die for any man," Freneau answered truculently.

"Just so that you mean what you say," Bigot told him, "there is a written account in a sealed envelope that tells of your scheme to substitute one prisoner for another. The envelope is presently in the hands of a certain Citizen

Gide, who has instructions to open it and read its contents should anything happen to me."

"I understand," Freneau said in a low voice.

Audubon did not understand, but it was neither the time nor the place to ask for explanations. Whoever Citizen Gide was, it was sufficient for the time being that Citizen Freneau was afraid of him.

They entered the grim anteroom of the prison, and Freneau went about signing the necessary papers that would release the two prisoners into his custody.

"And who will countersign the release papers?" the guard asked.

To Audubon's astonishment Bigot said, "I will."

"And who are you?" the guard questioned.

"A member of the Paris police," he said.

"Any proof of your identity?" the guard asked.

"Is my word good enough?" Freneau offered.

"As good as Samson's own," the man said, passing the documents to Bigot for his signature.

Several minutes later two men were brought blinking into the light of the anteroom. They could have been twins, and the guard remarked as much. They were younger than Audubon by five or more years, but because of their long incarceration they looked much older. The Marquis's eyes were blue, his lips sensual.

"Come along, you two," Freneau said, "I don't have all night to move you to your new home."

The two prisoners, flanked on one side by Bigot and the other by Freneau, moved slowly toward the door.

Audubon came up behind them and in a low voice said, "The faster you walk, men, the sooner you will be freed."

They started to turn.

"No," Audubon ordered, "just keep moving."

They quickened their pace, and a short while later the four of them were some distance from the prison. They stopped in a deserted street where not one light shone.

"Who are you?" the Marquis asked, looking at Audubon and Bigot.

"Tell them what they must know," Audubon said to Bigot.

"Please, gentlemen," Bigot asked, already moving into an even darker alley on the left side of the street, "will you follow me?"

"And when will you release me?" Freneau asked.

"Soon," Audubon replied. "Soon."

After a while Bigot came out of the darkness and announced that "the two men are on their way."

"Excellent!" Audubon exclaimed. "Now about Freneau—"

Bigot clapped his hand on Freneau's shoulder and said, "He will not cause any trouble."

"We must—"

Freneau suddenly stiffened and dropped to the ground.

"He is dead," Bigot told Audubon.

"But how—"

"I killed him," Bigot said, "or rather, this small pin tipped with curare did. He knew too much, Captain, much too much to be allowed to live."

17

The following morning Audubon and Joue sat in a café on the Place Michel. During the night the weather had changed, and the sharp bite of autumn was back in the air.

"Rain is on the way," Joue pronounced, indicating the upper portion of the window that held a fragment of leaden sky.

Without comment Audubon nodded. His experience with Bigot the previous night weighed heavily on him—indeed, so heavily that he had slept very little, and when he had, it had been a sleep beset by a myriad of disturbing dreams, none of which could he specifically remember but each of which had left sufficient residue to make him feel uneasy.

"How did your meetin' go last night?" Joue asked.

"The answer to that," Audubon replied, "would depend on one's point of view."

"That man—"

"His name," Audubon said, "is Remy Bigot."

Joue nodded and questioned whether Audubon and Bigot held different viewpoints.

"Decidedly," Audubon answered.

Joue shook his head but made no comment.

"He is a strange man," Audubon said with a sigh, "a very strange man." And then he lifted his mug and drank some of the coffee before he added, "Just when I think I am in control of a situation he does something to make me doubt that I ever was in control."

"If one of my men did that to me," Joue responded, "I'd

have to knock him about a bit until he learned who was in charge."

"I wish it were as simple as that," Audubon commented. "There is one kind of law aboard a ship and another kind of law on land. I am not sure which one is the better, but the one aboard a ship is straightforward and absolute . . . the one on land is neither. And this man Bigot is as shifty as any wind."

Joue broke a small roll and coated it with a thick layer of butter before he said, "If I were you, Captain, I wouldn't wait until the shifty wind blows into a storm."

"He is not the stormy type," Audubon told his first officer. "I would feel much easier if he were. . . . The trouble is, Joue, though he knows what I am doing, I cannot even begin to guess what he is doing, or what he will do. . . . He is like an iceberg: The danger is never from what is visible but is in what lies beneath the surface. Last night he killed a man, and when I took exception he told me that it was unnecessary for me to concern myself with such details."

"Did the man deserve killing?" Joue asked, breaking another roll and commencing to butter the halves the same way he had before.

"Last night when I took issue with Bigot about it," Audubon admitted, "I was positive that it was a senseless thing for him to have done, but now I am not sure."

With a shrug Joue said, "It's a bad thing, Captain, not to be sure."

Audubon had no choice but to agree; but to avoid any further explanation he did it silently with a nod. How could he possibly explain that it was Bigot's nonchalance that had disturbed him most.

Audubon finished his coffee and called for a second mug. The events of the previous night gave rise to several questions. . . .

Who was Gide?

And why was he so intent on meeting Gouverneur Morris?

Perhaps the most interesting enigma of all concerned Bigot's association with the Paris police. . . .

Audubon drank his second mug of coffee. As far as he was concerned, a shifting wind was not to be trusted, and though that was the conclusion he arrived at, he was at a loss to think of a way to protect himself and Joue from it. The best he might be able to do in any dire circumstance would be to kill Bigot before he killed him. Should it come to that, the Dauphin would be the loser, since alone neither one of them would be able to rescue the boy and transport him to safety. That much was quite clear to Audubon, and he wondered if Bigot saw the situation between them the same way.

"I've found someone who wants to sell his barge," Joue said as he began to eat the last roll on the table.

"How much?"

"A hundred livres."

"Is it sound?"

"Yes."

"Will he sell it to you?"

"No," Joue said. "I don't think he trusts a black man."

"He will when you show him your hundred livres," Audubon said. "Then he will not care what color you are. He will only see the color of the gold, and that will be all that matters. I tell you, Joue, if a man is a bastard, then it makes no difference whether he is a monarchist or revolutionary—he is still a bastard."

"I'll drink to that," Joue said, lifting his mug.

"You would drink to anything," Audubon responded.

"That's because practically anythin' is worth drinkin' to," Joue laughed.

"You are probably right," Audubon said, and lifting his coffee mug, he saluted him.

18

Bigot stood off to one side of the billiard room in the Little Tower inside the precincts of the Temple. The low-ceilinged room was about as long as it was wide. Two armchairs upholstered in blue-and-white Utrecht velvet stood on either side of a rosewood chiffonier. A large Boule desk had been pushed against one wall to make room in the center for a table and three chairs. The walls were decorated with several gilt-framed engravings, including two by Van Loo—the "Bain de Diane" and the "Coucher"—that Bigot recognized. There was a good-sized fire going in the hearth, and though the room had been quite cold when he and the other men had entered, it was rapidly becoming almost intolerably warm.

Most of the men stayed in the deeper shadows, preferring, it seemed to Bigot, to be spectators rather than participants in what would soon take place. But Citizens René Herbert and Pierre Chaumette were standing close to the table where the light from a single candle flickered uncertainly over their dissimilar forms.

Herbert was the shorter of the two and given to dressing like a dandy. His hands were very white and seldom still. Chaumette was not only taller, he was also broad-shouldered and handsome with classical features that were accentuated by black, flowing hair.

Both men were impatiently waiting for Simon to bring the Dauphin to them.

Gide had sent Bigot a message with Louise late that afternoon, counseling him to remain close to Chaumette or he would miss the opportunity to see at least part of the Temple for himself and have a firsthand look at the Dauphin; for despite Bigot's budding association with Simon, it had not yet reached the degree of ripeness that would have permitted him to ask the warder to be allowed to see the Dauphin. But Bigot's presence there with such influential men as Chaumette and Herbert would advance the value of his currency with Simon and might even provide the necessary leverage to move the warder from where he now stood to a more useful position. It was a possibility worth exploiting.

"I would rather be in a café than here," one of the men close to Bigot whispered. "I have an idea that what we have been called to witness is not going to sit well with me."

In a low voice Bigot said, "It must be done. . . ."

The man made a breathy sound but was obviously too put out to protest.

But from Gide, Bigot had learned that the Public Prosecutor, Fouquier-Tinville, had not been satisfied with the evidence against the Queen and had sent Herbert and Chaumette to procure what they could from the Dauphin to strengthen his case.

Simon's wife, Marie-Jeance, entered the room and set a decanter of wine and three glasses on the table. "Will there be anything else?" she asked loudly enough for everyone to hear.

"Nothing," Chaumette barked.

She tried to smile, failed, and hurriedly left the room.

Chaumette poured a bit of wine into two of the glasses, and then taking a small vial from his pocket, he emptied its contents into the wine that remained in the decanter. He passed the vessel to Herbert, who held it closer to the candlelight, studied it for a few moments, and with a strident laugh announced to the others, "That will help the little Capet to remember, so says Chaumette, our former medical student turned politician."

"He will remember everything you tell him to," Chaumette said with a nod.

"Let us hope so," Herbert responded. "Let us hope so." He set the decanter down on the table and faced the door.

The room had become uncomfortably hot, and several

of the men began to move from one place to another in the vain hope of finding a spot that would afford some relief from the heat.

But Bigot did not move. He had a perfect view of the table from where he stood and was not in the least bit willing to surrender it to someone else who would not have as much use for it as he had.

After a few minutes Herbert announced, "I think I hear them coming."

Several of the men complained of having to wait for the son of a whore, but Chaumette immediately silenced them as the door swung open and Simon entered the room, leading the Dauphin by the hand.

The child was rather thin, with large, intelligent green eyes, small, sensuous lips, and blond hair. He was quite pale.

Seeing the two men at the table, the child hesitated; but Simon gave the boy a none-too-gentle pull forward, telling him that the men had come to talk to him.

Bigot studied the boy. There was a startling resemblance between the child and Captain Audubon. There were some who claimed that the King had been unable to father children by the time Marie Antoinette had become pregnant with Louis Capet and that his real father had been her lover, Axel Fersen. But the boy did not resemble the Swedish nobleman as much as he looked like the man who would attempt to rescue him.

Bigot's lips curled into a half smile. Obviously there was some truth somewhere, or even some justice; but he for one could never think of where that *somewhere* would be. For him, and perhaps even for Captain Audubon, there was only the circumstance of the moment. . . .

Even as these cynical thoughts slithered through Bigot's mind he was very much aware of what was taking place at the table. The Dauphin was already seated, and Chaumette, too, had settled into a chair that he moved from its place in front of the boy to the side of the child. Herbert remained standing, his small, feminine face set in hard lines and beads of perspiration glistening on his forehead.

Chaumette looked up at Herbert and then with a nod asked, "What is your name?"

The Dauphin hesitated. His eyes darted to Simon, and

then in a small, fragilely piping voice he answered, "Citizen Louis Capet."

Simon grinned broadly and said, "That was the first thing I taught him. . . . I tell you it took some doin'. . . . Every time he'd give the wrong answer I'd give him the back of my hand."

Herbert glared at the warder but said nothing.

"Do you know who we are?" Chaumette questioned, gesturing to Herbert and then back toward himself.

The Dauphin nodded.

"Are you afraid of us?"

The child took a few moments to think, his eyes moving from Chaumette to Herbert and then back to Chaumette before he slowly shook his head.

By asking all sorts of questions Chaumette slowly put the child at ease, and from this interlude Bigot learned that the Dauphin had a passion for birds—he was allowed to keep many in cages in his room—and seemed to possess a talent, even at his young age, for drawing. The King had also possessed more than a hint of these two characteristics.

"Get on with it!" Herbert suddenly exclaimed.

"Perhaps," Chaumette answered, "you might do better since you have children of your own?"

Stung and flushing, Herbert accepted the challenge by picking up the decanter of wine and pouring some into a glass that he proffered to the boy, saying, "Here, little one, drink this and you will sleep like an angel." He smiled as he spoke and leaned close to the child.

Chaumette moved away from the table, stood up, and walked toward where Bigot was standing. "Do you mind, citizen," he asked, "if I share this spot with you?"

"Not in the least," Bigot answered, and taking a risk, he added, "Perhaps we can console each other?"

Chaumette looked at him for several moments and then asked, "Bigot, is it not?"

"Yes," Bigot answered, and then with a smile he said, "I never did have the proper opportunity to thank you for—"

Chaumette waved him silent and whispered, "What you did was appreciated."

Bigot nodded and wondered just how much of the two thousand livres he had paid to Gide ever wound up in

Chaumette's hands. Perhaps half?

"It is the child," Chaumette said, gesturing toward the table, "who needs some consolation, not us."

Bigot made no reply, but his heart began to pound. His relationship with Chaumette was going to prove more interesting than he had ever suspected it would. . . .

"Have another glass," Herbert said to the Dauphin when the child had just about finished his first.

"You will have him asleep," Chaumette called out, "before. . . ."

"I will handle this in my own way," Herbert screamed back.

"All of you," Chaumette said, stepping out of the shadows to address the others, "have heard the Deputy Prosecutor. The information he obtains is his and his alone. I will sign as a witness but not as one of the interrogators."

"I will accept full responsibility for the interrogation," Herbert shrilled, and turning his attention to the Dauphin, he asked, "Do you play with yourself?"

A murmur flowed out of the deep shadows where the other men stood, but Herbert disregarded it and repeated the question.

"I do not know what you mean," the boy said.

"Do you pet your tool?"

The boy looked at Simon, and the warder said, "I caught him at it, citizen, many times, and each time I beat him."

"Louis Capet, do you handle your penis?" Herbert pressed.

"Yes."

"And your mother taught you to do that?" Herbert said.

"Yes," the Dauphin said, "My mother—"

"You go too far," one of the witnesses objected.

"To convict a Queen, citizen," Herbert answered, "one must be willing to go to the moon and back again, or even to hell itself."

"And that is where we are this night," Chaumette whispered to Bigot. "We are in hell."

"You have seen your mother naked?" Herbert told the boy.

The Dauphin repeated that he had.

"She was with a man who was also naked?"

The boy nodded.

"Name him."

"I cannot remember."

Herbert supplied the Dauphin with names that included the Comte d'Artois and Axel Fersen. And then he asked, "And your mother taught you how to put your penis in her body?"

"My mother taught me how," the Dauphin answered.

"And sometimes there were other women in bed with you and your mother?"

"Other women, too," the child answered with a big yawn.

Herbert patted the boy on the head and said, "Now you can sleep like an angel, just like an angel. . . ."

19

It took several days for the story of Freneau's death to appear in the evening editions of the newspapers. Herbert's *L'Amie du Peuple* and *Le Père Duchesne* carried stories broadly hinting that the executioner's demise might not have been due to natural causes. From anonymous sources they had subsequently learned that the deceased had last been seen in the company of two men. The articles went on to probe the political significance of Freneau's death and naturally came to conclusions critical of Robespierre and his supporters.

Madame Berthoud's reaction to the news of Freneau's death was a mixture of surprise, incredulity, and heightened fear. She had not anticipated that Freneau would be killed. Frightened, yes. But not murdered . . .

She did not want to be responsible for killing anyone, even an evil man like Freneau. And though she wanted desperately to ask Audubon or Bigot what had happened once they had secured the freedom of her husband and the other man, she was absolutely certain that neither one would tell her anything.

Of the two men, Madame Berthoud concluded, Audubon would have been more likely to kill than Bigot, since he would be the one whose temper would require very little provocation to manifest itself in an act of violence.

Once home from the Temple, Madame Berthoud spent most of the evening doing those chores that were required

to keep her small room neat and clean. Then she undressed and took a great deal of time washing her body
with hot water and soap, though soap was very scarce and
from what she had recently heard would soon be almost
impossible to buy. When she was done with her ablutions
she slipped a clean white cotton nightgown over her head
and climbed into bed.

Tired, she closed her eyes and almost immediately de-
scended into the depths of sleep, but almost as soon as she
fell asleep, so it seemed to her, she was awakened by a per-
sistent knocking at her door. She opened her eyes and
frowned, more from a feeling of chagrin than anything
else. It was very late, probably past midnight, and she
would have to be up by first light to be at the Temple for
her work.

The knocking became louder, more demanding.

Suddenly she bolted upright, then, swept by fear, shrank
back against the headboard. She tried to find her voice but
could not. Enveloped by a cold sweat, she began to tremble. That the police might have discovered her involvement
in a plot to rescue the Dauphin was too terrifying to contemplate.

"Nicole?"

Who would use. . . . "Bigot?" she whispered.

"Nicole?" he called again.

Clearing her throat, she asked, "What do you want?"

"Open the door," he told her.

She hesitated.

"Open the door," Bigot repeated.

"All right," she answered. "All right." And leaving the
bed, she padded to the door. "You nearly frightened me
out of my wits," she said as soon as he was inside the
room.

Bigot went to the table and turned up the lamp.

"Is anything wrong?" she asked, suddenly full of fear
again.

He shook his head.

She studied him and said, "You do not look well."

"I have been worse," he said dryly.

"And what is that supposed to mean?" she questioned.

He stood at the window looking out at the night sky and
told her in a low voice, "If I look ill, it is because I am,

though not with any known physical malady."

"You are not making any sense," she said impatiently.

"Have you anything to drink?"

"Wine . . ."

"Something stronger?"

"Brandy."

"That will do," he told her.

She fetched the bottle from the closet and poured him a drink.

He drank most of it in two huge swallows, hardly pausing between one and the other.

"Now will you tell me why you're here?" she asked.

"To see you, Nicole," he responded, looking at her.

Suddenly she realized that she was wearing nothing more than a nightdress and that it not only exposed the tops of her breasts but was transparent when she stood in front of the low fire in the hearth.

"I came to see you," he told her in a low voice, "just to assure myself that everything is not ugly and there are a few things left in the world that a man might touch without feeling sullied."

Before she could reply, his arms were around her and he was pressing her to him.

"Are you still angry with me, Nicole?" he asked, moving his hand through her hair.

How could she answer that with his arms around her so and the scent of him filling her nostrils?

"I came to you," he whispered, "because I needed you."

Intuitively Nicole understood he had seen something that had deeply troubled him, and she asked him if he wanted to tell her about it.

He shook his head, and again telling her that he needed her, he pressed his lips to hers. His kiss was delightfully warm, and encircling his neck with her arms, Nicole gave herself up to the voluptuousness of his embrace. He moved his hands over her breasts, bringing her nipples to full bud. And then he slipped the nightdress off her shoulders, letting it drift to the floor. Naked, she was swept into his arms and set down on the bed.

"Nicole," he whispered, settling down next to her after hurriedly taking off his clothes.

She moved her hands over his nakedness and reveled in

the touch of his body. It had been so long since she had been with a man, so long since a man's warmth had mingled with her own, that she often despaired of ever again knowing the joy of it.

"You are lovely," he told her.

She felt his hands skim over her breasts, touching her nipples ever so lightly and then moving down her stomach to the thatch of her womanhood.

She sighed with pleasure, and finding his sex, she pressed it against her body.

He kissed her breasts, her neck, and without any embarrassment buried his face between her naked thighs.

Her body flooded with exquisite sensations, waves of feeling that rushed over her more and more urgently as his tongue probed her body until she moaned and thrashed about in a world of brilliant yellows and hot reds that seemed to flow out of the depths of her womb and pass before her closed eyes.

Bigot raised himself, and sliding between her open thighs, he entered her body.

Nicole uttered a deep sigh of contentment and told him, "You do not know how much I have longed for this to happen, Remy."

He repeated his own first name with a chuckle and slowly began to move.

She followed his motions, thrusting herself against him with wild abandon. His hands were on her breasts and then under her buttocks.

"Remy," she whispered, "oh, Remy!"

He sucked on her nipples, rolling one then the other between his teeth.

The tension in her became almost unbearable. She whimpered in ecstasy, and then suddenly something deep inside her body gave way. Shudder after shudder coursed through her, and she cried out, "Love me. . . . Love me. . . . Please love me!"

Bigot did not answer but rode her a few moments more until with a deep, guttural sound he announced the imminence of his own passionate climax.

The very next instant Nicole felt the hot surge pour into her. And that, too, thrilled her.

"Do you love me?" she asked when they finally separated and lay calmly side by side.

"I appreciate you," he said, touching her bare breast. "I appreciate you."

"And what of love?" she asked in a small voice.

"A man in my calling," he told her, "cannot love, at least not the way you mean it."

"Then you came here just to use me," she accused, moving out of his reach.

"No, Nicole," he responded, encircling her naked body with his arm. "I came here to be with you, and as you see, I am very much with you."

With a sad sigh she acquiesced to her own desires, and by moving back into his embrace, silently agreed to become his mistress.

20

"I am so pleased that you could come," Gouverneur Morris said. His French was quite good, Audubon noted as Morris limped toward him. A tall man with a somewhat large nose and a humorous but firm mouth turned down at the corners, Morris was a virile, attractive man whose bachelor bed seldom lacked a woman.

"It is a pleasure to see you again, Governor," Audubon responded, shaking his host's hand.

"Come now," the American laughed, patting Audubon's arm, "there is no need for two old friends to be so formal. We have the right to address one another by our given names. I had hoped you would be able to accept my invitation. You were the last person I expected to see at Meot's the other night."

Audubon nodded and looked past his friend into the room, which was huge—even for the salon of a house on the fashionable rue de la Planche. There were perhaps fifty or sixty people standing about, and there was still enough room left to fit double the number comfortably. Two enormous crystal chandeliers emblazoned with hundreds of candles illuminated the entire room, and a large hearth provided generous warmth against the blasts of cold wind that rattled the windows. Servants were everywhere busily dispensing food and drink.

Morris turned, and gesturing toward the other guests, he said with a characteristic mocking laugh, "This is a far cry from the times we knew together, eh?"

And Audubon responded, "Hardly the rough linsey-woolsey we used to wear."

Morris clapped his friend on the back and guffawed. "Come," he said. "I see some of my guests are wondering who you are."

The two men advanced into the room, and suddenly a woman exclaimed, "I thought my eyes were playing tricks on me, Captain Audubon."

"Madame de Beauharnais," Audubon said, turning to her. "What a pleasure to see you again." Joséphine's face was still doll-like, with small, delicately chiseled features and a full, sensuous mouth. For an instant he could not help but recall what an eager lover she had been during the long voyage from Martinique to France. There were fewer lines on her face then, and though she had already given birth to two children, she had been as wanton with him as if she had been no more than a woman of the streets.

"I had no idea you knew each other," Morris commented.

"Madame de Beauharnais and I," Audubon explained, "are old friends. . . . Her former home was Martinique, one of the islands I frequently visited."

A third man came toward them. He was tall, lean, and quite handsome, though his complexion had a decided yellow cast. "Tell me, Joséphine," he questioned, "what are you up to now?"

She laughed, and waving her closed fan at him, she said, "Citizen Barras, this is an old friend of mine, Captain Jean Audubon."

The two men shook hands.

"Perhaps," Joséphine de Beauharnais suggested, "we will have an opportunity to chat about old times."

"It would be my pleasure," Audubon answered.

Barras slipped his arm around Joséphine's waist, and looking fiercely at Audubon, he said, "Will you excuse us? A friend of mine is waiting for us before he tells his funny story."

"Do let us talk, Jean?" she said.

"We most certainly will," he answered, looking steely-eyed at Barras.

The two men nodded to each other, and Barras whisked

Joséphine off to the side of the room, where they melded into a small group of guests.

"He is a very possessive man," Morris explained as they started to walk again.

"Who is he?"

"Paul Barras. You mean you do not know him?"

"The name is familiar, but—"

"He is a member of the Committee of Public Safety. He was a viscount but went over to the other side when he saw that the Revolution had to come."

"And his relationship with her?"

"Obvious, is it not?"

"Yes," Audubon answered. "But where is her. . . ."

Morris drew his finger across his neck.

"I had no idea," Audubon commented. For some peculiar reason he was touched by Alexandre de Beauharnais's death. Perhaps it was because Joséphine had once told him as they lay naked in his berth that her husband was an ineffectual man, in and out of bed.

"It is hard to keep track of all those who—" Morris broke off abruptly and propelled Audubon toward a man who was standing with his back to the window. "That is Citizen Talleyrand. . . . Perhaps he is the most interesting in the room, with the exception, of course, of the two of us."

Audubon shook hands with Talleyrand, who asked him if he knew Barras.

"He knows Joséphine," Morris said, speaking for his friend.

"Then I would be wary of Barras," Talleyrand counseled. "Even now he is looking at you. . . . No, do not turn around to see. . . . Take my word for it that you have already stirred his curiosity, to say nothing of his enmity if Joséphine was foolish enough to mention your name to him before he ever set eyes on you."

Audubon managed a smile and said, "I myself, citizen, would bless their union."

"And perhaps," added Morris with mischievous lasciviousness, "take pleasure in looking upon it."

The three of them laughed, and Morris suggested they drink together.

"Another time," Talleyrand said with a wry smile. "Now

I am busily engaged in my continuous study of human nature."

Morris and Audubon continued to move around the room, pausing now and then for the host to introduce Audubon as "his old and dear friend." Though the men shook his hand and the women smiled at him, Audubon sensed their mistrust, and he finally said, "I think it would be better if I did not meet any more people. . . . I seem to make them uneasy."

"Shall we drink then?" Morris asked.

"Yes," Audubon answered, "I think that is what I would like to do now." That he was there was, as far as he was concerned, the end result of Bigot's insistence that he renew his acquaintance with Gouverneur Morris, and he heartily resented it. Nothing was there that could possibly be of interest to him or to Bigot.

Morris took two glasses of wine from a tray carried by one of the servants, and handing one to Audubon, he asked, "What shall we drink to?"

With a shake of his head Audubon told him, "You make the toast."

"To France," Morris said.

Audubon smiled, and touching his host's glass, drank.

"Now," Morris said, "tell me what an old sea dog like you is doing in Paris."

"I came for a commission. . . ."

"I might be able to help," Morris offered.

"No, no," Audubon said, "I already have an advocate for my petition."

Morris cocked his head to one side and told him, "But a word from Barras or some of the other people on the Committee—"

Audubon waved the suggestion aside and assured Morris that his commission would be granted momentarily.

They finished their wine, and Morris exchanged the empty goblets for two that were filled. "Now you must toast," he insisted.

Audubon toasted the United States.

"And now," Morris told him, "having fulfilled my duties as a host, I am going to leave you to your own devices. Sometime before midnight the dining room will be opened and a buffet supper served."

"I am sure I will get on very well," Audubon said.

Morris nodded, and limping, drifted away to mingle with some of his other guests.

Audubon had no intention of remaining until midnight. Had he been able to, he would have left immediately, but consideration for his friend's feelings prevented him from acting and he remained standing in one place for a considerable length of time.

Perhaps because Joséphine was the only person other than Morris that he knew, or perhaps because he saw Barras look at him from time to time and he was disinclined to be frightened of any man, even as powerful a man as Barras, Audubon drifted across the room until he stood at the periphery of the group surrounding Joséphine and her new lover.

Barras was laughingly telling his audience, "Citizen Herbert was too out of sorts to accept Gouverneur Morris's invitation. But who could blame him after his rebuke from Robespierre? Imagine yourselves in his position. . . . The poor man goes to the Temple at Fouquier's behest and extracts a confession from Louis-Charles Capet that will surely put his mother's head on the guillotine and, mind you, argues with Chaumette while he is there, only to have Robespierre shout about him, 'That fool . . . It is not enough that Antoinette should be a Messalina. That idiot must make her Agrippina.' Poor, poor Herbert, how he must be suffering."

Everyone laughed, and then someone wanted to know what the boy had told Herbert.

But Barras shook his finger at him and said, "That I cannot tell you, but if you happen to know enough ancient history you will remember that Agrippina lay with her son."

A gasp of disbelief burst from his audience.

Barras shrugged, and looking straight at Audubon, he asked, "What do you think about that, Captain?" There was a smile on his handsome face but a challenge in his tone.

"I would think," Audubon said slowly, "that I am in no position to have any thoughts on the matter."

The smile left Barras's face, and he asked, "Do you think Marie Antoinette capable of such—"

"Perhaps," interrupted Audubon, "your question would be better put to a woman than a man since another woman might give you a more honest answer than I."

Barras's yellowish complexion became slightly suffused with a reddish tinge. "Tell us, Captain," he asked, "what do you think you are in a position to tell us?"

Audubon smiled and answered, "About the sea, about ships, and perhaps something about the men who sail them. . . . I have spent a lifetime at sea, citizen, which is substantially longer than—"

"Captain," a woman called from directly behind him, "the only ship Citizen Barras knows anything about is the ship of state, and that kind of knowledge hardly qualifies him to know anything about real ships and the men who sail them."

She spoke with a light laugh on her lips that made all within hearing laugh, too.

Barras graciously admitted that what the lady had said was true.

Audubon, too, agreed with her, and turning, he saw she was smiling at him. . . . He also saw that she was physically well-fashioned, with ample breasts bared to the nipples by the cut of the blue off-the-shoulder gown she wore. Her waist was narrow and her hips wide. Her eyes were brown and heavy-lidded. She had mink-colored hair, a small mouth, a strong chin, and a graceful neck.

She nodded to him and said, "I would so like a glass of wine, Captain."

"And in exchange," he asked, "would you give me your name?"

"Madame Adèle Flahaut," she told him.

"Jean Audubon," he said.

"The wine, Monsieur Audubon, please?"

"The wine," he repeated with a laugh and went off to fetch it.

21

Audubon lit his pipe and sent a narrow white column of smoke toward the low ceiling. Impatiently he asked Joue, "Do you see Bigot?"

"Not yet, Captain," his first officer answered.

"Blast that man," Audubon complained. "He either comes up on you and takes you unawares or he is late." He was annoyed with the constant din in the place.

Joue shrugged.

"I tell you, Joue, and I will tell him, too, when I see him, I resent both methods of—"

"He has just entered," Joue said, looking toward the large front door.

Bigot threaded his way through the café's tables until he reached Audubon's. Then he summoned a waiter and asked for another glass and some cheese.

When Bigot was finally seated he smiled at Audubon and said, "I am sorry that I kept you waiting, but a police matter required my attention."

Audubon said nothing.

Bigot turned his attention to Joue and asked, "Have you purchased the barge yet?"

"He has," Audubon answered. "We will move our belongings there tomorrow."

Bigot shook his head.

"And why not?" Audubon answered.

"You must stay where you are, on the rue Hyacinthe," Bigot told Audubon. "Joue will move to the barge, but I think it would be wiser for him to make as many trips up and down the river as possible before we use it to transport another kind of cargo."

Audubon looked to Joue for his consent.

"I'll do whatever you say, Captain," the man said.

Audubon nodded.

"Then that is settled!" Bigot exclaimed with evident satisfaction. "Now what have you to tell me about your soirée at Gouverneur Morris's house the other night?"

"There is not much to tell," Audubon responded, "except that Citizen Barras said that Herbert had incurred Robespierre's displeasure by obtaining a confession from the Dauphin that would surely destroy the Queen."

Rubbing his chin, Bigot asked, "Did he reveal the nature of the confession?"

"That she was mistress to her own son," Audubon answered.

"Interesting," Bigot commented, never betraying that he had been witness to the event Barras had spoken about.

"Barras took an intense dislike to me," Audubon said.

"Oh, you had words with him?"

The waiter came to the table with Bigot's glass and cheese.

"Over a woman," Audubon said as soon as the waiter was out of earshot. "I was acquainted with his current mistress, Joséphine de Beauharnais." And he explained that he had had business dealings with Joséphine's family before she had become Madame de Beauharnais.

Bigot listened and surmised that Audubon had had dealings other than business with the woman and that she had foolishly given Barras some intimation of it.

"I remember her," Joue said when Audubon had finished. "She was a real beauty."

"She still is," Audubon told him.

"And her husband? Where is he?"

"Guillotined."

Bigot was quiet for several minutes. His sources had revealed that Barras was in close communication with Fouché. They might well be laying the groundwork for stronger opposition to Robespierre. He cast his eyes on Audubon and asked, "What kind of woman is this Joséphine?"

Audubon shrugged.

"Do you think she can be trusted?"

"It depends on what you would trust her with," Audubon answered.

"I would like an introduction to her," Bigot told him.

Audubon was about to protest, but Bigot said, "I must remind you again that once you leave Paris I will remain behind and there will be a great many things that I must attend to. Madame de Beauharnais might make my work easier, especially if she holds some sway over Barras."

"I will see that you meet her," Audubon replied.

"I will meet Barras through other channels," Bigot said and then asked, "And was there anyone else of interest there?"

"A Monsieur Talleyrand."

"He too, eh?" Bigot exclaimed.

"He was there," Audubon said, "but from what I could see he had practically nothing to do with the other guests."

"I would not be too sure about that," Bigot said.

Audubon looked at him questioningly, but Bigot did not elaborate. Instead he again asked, "Was there anyone else?"

"No one of any consequence."

"I assure you, my dear Captain," Bigot told him, "a person who may seem of little or no consequence now could easily develop into someone of inestimable consequence at a later date."

Audubon ground the pipe bit between his teeth. He was not about to reveal his newly made friendship with Madame Adèle Flahaut.

"But if you say," Bigot told him, "that you had no other encounters of any consequence, then naturally I must take your word for it."

"So that is the way the wind blows," Audubon commented, taking the dead pipe from his lips.

It was Bigot's turn to look at him questioningly.

Audubon shook his head.

"And what is that for?" Bigot asked.

"Do not trifle with me," Audubon told him in a level voice. "You know exactly what took place at Morris's house."

"Only from an observer," Bigot admitted with a hint of

a smile playing on his lips. "It is always much better to have a report from a participant."

Audubon nodded, but the very next instant his arm shot across the small table. Before Bigot could offer any resistance Audubon had grabbed hold of him by the front of his coat, pulling him to his feet and halfway across the table, upsetting the glasses and wine bottle.

Those customers who saw what was happening leaped to their feet and crowded around the table while Bigot, twisting and turning like a hooked fish, smiled and said in an unsteady voice to those who had surrounded them, "A wager, citizens, a wager between friends." He looked imploringly at Audubon.

"A wager," Audubon growled, releasing his hold on Bigot.

"You see," he explained, "it was nothing more than a wager, and my friend has won it."

The spectators moved slowly back to their own tables.

"I warned you," Audubon said, "never to have me followed."

"You were not followed," Bigot answered, adjusting his coat and jacket.

"Then how did you know—"

"Because," Bigot told him sharply, "it is my business to know." And pointing a thin finger at Audubon, he said, "It is also my business to warn you to be careful of what you say to Madame Flahaut."

"And why the warning?"

"Be careful," Bigot told him. "Do what you will with her, but do not give her any reason to suspect your real reason for being in Paris."

With a grimace Audubon asked, "Then her intervention on my behalf was—"

"Suggested by Talleyrand," Bigot said. "He is her lover, or one of them. . . . I repeat, do what you will with her, but do not do or say anything that would betray your purpose, Captain."

Audubon swore under his breath.

"There is something else we might as well settle right now."

Audubon nodded.

"Once you have the boy," Bigot told him, warily

watching for the slightest movement that would betray Audubon's intention to haul him across the table again, "you will rendezvous with a British frigate and deliver the child into the hands of the captain."

Audubon's eyes went wide with surprise. It took several tries for him to find his voice, and when he finally did, he asked, "Why was I not told of this before?"

"I have just received word about it," Bigot said with a shrug. So far Audubon was not showing any signs of an imminent display of violence.

"Word from whom?"

"My superiors."

"From General Charette?"

"I am sure he was informed," Bigot said.

"I do not like it," Audubon told him, chewing on the stem of his pipe, "I do not like it in the least. Our countries are at war."

"True enough," Bigot answered. "But we are fighting the revolutionaries, not those who are our friends. Your people in Vendée are fighting them, too."

"Am I your friend, Bigot?" Audubon asked.

"I can very well ask the same question."

"And I would answer," Audubon said, "with a simple 'no.' We are not friends."

"Enemies then?"

Audubon shook his head and told him, "I would rather say that we are poorly matched—"

"Regardless of what we are," Bigot interrupted, "what difference does it make as long as we successfully conclude our enterprise?"

"If you were in my place," Audubon questioned, "would you be so willing to do what your orders ask me to?"

"England will return the Dauphin to France," Bigot said. "Your people will be given the rightful heir to the throne."

"And do you care about that, Bigot?"

Bigot smiled and said, "Only in as much as it is my assignment. Like yourself I am a professional."

Audubon nodded, and looking straight at Bigot, he said in a low voice, "But I am also a Frenchman."

"Which is exactly why," Bigot responded smoothly, "you should see what England intends to do."

"I do indeed see what England intends to do," Audubon said with a smile. "Believe me, Bigot, I do indeed see that England would like to govern France, or at least the Royalist part of it, through the Dauphin."

Bigot gestured with his hands and said, "That is a political matter, and I am not a political man."

Audubon shook his head but did not speak.

22

Audubon had no clear understanding of why he chose to attend the Queen's trial. Perhaps it was because Joue was already working on the barge and he was alone and bored; or it might have been that he was seeking something to distract him from thinking about Madame Flahaut, who was very much in his thoughts; could it also have been simple curiosity about the mother of the Dauphin?

The trial took place in the Hall of Liberty, formerly the Grand Chamber of Parliament, in the Palais de Justice, a huge structure with the cathedral of St. Chapelle a part of it. The walls of the trial room were newly decorated with various paintings depicting the rights of man. These replaced the tapestries and paintings that had previously hung there.

The gallery was crowded with spectators, many of whom had gained something of a reputation as sansculottes. And there was a large deputation of those harpies, the *tricoteuses,* who spent most of their time at the Place de la Révolution knitting while watching the guillotine do its work.

A carnival-like atmosphere prevailed in the dimly lit chamber before the prisoner was brought in. The many bawdy exchanges among the spectators in the gallery indicated how much the people knew about the Widow Capet's former amours.

Shortly before eight o'clock, the President of the Court, Armand Hermann, took his place at a table whose legs were carved griffins.

The three judges joined him at the table; one was Coffunbal, a former clerk, a former errand boy, a former police officer, a former lawyer, and a former doctor. The second was the former deputy, Deliege, who wore a wig and was alleged to be the bastard son of Louis XV. And the third judge was a man named Donze-Verteuil, who was past sixty and whose fat round face practically obscured his small mouth.

There was a pause of several minutes before Fouquier-Tinville entered carrying a portmanteau. His appearance immediately brought silence to the room. He was a big, strong-looking man with a bull-like neck and broad shoulders. His hair was dark and smooth. His face was full and pitted with smallpox scars. He had a high forehead, a Roman nose, and pronouncedly arched eyebrows.

Without looking at the judges or the spectators, Fouquier went to his simple desk, sat down, and immediately began studying the papers he had brought with him.

At eight o'clock the Queen was brought into the courtroom. Instantly a low murmur, like the sigh of a winter wind lost under the eaves, came from all parts of the gallery.

Audubon leaned forward. Though she was only thirty-seven, the Queen's hair was completely white and her complexion pallid. She was very thin; because her face was so sunken she looked like a sad old woman. She wore a simple black dress, and by adding "weepers" to a lawn bonnet and fixing a crepe veil under it, she had provided herself with a widow's headdress.

The guards escorted the Queen to a small platform where an armchair had been placed so that she could be seen by everyone in the court.

Claude Chauveau-Lagarde and Tronson du Couray, the Queen's lawyers, stood on either side of her. Chauveau-Lagarde was famous for having defended Charlotte Corday, Marat's assassin, some months before.

While the witnesses took the oath the Queen remained standing. By Audubon's count, forty-one people were there to testify against her.

Finally the court usher addressed Marie Antoinette. "The accused may be seated," he told her. "Now state your name, surname, age, position, place of birth, and residence."

And she answered in a calm voice, "My name is Marie Antoinette Lorraine d'Autriche, aged about thirty-eight, widow of the King of France, born in Vienna. At the time of my arrest I was in the session hall of the National Assembly."

Fabricuis, the court clerk, then looked toward Fouquier, the Public Prosecutor, who said in a low but very distinct voice, "You may read the indictment against the Widow Capet."

The indictment was eight pages long, and Fabricuis's voice was barely audible, though Audubon was sure the Queen was able to hear it quite plainly.

Throughout the reading, the Queen looked distracted to him, almost as though she were listening to something she had heard previously, and he noticed, as he was sure others did, that she moved her fingers on the arm of her chair as if she were playing the pianoforte.

As soon as Fabricuis had finished, Citizen Hermann announced, "This is what you are accused of. Pay careful attention. You will now hear the charges brought against you."

The first witness was called. He was a former linen draper and presently a deputy to the Convention. He gave a detailed account of the feasts and orgies that had taken place in the town of Versailles among the Queen's guard.

The Queen told the court that she had no knowledge of the facts presented to the court by the witness.

As witness followed witness to the stand, Audubon soon realized that Marie Antoinette was being tried for things she might have been guilty of as well as those imputed to her by rumor. By clever maneuvering Fouquier made it seem that the Queen was guilty of sending French gold to Austria, that she was a Lesbian, and that all her children were bastards.

Fouquier pressed her to answer his questions without giving her time to think.

Chauveau-Lagarde tried desperately hard to defend the Queen, pleading with the Public Prosecutor to give the accused time to speak. But Fouquier brushed the plea aside with a wave of his hand and demanded to know, "Where did you get the money to have the Petit Trianon built and furnished? It must have cost an enormous sum."

This time the Queen responded quickly. "Perhaps it cost

more than I had expected. The expenses for it grew rapidly."

Fouquier gave a loud, disdainful cough that immediately precipitated a flurry of laughter from the gallery.

As the morning wore on, a great many of the spectators became restive and the *tricoteuses* shouted for the accused to remain standing when she answered the questions put to her, so that they would not miss anything. But the President of the Court threatened them with expulsion if they did not remain quiet.

And then Fouquier summoned Herbert to testify against the Queen.

Audubon studied the man. He did not look any more or less evil than anyone else.

Herbert cleared his throat, and then in a high-pitched voice he told the court of his suspicions about Toulan, one of the guards at the Temple, who in his opinion had been too sympathetic to the Widow Capet. He said that he had found many counter revolutionary articles in her personal belongings. Then he accused the Queen of defiling her own son, detailing the young Capet's confession, made in front of witnesses. Herbert named those who were with him on the night of October 6.

Audubon almost jumped to his feet when Herbert mentioned Bigot's name.

Herbert went on to say, "There is reason to believe that this criminal intercourse was not dictated by pleasure but in the calculated hope of enervating the boy, who they still thought was destined to occupy the throne and whom they wished to dominate morally as a result of their scheme. As a result of the efforts he was forced to make he suffered a hernia. But since he has been taken from his mother his constitution has become robust."

The President asked the accused, "What reply do you have to this deposition?"

Her voice trembling, the Queen replied, "I have no knowledge of the incidents of which Herbert speaks."

The President was not going to pursue the matter, but one of the jurors rose and said, "Citizen President, would you draw the attention of the accused to the fact that she has not answered the charge made by Citizen Herbert on the subject of what passed between her and her son?"

A look of displeasure passed over the President's face.

He even shook his head, but finally he turned to the Queen and repeated his question.

The Queen slowly got to her feet, looked at Herbert, then at Fouquier, and finally, turning to the gallery, she cried, "If I did not reply, it was because nature recoils from such an accusation against a mother." And then, flinging her arms out toward the spectators, she shouted, "I appeal to all who are mothers in this room!"

The effect of her appeal was instantaneous. People were shouting, "Bravo . . . Bravo . . ." Others were clapping and stamping their feet, even some of the *tricoteuses* were shouting their approval. Carried away by the enthusiasm of those near him, Audubon, too, shouted his approbation.

For a few moments the session had to be suspended. But when order had been restored, the President of the Court began a line of questioning that tangentially touched on the royal family's flight from Paris and subsequent capture at Varennes.

Silence fell over the gallery.

To Audubon it seemed as though everyone in the room was holding his breath, himself included.

And then the President asked, almost nonchalantly, "Who provided you, or caused to be provided, the famous carriage in which you went away with your family?"

"It was a foreigner," the Queen answered.

"Of what nation?"

"Sweden."

"Was it not Axel Fersen, who was living in Paris in the rue du Bac?"

"Yes," she answered.

Practically en masse the people in the gallery breathed freely and engaged in derisive comments. It was obvious that the sympathy the Queen had gained by her emotional appeal to the mothers in the room she had now lost by openly admitting her connection to Count Axel Fersen.

After a recess of two hours the session resumed. Audubon was back in the gallery listening to a parade of witnesses present their damaging testimony against the Queen. And what they did not impute to her the Public Prosecutor's questioning did.

Darkness spread across the large windows of the chamber, and the proceedings were halted long enough to allow attendants to mount additional candles and circular metal reflectors in the sconces along the walls. But the light in the room remained exceedingly dim, especially toward the front, where the accused and the court officials sat.

At eleven o'clock the President declared the court in recess until nine o'clock the following morning.

When Audubon left the Hall of Liberty his head ached and he was very tired. As far as he was concerned, Fouquier, either through direct questioning or by having Hermann present his questions to the Queen, was attempting to place all the ills that had fallen on France in the previous years on Marie Antoinette's fragile shoulders. Even he, who in the discharge of his duty as captain of a ship was sometimes called upon to sit in judgment of one of the crew, would ask for more evidence of malfeasance before passing sentence than Fouquier had demanded from those who had testified against the Queen.

By the time Audubon entered his room he had just about decided not to return to the trial the following day. He drank several glasses of cognac. As a feeling of warmth spread through him, his thoughts slipped away from the plight of the Queen, and he began to think about Madame Flahaut.

23

Audubon breakfasted in the café close to his lodgings. He sat alone at the table near the window where the small portion of the framed sky was slate gray. He was in a foul mood, and there was a sour taste in his mouth from all the cognac he had drunk the previous night.

From the snatches of conversation that drifted to him from other parts of the room, Audubon was aware that everyone in the café was talking—as doubtless was everyone else in Paris—about the Queen's trial. There seemed to be a division of opinion, from what he could make out. Some felt that Marie Antoinette should be sent back to Austria.

"Let her brother take care of her," Audubon heard one man declare.

Others felt that she should be tried and sentenced to prison for a period of years.

Oddly enough, none of the patrons in the café mentioned the death sentence, which made Audubon wonder if that was the prevailing attitude of the people.

Then one fellow declared, "And this business that Citizen Herbert brought up about her and her son is going too far, I think. . . . I wouldn't deny that she was a whore, perhaps even a Lesbian, but when was it a crime in France to be one or the other. . . . And besides, where would we men be if there weren't whores to give us what our wives won't?"

There was general agreement, and the same man said, "If the Widow Capet is guilty of anything, it is foolishness, and most women are guilty of that, too."

This comment caused the voluble man's companions to laugh heartily. Then one of his friends cautioned him against voicing his opinion so freely. "Even the Queen's lawyers are being taken to task for defending her," he said, and picking up the morning edition of *Le Père Duchesne*, he read, "Is it possible that there should exist scoundrels bold enough to defend her? And yet two babblers from the law courts have that audacity. . . . I myself saw those two devil's advocates not only dance like cats on hot bricks to prove the slut's innocence, but actually dare to weep for the traitor Capet and say to the judges that it was enough to have punished the fat hog and that his whore of a wife should be pardoned."

For several moments the men remained silent; but then one who had not previously spoken said, "Herbert has been demanding her head all along. Perhaps he'll finally get it, though I don't see what good it will do him."

Audubon dropped several coins on the table and left the café. Despite his resolve not to attend the day's session of the trial, he headed for the Palais de Justice, and because the court was already in session he had to bribe several guards to gain entrance to the Hall of Liberty.

For the most part the second day of the trial was a repetition of the first. Fouquier and Hermann neatly divided the task of tearing apart what was left of the Queen's reputation. And then, to Audubon's surprise, one of his former commanders, Admiral d'Estaing, came forward to testify against the Queen. In his nasal voice he told the court that because of the Widow Capet's intrigues and interference in matters that did not concern her he had lost a promotion.

"Do you deny this?" the President asked.

"If the Admiral did not receive his promotion," the Queen responded, "it was because he lacked the necessary qualities to be given more responsibility than he already had."

Audubon knew Marie Antoinette's response was true. The Admiral had proved himself inept when he had commanded a squadron against the British during the American Revolution and had suffered heavy losses in several different actions off the state of Rhode Island.

The President thanked D'Estaing for his testimony and then called for the next witness.

At four thirty a short recess was called—not so much

for the Queen's benefit, Audubon was sure, as to give the members of the court a chance to eat, drink, and stretch their legs.

When the session resumed, additional candles were already in place. More witnesses were called.

Suddenly, as he was wont to do, the President of the Court switched his line of questioning—he was having difficulty trying to sustain the accusation by Citizen Michel Gointre that the Queen had had forged assignats made—and asked, "At the time of your marriage to Louis Capet, did you not conceive the project of uniting Lorraine with Austria?"

"No," Marie Antoinette replied.

"You bear its name."

"Because one must bear the name of one's country."

Again the President changed the direction of his questioning and asked, "Did you not investigate feeling in the departments, districts, and municipalities?"

"No," she answered, shaking her head. "I did not."

Immediately, Fouquier was on his feet, disputing the answer she had given. "There was found in your desk a document proving this fact conclusively," he roared, "in which are written the names of the Vaublancs, Jaucourts, and others."

Marie Antoinette denied having written anything of the kind.

"Have you nothing more to add in your defense?" Hermann questioned.

For the first time since the trial had begun, the Queen stood up and without the slightest hesitation said, "Yesterday I did not know the witnesses. I was ignorant of what they would testify. . . . Well, no one has uttered anything positive against me. I end by remarking that I was only Louis the Sixteenth's wife, and I was bound to submit to his will."

Her remark was undeniably clever, and everyone expected Fouquier to launch an immediate attack, discrediting it. But he said nothing.

The President then ordered another short recess. The bells began to toll. It was midnight.

When the session was resumed some two hours later, Fouquier stood up, and looking at the jurors, tongue-lashed them for their willingness to listen to the lies of the Queen. And then he turned toward her and roared, "I look at you, Widow Capet, as a declared enemy of the French nation—as one of the principal instigators of the disturbances in France during the past four years to which thousands of French have fallen victim."

His accusation gained applause from the gallery.

Marie Antoinette's lawyers followed the Public Prosecutor's address, and he became so enraged at the eloquence of their defense that he ordered the arrest of both men, to the outrage of many of the people in the gallery.

When the proceedings were resumed, Hermann presented the court with the indictment. "Today a great example," he began, "is given to the universe. Nature and Reason so long outraged are at last to be satisfied. Equality triumphs. . . ." He continued for several minutes to describe the Queen's crimes, her perfidy to Louis Capet, to France, and to the many people who had trusted her. "I end," he told the court, "with the general reflection that I have already made to you: It is the French people who accuse Marie Antoinette. All the political events of the last five years testify against her."

Hermann paused to drink some water from a glass in front of him on the table. Then he said to the jurors, "There are four and only four questions with which you must concern yourselves in order to reach a verdict. First, is it established that there were intrigues and secret dealings with foreign powers and other external enemies of the Republic, which intrigues and secret dealings aimed at giving them monetary assistance, enabling them to enter French territory and facilitating the progress of their armies there? Second, is Marie Antoinette d'Autriche, widow of Louis Capet, convicted of having cooperated in these intrigues and of having kept up the secret dealings? Third, is it established that there was a plot and a conspiracy to start civil war within the Republic? And last, is Marie Antoinette d'Autriche, widow of Louis Capet, convicted of having taken part in this plot and conspiracy?"

It was three o'clock in the morning when the jurors left the Hall of Liberty to deliberate.

Audubon waited until the gallery was practically empty before he went down to the waiting room where small groups of spectators like himself were waiting for the Pres-

ident's summons that would call them back to the chamber
to hear the verdict. The room was dark and very cold.
People were rubbing their hands and stamping their feet in
order to keep their extremities warm.

Audubon leaned against one of the walls. His eyes
burned from lack of sleep. He was hungry, uncomfortably
cold, and he could hardly think; but he was determined to
stay until the jury returned a verdict—even if it meant
going without sleep for several nights more.

At four o'clock in the morning the President's bell
sounded and Audubon and the other spectators trouped
back into the gallery of the Hall of Liberty. As soon as
the gallery was filled and the doors to the halls closed,
Hermann asked the people in the gallery to be calm,
regardless of the verdict, and then he warned them that
the law forbade them to make any sign of approbation
and that a person once overtaken by the law, with whatever crimes she might be covered, belonged only to
unhappiness and humanity.

The Queen was brought into the courtroom and went to
her place on the platform. Her two lawyers were brought
back into the room under guard.

Hermann was handed the jury's verdict, and addressing
the Queen, he said, "Marie Antoinette, here is the jury's
declaration. . . ." He paused and then added, "Yes, to all
the questions."

Fouquier was on his feet demanding that the accused be
condemned to death in accordance with Article I of the
first section of the first chapter of the second part of
the penal code. And he read that particular section of the
penal code to the court. Fouquier then strengthened his
call for the death penalty by quoting Article XI of the first
section of the first chapter of the second part of the same
code. "All conspiracy and plots tending to disturb the State
by civil war, by arming citizens one against the other or
aimed against the exercise of the legitimate authority, shall
be punished by death."

"Marie Antoinette," the President asked, "have you any
objection to make to the application of the laws invoked
by the Public Prosecutor?"

The Widow Capet shook her head.

And then Hermann pronounced the death sentence, ordering it to be carried out that day "in the Place de la Révolution and printed and displayed through the Republic."

The Queen left the platform and crossed the hall. It was obvious that she was unaware of what she was doing. In the past few minutes Audubon had watched her wilt. Even the *tricoteuses* were silent as she raised her head, looked at them, and then, turning, allowed herself to be escorted from the room.

Audubon shuffled out of the gallery with the others and walked silently away from the Palais de Justice and through the deserted streets to the Place de la Révolution to await the coming of the Queen.

24

News of the Queen's impending execution spread rapidly through Paris, bringing thousands of people into the cold gloom of the predawn darkness. They filled the Place de la Révolution and lined the streets all the way back to the gates of the Conciergerie.

Many came with torches whose flickering flames punctuated the night with yellow spears. Hawkers did a brisk business, selling wine, brandy, and cognac. And here and there people lighted small fires to stave off the sting of the cold.

Audubon stood in the Place de la Révolution with the other spectators who had been in the gallery when the Queen's sentence had been handed down. They were close to the scaffold, which loomed up in front of them more sinister than the natural darkness that lay over it.

Except for the hawkers bawling their wares the people were quiet, despite their numbers. They spoke to each other in whispers and not more than a few words at a time.

Audubon heard one woman nearby tell another, "I thought she'd get away with it. She gave clever answers. I didn't think it would come to this."

And much later, when the darkness was becoming a cinereous light, a man asked his companion, "Do you think this is the right thing?"

"She is guilty," came the gruff answer.

A third person added, "It's best for all of us if she dies."

"There's still the little Louis Capet and his sister," the first man said.

"Rest easy, citizen," the second speaker replied, "the government knows what to do with them. . . ."

The mention of the Dauphin made Audubon strain to hear more. But the conversation did not continue. Audubon had not previously thought about the boy in any way other than as something to be removed from one place and transported to another. Though he was aware of the boy's royalty, it did not awe him as it obviously did Madame Berthoud. If he was impressed by anything, it was the seeming impregnability of the Temple. But the few words he had just overheard served to remind him that what he would attempt to rescue was not an object, not a thing but a flesh-and-blood human being with a great many enemies and very few friends. For a child to be in that position seemed both ludicrous and sad, and for the first time since he had agreed to undertake the mission Audubon found himself wondering what would happen to the Dauphin if he should fail.

With a shrug, Audubon recognized that the possibility of failure loomed greater than success. Thus far neither he nor Bigot had come up with any scheme that would even suggest a feasible plan for gaining access to the boy, let alone freeing him. But he was a patient man. From his years at sea Audubon had learned to wait for the wind to come and end the calm. . . .

The hours passed, and detachments of troops marched into the Place de la Révolution to surround the scaffold and clear the way for the Queen's tumbrel.

Audubon bought a bottle of wine and a bagful of hot chestnuts.

As the light became stronger the torches were quenched and dark columns of smoke rose from the chimneys of the buildings around the Place de la Révolution. But the sky remained gray, and in the direction of the Seine wisps of mist hung above the water.

The bells tolled eleven, and a few minutes later Audubon and those near him sensed that something was happening at the far end of the square, where the rue de la Révolution intersected the rue St. Honoré. . . . And then, like the whisper of a wave, the words "She comes. . . . She comes. . . . Marie Antoinette comes. . . ." rolled across the square until the murmur gained in volume and became a shout.

The people surged forward, but the soldiers crossed their bayonets and held them back.

The better part of an hour passed before the tumbrel, drawn by two plow horses, turned into the rue de la Révolution and slowly made its way into the square.

"Who's that with the whore?" a *tricoteuse* shouted.

"A filthy priest," a man answered.

The tumbrel was preceded by Grammont, the actor, carrying a sword and riding a black horse. The cart itself was surrounded by police, and pikemen brought up the rear. Only when the cart gained the square did Audubon realize that to increase the Queen's humiliation she had been seated with her back to the horses. The cart stopped and then started with a jerk that nearly caused the Queen to lose her balance.

A woman in the crowd cried out, "Death to the Austrian bitch!"

Halfway to the scaffold Grammont stood up in the stirrups, and wildly brandishing his sword above his head, he shouted, "Here she is, the wicked Marie Antoinette! She is done for, my friends."

The Queen sat very still. She was dressed in black and wore a bonnet.

The tumbrel stopped some twenty paces from where Audubon was standing. The Queen's face was ashen, though it seemed to him that her cheeks were red with fever.

Marie Antoinette left the tumbrel alone, turned around, and seemed to falter when she caught sight of the wooden collar that would soon be placed around her neck.

After a moment she hurried up the steps, losing one of her shoes in her haste. She paused again to speak to the executioner and then looked around at the people in the square.

Suddenly the assistants took hold of her. The bonnet fell from her head, revealing that her white hair had been cut. The men dragged her to the plank and tied her to it. The plank was tipped into place and the wooden collar placed around her neck. . . .

The knife dropped!

An assistant executioner picked up the bloody trophy,

and holding it up by its white hair, gained the applause of the multitude as he carried it around the scaffold.

Audubon turned and pushed his way out of the Place de la Révolution. Though he had seen many people die, few of those deaths had ever put him in such a black mood as had the one he had just witnessed. Those who stood in his way he rudely pushed aside, and he would gladly have welcomed a fight with anyone foolish enough to challenge him.

When he reached the Quai des Tuileries he stopped and looked down at the river. What was he to the Queen or she to him that her death angered him so? Audubon did not know, at least not in any way he could define to himself.

He shook his head and started to walk again along the quay. A sudden gust of wind buffeted him, and turning up his collar, he quickened his pace. The sky was beginning to blacken with rain clouds.

© Lorillard 1975

C'mon

Come for the filter. **You'll stay for the taste.**

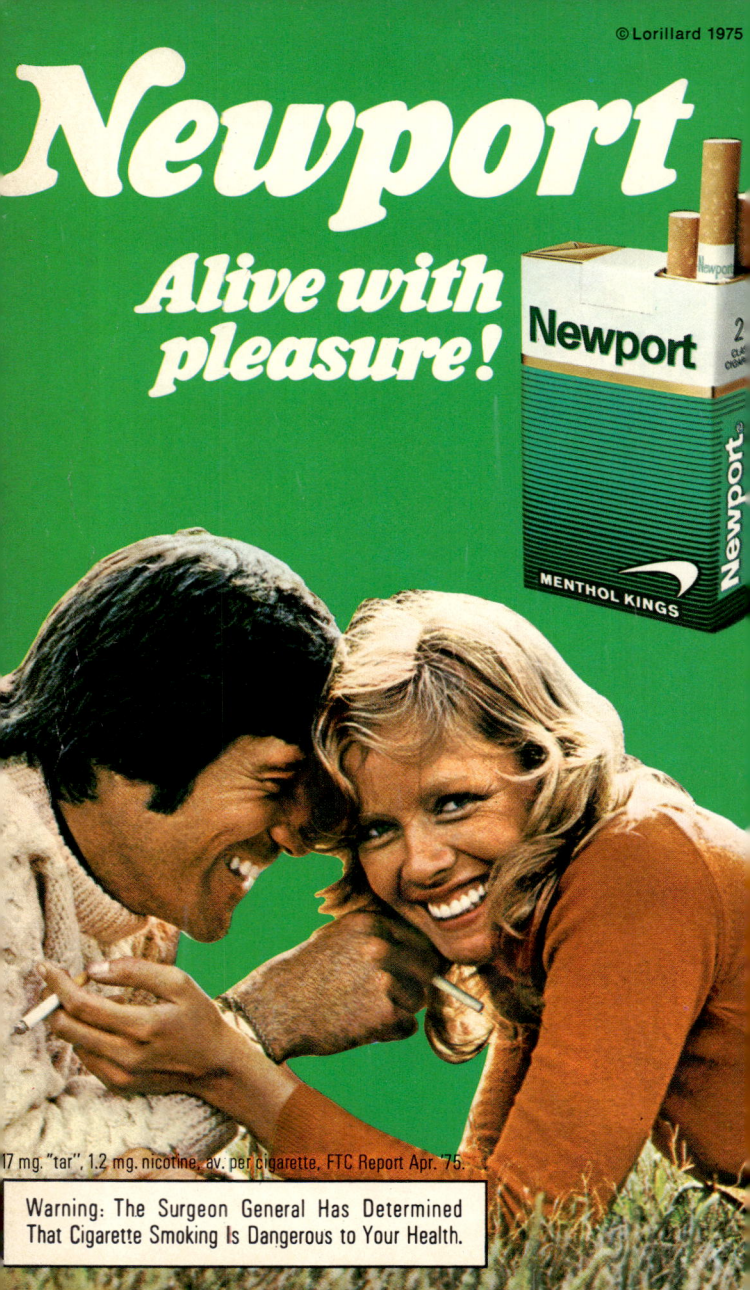

© Lorillard 1975

Newport

Alive with pleasure!

Newport
2
CLA...
CIGA...
Newport®
MENTHOL KINGS

17 mg. "tar", 1.2 mg. nicotine, av. per cigarette, FTC Report Apr. '75.

25

Bigot hurried along the rue du Bac. It was late evening, a November rain was falling, and the cold was bone-chilling.

Despite the inclemency of the weather, he took the usual precautions to make sure he was not being watched. When he was completely satisfied no one was following, Bigot approached the bookshop. Its window was so steamed that he could hardly tell if there was a light in the shop. He pulled the bell cord and waited impatiently for Louise to open the door.

"It is Bigot," he announced as soon as he heard her come close to the door. A moment later he was inside the shop. He looked questioningly at the young woman.

She shrugged, and with a gesture of her head to indicate Gide was in the room upstairs, she whispered, "He is in a bad humor."

Bigot nodded, reached out, touched her cheek, and quickly let his hand slip down her neck until it rested on the exposed tops of her breasts.

With a laugh she brushed it off and complained, "Your hand is cold."

"And what better way to warm it?" he responded.

"There is a better place than that," Louise said, looking at him boldly.

"Is that an invitation?"

"I am sure," she laughed, "that you do not need me to tell you what it is."

Bigot chuckled and quickly climbed the stairs to the

floor above, where he found Gide sitting in a large chair, staring into the fire.

Scowling, Gide looked up but did not say anything.

Bigot was not in the least perturbed and commented, "If it gets any colder we will have a very early snow."

"Bah!" Gide exclaimed, hurling his bulky body out of the chair.

Bigot slowly faced him.

"It is taking too long," Gide said gruffly. "It is taking too long."

Bigot raised his eyebrows.

"I am being pressed," Gide told him.

Bigot slipped off his wet coat, and spreading it out over the back of a chair close to the hearth, he said, "Then by all means, my dear Gide, let Robespierre go into the Temple and get the boy."

"But—"

Bigot held up his hand and said, "If Citizen Robespierre thinks that it is taking too long, then by all means let him shorten the time. He has the authority to order that the boy be brought to him, though I am sure his enemies would like that. . . . Just think of what a man like Fouché would do, eh? Robespierre for all his power is powerless to act. He must depend on men like us to do what he cannot."

"He does not understand that it takes time," Gide responded. "He is a man with a strong philosophical bent who does not appreciate, much less consider, the practical side of the problem."

Bigot gave a snort of disdain and said, "It is not a simple matter of using a battering ram to breach the walls of the Temple, or, for that matter, even of fighting one's way in and then out."

"That much he understands," Gide commented.

"If he understands that," Bigot said, "then he must also understand that another way must be found."

"He will not like waiting," Gide said.

"Who does?"

"You cannot tell me anything more definite?" Gide asked.

"Only that once all the pieces are in place," Bigot replied, "the Dauphin will be taken out of the Temple."

Gide uttered a weary sigh and sat down again; he filled

his glass with wine, offering Bigot another as well.

Bigot moved to the hearth before he said, "I want an introduction to Barras."

Instantly Gide began to cough and became red in the face.

"I have already had the pleasure of meeting Madame de Beauharnais," Bigot told him.

"Then why not ask her?" Gide questioned, still choking.

"It would be more appropriate—"

"You mean," Gide said, striving to keep his voice from degenerating into a fit of coughing, "that coming from someone else it would be more advantageous to you."

"Precisely!"

"He is not a friend," Gide commented with a frown.

Bigot smiled and said, "There are few who are."

"Suppose," Gide said, "I manage the introduction for you. Will you tell me—"

Bigot did not let him finish. "I am not here to bargain with you, Gide," he said, "or to play the childhood game of you-tell-me-what-you-know-and-I'll-tell-you-what-I-know. . . . If you will not have me introduced to Barras, I will find another way—and as a last resort there is Madame de Beauharnais. Will you provide me with an introduction?" Bigot pressed.

"He is very dangerous."

Bigot nodded.

"He is most definitely one of Fouché's men."

"As are several others," Bigot answered.

"I have a man in my employ," Gide said, lowering his voice, "whose name is Robillard."

"Should I know the name?" Bigot questioned.

"No," Gide answered. "He has never been engaged in anything like this before. But he has," Gide said with a ghost of a smile on his heavy lips, "an enormous greed."

"You mean he prefers to be paid from two different sources," Bigot said.

Gide nodded.

"Does he know that you know more than you should about him?"

"Sometimes I think so," Gide admitted with a shrug. "Anyway, it does not matter, since I never use his information without cross-checking it with several other agents who are not quite so greedy."

"And this Robillard will introduce me to Barras?" Bigot asked.

"Yes."

Bigot moved away from the hearth and went to the window. The glass was too fogged for him to see into the street without first wiping away the film of water that obscured his view, and he had no intention of doing that. He faced Gide again and asked, "Will he become curious?"

"Probably."

"If he becomes too curious," Bigot told him, "you might lose an agent."

"It would not be much of a loss as far as I am concerned."

"And his other employer?"

"I think Fouché would miss him somewhat more than I would."

Bigot went back to the hearth, and watching the flames gnaw their way around the end of a stout faggot, he asked, "Do you want me to get rid of him?"

"Only if he gets in the way," Gide answered.

Turning around, Bigot questioned, "And there is no one else?"

"No one quite as close to Barras," Gide told him. "He is the courier between Barras and Fouché."

"Are you certain?"

Gide nodded and said, "I will arrange a meeting between you and Robillard. I have no doubt that you will be able to convince him of your desperate desire to meet with Citizen Barras. And as for Robillard, he will be very impressed with your association with the Paris police—and your generosity." Gide rubbed his fingers together to emphasize the financial arrangements that would have to take place between Bigot and Robillard.

"How much, would you say?"

"A hundred livres," Gide said, "should be enough."

"And what reason will you give him for our meeting?" Bigot questioned.

Gide began to laugh, softly at first and then very loudly as he said, "Suppose I tell him that you are suspected of being a foreign agent?"

Bigot looked at him, and then he, too, roared with laughter.

"What's going on up there?" Louise called from the foot of the stairs.

"Nothing, my pet," Gide shouted, "absolutely nothing!"

"You can tell Citizen Robespierre," Bigot said, "that I am about to fit another piece into place."

"Barras?" Gide questioned.

Bigot nodded.

26

The snow held off until the middle of December, and then just enough of it brushed the city to transform even the meanest streets into scenes of exquisite beauty.

In the Place de la Révolution, the morning of the first snow, the white covering was quickly drenched with streaming blood as the victims were fed into the guillotine's insatiable maw. But the crowds who had gathered there in the previous months to watch the daily bloodletting were now considerably thinned. Even those screaming hags, the *tricoteuses,* were fewer in number than before.

The people of Paris were struggling not only to keep warm but also to keep their stomachs filled. For most, bread was a luxury. Potatoes were even more difficult to come by than bread, and any kind of meat was impossible to get.

Such difficult conditions in the early part of the winter made the people fearful of what the depths of the season would bring when the days would be shorter, with little or no sunshine, and the snow and bitter cold would lay siege to the city and the surrounding countryside.

Here and there these fears were voiced. Audubon, who was vexed by his own situation, would hear some discontented person grumble about the government and wish that the Revolution had never taken place. This attitude reflected his sentiments, which did not stem from poverty and want but came rather from a profound feeling of ennui and from his deepening desire to sleep with Madame Flahaut.

When he was not involved in some erotic reverie about Madame Flahaut, Audubon was seething about Bigot, who was busy spinning a web of such incredible dimensions that it seemed impossible that he could keep track of all its various threads.

To Audubon it seemed that their purpose had become greatly attenuated in the months he had spent in Paris, and he said as much to Bigot when they met in the Café Grotte Flamande, famous for its beer.

Bigot had brought Madame Berthoud with him and asked, "Is that what you think, too, Nicole?"

She gave a slight shrug and answered, "It does seem as though it is going on for a long time."

Audubon said, "I do not see that we have made any progress. I have gone back to the Temple, I do not know how many times, and each time I go I only reinforce my first impression of its impregnability."

Bigot agreed and then added, "But only if one thinks of storming, and my dear Captain, I have no intention of doing something as foolish as that." Bigot leaned forward and said, "I promise you that your patience will be rewarded. . . . Trust me!"

Audubon said nothing. For Bigot to ask to be trusted approached the absurd.

"You have my word on it," Bigot said, extending his hand toward the obviously dubious Captain.

More out of courtesy than belief, Audubon grasped the proffered hand. And then, standing, he bade the two of them good evening. Before either one had the chance to speak, he was away from the table.

Bigot's attitude had greatly vexed Audubon, and though Madame Berthoud looked happy, Audubon was bothered that she had given herself to an Englishman.

It was not yet nine o'clock. In the better restaurants those who could still afford it were just sitting down to sumptuous dinners. As always, if a man had the price, he could get all the food he wanted. But for the wretches Audubon saw gathered at the fires in the streets or cowering from the bite of the wind in doorways or alleys, a potato seemed too much to hope for.

Just before he reached the Pont Neuf Audubon saw an unusually large crowd, not around a fire, but about an old woman who in a screechy voice was importuning any one of the onlookers to risk a sou to know the future. Fortune-tellers were plentiful on the streets of the city, and Audubon, like all men of the sea, both admired and feared those whose powers permitted them to see what ordinary men could not.

Curious to see if she would entice anyone to have his fortune told, Audubon stopped. The woman was very old, and in the dim reddish light that reached her face from the small brazier of glowing charcoal, he saw the hairs on her chin, the cracked, leathery look of her skin, and her small, bright, rodentlike eyes.

"What," she screeched, stamping her ill-shod feet, "there's no one man enough to hear what I have to say about him? My last husband said that the trouble with France is that she lacks men. Now the poor dear lacks his head."

The crowd chuckled, and she did a little jig.

"Can't talk about the government 'cause it's the only one we have. . . . It's like talkin' against your mother and father. . . . You didn't pick them, but you sure as the devil can't change them, now can you?"

Audubon enjoyed her patter. It made him smile, and that in itself was a good thing, considering how angry he had been before he had stopped.

"I tell you," the old woman went on, "when I was younger I was not much better-looking than I am now. . . . My first husband always said I was a sight for sore eyes. He still says that whenever I conjure his spirit from the depths of hell. . . ." She did another little jig and sang, "Tra-la . . . Tra-la . . . Tra-la . . . la . . . lee." And then she said, "There's a man of the sea here. . . . I can always feel when a sailor is close. There's something about them. . . ." Her small eyes moved over the crowd, and she started toward Audubon.

He backed away.

"Come, come, dearie," she coaxed, turning the attention of everyone around her to him. "Come, I'll tell your fortune for nothing. . . . I would have married a sailor man, but after a night with me he said he'd risk the wildest storm at sea rather than spend another night listening to my snoring."

Unable to escape, Audubon sheepishly allowed the

crone to lead him close to the feeble light coming from the brazier.

"Don't be bashful," she cooed. "My days of wantonness are long gone, but if I were younger I would make you an offer."

The audience delighted in her comments.

"A man like you shouldn't be without a woman," she teased, taking his hand in hers. "Now let's see what your hand tells me. . . . Come, come, don't be bashful, show Mother Bertoise your palm. . . . I tell you, if my tit was still worth holding, I'd give it to you to hold! Truth is, sailor, I'd give you a lot more to hold."

Even Audubon could not stop himself from laughing. And now that he was close to her, he could see that despite her self-deprecating remarks she must once have been a beautiful woman. Her bone structure was quite delicate, and under her kerchief there was a head of pure-white hair.

"A man of many adventures," she said, looking down at his hand. "One of character and patience . . . Yes, and of authority, too." She looked at him and asked, "You're a—"

"Captain," he told her in a low voice.

"A Captain!" she repeated loudly. "It's all here in the palm of your hand."

The audience was impressed, and several people asked her to tell more.

She whispered to Audubon, "Is it all right?"

"Yes," he answered with a nod. He, too, was impressed now and curious to see what else she might tell him.

"This portion says that you have had your share of fighting. . . . Is that true?"

"Against the English," he answered.

She traced a line with her dirty fingernail and said, "You will have a long life."

He thanked her for that prediction.

"You are married but not in love with your wife," she told him. "But one can hardly hold that against you, since few men are. . . . But there are two other women in your life."

"Only two?" Audubon laughed.

"And I see something very strange," she said.

"And what's that, old lady?" Audubon asked, thoroughly enjoying himself.

"Danger," she whispered. "Great danger."

Someone in the crowd yelled, "Louder ... Speak louder."

"She says," Audubon laughed, "that she sees great danger."

"Don't laugh, Captain," the hag told him.

"Not at you," he responded, "but my very calling is dangerous."

"Not from the sea," she said. "The danger comes from those who pursue you."

Audubon tried to pull his hand free, but her bony fingers were like claws and they held it fast.

"You have something," she said, "that others want. They would kill you to get it."

"What does he have?" a man standing close by asked.

Audubon looked at him. Though he did not know him, he nonetheless looked familiar. He was of middling height, heavyset, with a strong face.

"He's traveling with others," the woman said. "It all has to do with—"

"Well, what?" the familiar-looking man pressed.

Audubon wrested his hand from the old woman's grasp and said, "A business trip, is that what you saw there?"

She did not answer.

The same man asked, "Tell us what you saw there, Granny."

"I cannot lie," she said, looking at Audubon, "or the powers I have will leave me. ... His business is connected with the King."

Without hesitation, Audubon turned and bolted through the crowd. He ran until his lungs felt as though they would burst, until his body was wet with perspiration. He ran until he lacked the strength to continue. Then, leaning against a wall, he remembered having seen that same chunky man on several other occasions during the past few days. He was sure the man was not one of Bigot's. . . .

27

For a few days following the incident with the chunky man and the fortune-teller, Audubon was wary. And whenever he turned a corner he looked over his shoulder to see if he was being followed. But he could see no one who remotely resembled the man. . . .

Eventually, deciding that he had been mistaken, Audubon let the events of that evening slip out of his mind and devoted himself to making Madame Flahaut his mistress.

By Christmas he was on a first-name basis with her, but despite his importunings the most Adèle would exchange with him was an embrace and a kiss.

"You know," she said one afternoon as they sat on a love seat in the parlor of her lodgings on the rue Perdue, "I hear all sorts of rumors about you."

He raised his eyebrows questioningly.

"People are trying to guess who and what you are," she told him.

"I am Jean Audubon—"

"No, silly," she responded, placing her small hand over his mouth.

Gently he removed it and said, "I will tell you, Adèle, what I have told no one. . . . *I am that I am.*"

She gave him a quizzical look.

"Could I be anything else?" he asked, realizing she did not recognize the biblical quote.

"It has a familiar ring," she commented with a laugh, and the laughter made her thinly covered breasts quiver.

"I must leave," Audubon responded, and kissing her hand, stood up.

"Will you be at Gouverneur Morris's party tomorrow night?" she questioned, getting to her feet and smoothing out her yellow silk negligee, through which all of her body was revealed.

Audubon nodded, and feasting his eyes on what he saw, he wondered how much—if any of it—the rest of him would ever enjoy. Still, he would have to admit that, though Adèle was purposely provocative in his presence, he did find pleasure in looking at her exquisite body.

"You are staring too hard," she pouted. "You will make me self-conscious of the freedom I feel with you."

Audubon swept her into his arms and kissed her passionately on her lips. She responded with some vigor, pressing herself against him and encircling his neck with her arms.

"I want you, Adèle," he whispered into her ear.

She eased herself out of his embrace. Her face was flushed, and her nipples pushed against their thin covering. "Not now," she told him in a choked voice. "I have things that must be done."

He nodded and suppressed the desire to take her into his arms again.

Adèle turned her back to him, and after a moment or two she asked, "And your friend Bigot, will he be at the party, too?"

"Probably," Audubon replied.

"There are rumors about him, too," she told him.

"Oh?"

"Does that surprise you?" she asked, facing him again.

Audubon shrugged.

"The two of you make an extremely odd pair."

"I am sure of that," he responded. "But why the questions about Bigot?"

She walked slowly to the hearth at the far side of the small room and with a shrug said, "Since you brought him to one of Morris's soirées some months ago, he has become practically a constant visitor. He is even at some social functions that you are not, and he is on very friendly terms with Barras and Herbert. It is even rumored that he has the ear of Robespierre."

"And what is all that supposed to mean to me?" Audubon asked, quite taken with the way the light from the fireplace silhouetted her seminudity.

"It is just that the two of you are so completely dissimilar," she said. "People have a tendency to note such discrepancies, Jean."

"I do not doubt it," he commented. "But even more peculiar than my friendship with Citizen Bigot is my relationship with a man named Joue. You might mention it whenever someone asks you about me and Bigot."

"You are not being very clear," she told him.

"Joue is black."

"What?"

"His mother was an African princess," Audubon explained.

There was an incredulous look on her face.

"You see, Adèle," he said, advancing toward her again, "as I told you before, I am what I am."

She held him away from her and in a low, throaty voice told him, "I really do have things to attend to."

Audubon nodded graciously, and taking her hand, brought it to his lips. "I hope to kiss much more, Adèle," he told her.

"Yes," she whispered, "I know."

Audubon released her hand, bowed slightly, and turning around, hurried out of the room.

Minutes later he was on the street. A heavy, wind-driven snow was swirling out of the twilight sky. He pulled up his collar and with his head lowered hurried to the Café Belle Nuit on the nearby Place Maubert. Though he had no doubt that Adèle's question about his relationship to Bigot stemmed from a source other than herself—probably Talleyrand—Audubon was nonetheless confident that her reaction to his embrace had not been in the least simulated. Her passion had been quite obvious. And the very fact that she was obviously involved in some intrigue to discover who he was added a definite fillip to the game they were playing.

28

Though the Revolution had abolished Christmas, no one
who was at Gouverneur Morris's house on the rue de la
Planche doubted what was being celebrated. The huge
ballroom was decorated with boughs of holly and ever-
greens. There were large vases filled with brightly colored
flowers. And on various portals throughout the house,
there were sprigs of mistletoe, whose purpose Morris took
time to explain to his many guests.

There were, in addition to the many tables resplendent
with all kinds of food, from succulent roast pigs to delicate
cheeses from the provinces, large silver bowls of wassail,
which to Audubon spoke with silent eloquence of the ines-
capable bond between the Americans and the English.

A quintet played lovely minuets and gavottes for those
guests who enjoyed dancing.

Audubon knew practically everyone there, if not by
name then by sight, since Morris had at one time or another during the past months introduced him to them.

Many of the guests had been members of the aristocracy
who had renounced their former lives to save their heads.
Some had changed their names. And some were just men
and women who had attracted Gouverneur Morris's curiosity.

He saw Barras, Herbert, and Chaumette talking together
near a window. Talleyrand was poised near a table, de-
vouring a canapé. And Bigot, with Madame Berthoud on
his arm, had just entered the room.

Audubon had started toward Bigot when he suddenly

saw the chunky man who had pressed the old fortune-
teller with so many questions. The man followed Bigot
and Madame Berthoud into the ballroom.

"It is a terrible night," Bigot said, coming up to Audubon. "We would have been here sometime ago, but I
could not get a hack."

"There is a man who came in practically on your
heels—"

Bigot nodded.

"You know him?"

"His name is Robillard," Bigot said casually.

"Is he one of yours?"

"Hardly," Bigot answered.

"Several days ago—in fact, when we last met," Audubon explained, "he followed me."

"I imagine," Bigot chuckled, "that he became bored
with following me."

"Is he following you now?"

"Yes . . . I even think I would miss him if he stopped,"
Bigot said. "Would you like to meet him?"

"But—"

"It is all very amicable," Bigot said. "He knows I know
that he is following me. He has his assignment, and I have
mine. As long as he does not interfere with mine, I will not
interfere with his. Besides, if I tried to stop him, it would
only anger Fouché and I really would prefer not to do
that."

Audubon looked at Robillard. The man not only gave
him a nod of recognition but also smiled at him. Of the
two, it was the smile that he found the more disconcerting.

"He seems to remember you," Bigot commented.

"I did not think he had forgotten," Audubon responded.

"I am famished!" Bigot exclaimed. "Would anyone care
to join me?"

Audubon declined. At that moment he would have very
much enjoyed a good long drink of Scottish whisky.

"What about you, Nicole?" Bigot asked.

"Not just yet," she answered.

"While I gorge myself," Bigot told them, "why not take
advantage of the music and dance?"

Nicole looked questioningly at Audubon.

Remembering they had met at a ball, he said, "It would
be my pleasure." He offered her his arm, she smiled at

him, and together they moved to the center of the floor where the dancers were executing the graceful steps of a gavotte.

"Bigot seems to be in excellent spirits," Audubon commented, noticing that though her blue gown was not elaborate it fitted her well enough to draw admiring glances from several of the men they passed.

"I think it is because we are nearer to our goal," she whispered.

"Are you happy?" Audubon questioned, although the very next instant he was sorry he had asked.

Her eyes avoided his, and she answered, "I have never really known happiness, but he gives me companionship and—"

"I am sorry I asked," he told her hastily, not wanting to hear any more of her explanation.

She did not attempt to complete what she had started to say. When the music ended, Audubon escorted her off the dance floor, and as they started toward Bigot she said, "Be careful, Captain."

"And what does that mean?"

But she only shook her head and repeated her warning.

When Audubon returned to Bigot he was engaged in a lively conversation with Talleyrand about the situation in Vendée. "You come from there, Audubon," Bigot commented, "tell us what you think of the war."

Audubon glared at him, waved the question aside, and making some excuse, hastily removed himself to another part of the room. Bigot possessed an absolute talent, as far as he was concerned, for infuriating him. He could not understand why the man always insisted on living inside the dragon's mouth. Scowling, Audubon shook his head.

"I had hoped for a better greeting from you," he heard Adèle say. And then she drifted into his line of sight from the left.

He turned slightly toward her and said, "I have a much better greeting for you."

"Ah, so you say!" she exclaimed, offering him her hand.

Audubon kissed it and then took a long look at her. She was dressed in a rose-pink gown, complete with panniered skirt and a décolletage that showed her ample cleavage to best advantage.

"How do I look?" she asked.

"I would rather feast on you than the food," he answered.

"Now that is a compliment I have not heard in a long time," she told him, touching his chest with the tip of her fan.

"Would you like to dance?" Audubon asked.

"Very much."

"My arm," he said.

"Now tell me why you were scowling so," she said, "when I first saw you."

"Because," he told her, "my passion for you is unrequited."

She laughed and began to move in time to the music.

29

When Audubon returned with Adèle to her lodgings on the rue Perdue the bells were just tolling three. The party at Gouverneur Morris's house had lasted until after two.

"It was a lovely night," she commented, dropping her cloak over the back of a chair and facing him.

Taking her in his arms, Audubon nuzzled her brown hair and told her, "You are lovely."

"Is that why you wanted to see me home?" she asked with a laugh.

Audubon kissed her, pressing his lips hard against hers until they parted and their tongues met.

"I have not been kissed that way for so long," she gasped when their mouths parted, "I had almost forgotten how delicious it is."

He held her close to him and felt her body strain against his. "I want you," he said passionately.

"I know you do," she told him, touching his cheek.

Audubon kissed her neck.

Adèle clung to him.

Audubon lifted her into his arms and carried her into the bedroom, to the canopied bed. Still holding Adèle in his arms, he buried his face in the décolletage of her gown and enjoyed the soft warmth of her breasts against his cheeks. Then he set her down and asked if she would prefer to be alone while she undressed.

"What would you prefer?" she responded.

"To help you," he said.

She nodded.

Audubon helped Adèle slip out of her gown, baring her breasts.

She turned toward him.

He took her in his arms. Her breasts were delightfully warm to his hand. Her nipples were pink and hard. He kissed them and then began to remove her petticoats.

When Adèle was completely naked he lifted her into his arms again and then set her down on the bed. Immediately she scrambled under the blanket.

Audubon laughed, and wasting no time, he removed his clothing and slipped into bed next to her. The heat of her body flowed out to him. He kissed her, enjoying the slippery luxury of her tongue, which she did not hesitate to give him.

"Tell me, Jean, why this means so much," she whispered, sliding her hands over his body.

"I am not wise enough to answer," he replied.

"Such an insignificance to be so significant is truly a puzzle," she whispered, kissing his nipples lightly.

Audubon stroked her naked back. . . . He was not given to thinking about the philosophical implications of sex. It was enough for him to enjoy it. He did not question the mysterious alchemy that had brought him to bed with Adèle. He accepted it as inevitable.

"You are a very hairy man," she told him, playing with the growth of hair on his chest.

"Does it bother you?" he asked, squeezing her bare buttocks.

"It is a sign of virility."

He laughed, and rolling Adèle onto her back, he kissed her breasts, teasing each nipple with his tongue.

"I like that," she whispered.

"And this, too?" he asked, caressing her sex.

"Especially that," she told him, taking hold of him.

Audubon enjoyed her delicate movements, and wanting to give her as much pleasure in return, lowered his mouth to her sex. In moments she was moaning with delight.

"I want to hold you in my mouth," she said throatily.

The pleasure she gave him made his blood race. The movement of her lips on him was almost too exquisite to stand.

"You know," Adèle commented, ceasing her ministra-
tions in order to speak, "I knew we would become lovers
tonight."

Audubon stopped and looked over his shoulder at her.

"A woman knows those things," she said.

He reversed his position, and settling down beside her,
he placed his hand between her thighs and asked, "What
else does a woman know?"

She laughed and said, "There was another woman interested in you at the party."

"Only one" he questioned.

"The one you were dancing with as I entered the room,
the former Marquise de St. Pierre, who now calls herself
Madame Berthoud."

"She would be the last one to be interested in me," Audubon laughed. "The very last."

"Every time she saw us together," Adèle said, "she
looked daggers at me."

"I was not aware of it."

"That is because you are a man," she gasped.

"A fact," he said, teasing her sex even more, "for which
you must at this moment be truly thankful."

"Oh, Jean," she exclaimed in a breathy voice, "oh,
Jean!"

Audubon eased himself between her bare thighs and entered her.

She flung her arms around his neck and at the same
time arched her body to meet his thrusts.

From the moment he coupled with her, Audubon felt
the wonderful rippling movement deep inside Adèle's
body. He bent his head and put his lips to her nipples.

Adèle made low, throaty sounds, and she said, "This is
my gift to you."

"I would want no other," he responded.

Circling his neck with her bare arms, she whispered,
"Fast, Jean. Oh, yes . . . Yes . . . Like that!"

Audubon enjoyed the softness of her body under his.

"And what is your gift to me, Jean Audubon?" she said
as her body strained against his and then collapsed as
spasm after spasm took hold of her.

Moments later Audubon's own ecstasy quenched the
light in his brain with a blaze brighter by far than the trop-
ical sun at noon, an efflorescence of pleasure that bloomed

from the depths of his physical being, filling him with the scent of Adèle's body.

"And what is your gift to me, Jean?" she asked again, her voice softer.

He rested his head on her naked breasts and said, "What can I give more than I have given?"

Adèle stroked his hair.

"Tell me what you want," he said, "and I will get it for you."

"I do not think you will."

"If it is within my power to give—"

"You will not," she said.

"Why are you so sure?"

"Because," she explained, "I have already asked, and you have refused to tell me who you really are."

Audubon sat up.

"You see," Adèle told him, "you are angry because I asked."

He looked down at her. Her head was resting on a pillow, and even in the darkness he could see the soft flow of her long brown hair, the movement of her bare breasts, and lower down, the triangle of her love mound.

"Are you angry?" she asked, placing her hand on his arm.

"No," he said, settling down in bed again and placing his hands behind his head.

"You are!"

"Go to sleep, Adèle," he said with a sigh. "I have already answered your question."

"But—"

"Go to sleep!"

Adèle turned around and drew the blanket over her head.

Audubon lay staring at the canopy above him and just before drifting off to sleep found himself thinking about Nicole Berthoud.

30

Several days after Audubon and Adèle had become lovers he spent the afternoon with her, and when he left her lodgings a cold, wind-blown rain was falling. The streets were dark, punctuated here and there by a yellow glow coming from a lamp or candle in a window.

Audubon turned up his collar, and with his hands thrust deep into his pockets he walked quickly toward the Pont de la Tournelle, which would take him to the Ile de la Fraternité, across the Pont Mare, and finally to Port Mare, on the other side of the river, where he would meet with Bigot and Madame Berthoud on Joue's barge.

Adèle's scent, a mixture of the floral perfume she used and the natural odor of her body, still clung to him, causing him to wonder if he had left some similar trace of himself with her.

Not that it really mattered, since he held no illusions about her. With a characteristic shrug Audubon accepted the fact that Adèle was sharing Talleyrand's bed when she was not with him. Though her original purpose had been to extract information from him, Audubon took a certain measure of satisfaction in knowing that he had managed to deflect her intent. They came together now not for what he could tell her about himself or Bigot but rather for the pleasure he could give her, which was obviously more than she was able to experience with whomever else she bedded. Pleased with his own prowess, Audubon smiled and hurried across the Pont Mare.

Joue's barge was the last in Port Mare, closer to the

Quai du Mail than it was to the bridge. Two structures rose from its deck. The one forward housed the four tow horses, while the one aft, near the tiller, provided a passageway into the cabin below decks.

Audubon boarded the barge, making his way along the makeshift gangway from the quay to the deck. A moment later he eased himself down the steps of the narrow companionway and into the large open space of the main cabin, where Bigot, Joue, and Madame Berthoud were seated at a table, over which a single lamp hung from a massive crossbeam.

Audubon mumbled a greeting, and then, reaching for the bottle of wine on the table, he filled a mug before removing his coat and taking his place next to Joue.

"We arrived earlier than I expected," Bigot said.

Audubon nodded and drank until the mug was empty. He glanced at Madame Berthoud. Though the light in the cabin was dim she looked paler than usual and there was redness about her eyes that suggested she had been weeping. Audubon wondered if Bigot was mistreating her. But it was none of his affair. Reaching for the wine, he filled his mug again, but he did not drink; instead, he took his pipe, filled it with tobacco, and began to smoke.

Bigot cleared his throat and said, "All the pieces are in place, Captain."

Audubon removed the pipe from his mouth, and pointing the stem at Bigot, he asked, "Are you telling me that you have found a way to get in and out of the Temple without being discovered?"

"Yes," Bigot replied.

Audubon started to smoke again.

Bigot took time to pour some wine into a mug and drink some before he said, "The boy can be gotten out—"

"By whom?" Audubon questioned.

"At least two different people," Bigot answered evasively.

"I will let that pass for now," Audubon told him with a wave of his hand. "But tell me, Bigot, something about all the pieces that have taken so many months to be put into place?"

"Your only concern, Captain, is the boy."

Audubon nodded, and putting his hand on Joue's shoulder, he said, "We leave tonight for home."

"Aye, aye, sir!"

Bigot was on his feet, and pointing his finger at Audubon, he said, "I swear, Captain, I will have you—"

Audubon launched himself across the table, sending the bottle of wine and the mugs crashing to the floor. He grabbed hold of Bigot. In an instant the point of his dirk was against Bigot's throat.

Madame Berthoud screamed.

"Shut up!" he ordered, and then to Bigot he said, "You should know better than to threaten me."

"It is you who threatened—"

"For all your cleverness, Bigot," Audubon told him in English, "you are a bloody fool." And letting go of him, he sheathed his knife and sat down.

Madame Berthoud was whimpering softly.

"Either stop that," Audubon told her harshly, "or leave."

Bigot straightened his clothes and resumed his place at the table.

"I want to know the pieces," Audubon said.

"And if you are captured," Bigot asked, "what then?"

"That is what you must risk."

"There are many other people's lives—"

"The pieces, Bigot," Audubon demanded. "Either I know all of them or Joue and I leave Paris tonight."

Bigot hesitated. To have his mission fail after he had done so much to make it successful was totally unacceptable. With a deep sigh he said, "I will tell you, but if there were time enough to replace you, Captain, I most assuredly would do that rather than accede to your demands."

"There are times," Audubon responded in a less harsh voice, "when we do not have a choice. For you, at least, this appears to be one of them."

"So it would seem," Bigot acknowledged dolefully.

"The pieces!" Audubon exclaimed, hardening his voice.

"Three days from today," Bigot explained, "Simon will no longer be the boy's warder. For some hours that same night neither he nor his wife will be in the precincts of the Temple, that is to say, they will not be there in any official capacity."

Audubon nodded.

"You understand," Bigot questioned, "what this hiatus means?"

"I would rather not trust my own interpretation," Audubon responded, relighting his pipe.

"Suppose," Bigot suggested, "that the husband and his wife returned to the Temple in order to collect a few bundles of clothing they had left behind, and that the boy happened to be hidden in one of the bundles?"

"And they will be able to walk past the gate guards without being challenged?"

With a shake of his head Bigot answered, "They will indeed be stopped, and the guards will search the contents of the various bundles, and then Simon and his wife will be told to move on."

"Then the guards—"

"Bought," Bigot answered, "as was Chaumette, who agreed to dismiss Simon, and as was Simon, who, for much less of a consideration than Chaumette demanded, became angry enough to go along with my scheme."

"You mean he knows he is going to be dismissed?"

Bigot smiled and said, "As a good friend to him, could I do less than warn him about his fate?"

"And did you happen to mention what his fate might be if he were caught?"

"A matter of no consequence," Bigot said.

"To you or him?" Audubon asked, leaning back against the bench on which he sat.

"He will not be going anywhere near the Temple," Bigot said, "but you will."

Audubon chuckled softly, and slapping Joue gently on the back, he said, "Now that is a wind I did not expect, did you?"

Joue shook his head.

"What about you, madame," Audubon asked, "did you know about it?"

"She is going with you," Bigot said.

"The devil she is!" Audubon flashed.

"It is either her or Marie-Jeance, Simon's wife."

"I told you what the Captain's response would be," Madame Berthoud said quietly.

"You have your choice," Bigot said, somewhat pleased to have presented Audubon with what in his own country was known as Hobson's choice—really no choice at all but rather the necessity of settling for one of two equally distressing prospects.

"Madame Berthoud," Audubon growled after a long hesitation.

"Excellent!" Bigot exclaimed almost gleefully.

"In other words," Audubon said, "we will be expected. . . . That is to say, Simon and his wife will be expected."

"Precisely."

"And from there we will make our way here?"

"Yes," Bigot answered, "and by morning you will be on your way."

"So you managed to buy our way in and out," Audubon commented.

"That is why," Bigot explained, "it has taken so long."

Audubon turned to Joue and asked, "What do you think of it?"

"It might work," Joue replied.

"And you, Madame Berthoud," he asked, "what do you think of it?"

"I think it has a good chance of succeeding," she answered without raising her eyes to meet his.

Audubon leaned forward, and looking straight at Bigot, he said, "I want to hear more, Bigot, I want to hear a lot more before I agree to—"

"But there is no more," Bigot maintained vociferously.

"Then I misjudged you," Audubon told him.

Bigot looked at him questioningly.

"Unless, of course," Audubon said, "you think I am a fool?"

Bigot was about to object, but Audubon asked, "How does Gide fit into all of this? There is no need to be surprised that I know the name, since you yourself mentioned it the night we freed Madame Berthoud's husband. The name, as I remember, caused Citizen Freneau to become extremely distressed. Now suppose you tell me who Monsieur Gide is and what his role is in this affair."

"I cannot compromise—"

"Bigot," Audubon said almost conversationally, "I do not like you, and I am sure you harbor no love for me, but as you once pointed out we are professionals. There are too many flaws in your plan. If I see them from where I am, those who would prevent us from taking the boy will also see them. Now it is up to you to prove to me that these flaws do not exist, or if they do, that they are indeed very, very small—practically infinitesimal."

"Gide is one of Robespierre's agents," Bigot said.

"Then it was through him that you gained your position with the police and your introduction to Chaumette . . . and probably Barras?"

Bigot nodded. He had greatly underestimated the Captain's quick intelligence.

"And in return," Audubon asked, "what were you to give for all these favors?"

"Joue," Bigot questioned, sweating, "is there more wine aboard?"

"I could do with a drink myself," Audubon said.

Joue brought another bottle to the table, and the mugs were picked up from the floor.

Audubon poured a drink for everyone and suggested that Bigot answer his question.

"In return we were to give him the Dauphin," Bigot said. "But Gide will be put out of the way."

Madame Berthoud gasped and shrank away from Bigot's side while Joue made a low whistling sound.

"All right," Audubon told him, "so much for Gide! I already know about Chaumette and Simon and his wife, but now I am interested in Barras. How does he become one of the pieces?"

"For a substantial consideration Barras has agreed to replace Chaumette. I have a fine relationship with him and his mistress."

"And what was the consideration?"

"Money."

"The other consideration?" Audubon said, gesturing toward himself, as though the action would cull the answer from Bigot.

"To deliver the Dauphin to him," Bigot said.

Madame Berthoud uttered a small cry of horror.

"And Barras is one of Gide's men?"

"He is one of Fouché's agents," Bigot explained, "pretending to be loyal to Robespierre. . . . Fouché would like to get his hands on the Dauphin, if for no other reason than to use him as a club against Robespierre."

Audubon paused to sip at his wine and then commented, "There are a great many pieces—many more than might be practical."

"But you do see how they interlock?" Bigot asked, wiping the perspiration from his forehead.

"To your benefit, Bigot," Audubon said. "I do indeed see the value of what you have done."

"I have even provided for a decoy," Bigot said, anxious to prove to Audubon that, though he had every intention of betraying Gide and Barras, he remained honest with him. "The morning after you take the boy from the Temple a certain Monsieur Jenais O'Jardia will leave Paris accompanied by a young boy disguised as the Dauphin—"

"That is it!" Audubon exclaimed, leaping to his feet. "That is where the biggest flaw is, where we need one more piece to complete the puzzle."

Bigot shrank back.

"The boy," Audubon all but shouted. "The boy must be replaced by another."

"I do not understand," Bigot said.

"If we leave nothing in the room where the Dauphin was, then by morning the guards will discover he is gone. But if there is another boy, someone closely resembling the Dauphin, it will take some time before they discover what has happened."

"You mean you want to substitute another child for the Dauphin?" Madame Berthoud questioned with disbelief.

"You could bring him in a sack and take the Dauphin out the same way," Bigot commented.

"It might take the guards a few hours to sort out what had happened," Audubon said, "and by then we would be well downriver and no one would be any the wiser."

Bigot warmed to Audubon's suggestion. "It will certainly confuse everyone, especially when Monsieur O' Jardia is apprehended sometime the same day or the one following."

But Madame Berthoud objected, demanding to know what would happen to the boy once he was discovered.

"Absolutely nothing," Bigot responded. "He will be regarded as the innocent victim of the conspirators. He will be freed. You have my word on that, Nicole."

"To involve an innocent child," she countered, "lacks all human decency."

"Our mission," Bigot said angrily, "has absolutely nothing to do with human decency. We are to get the Dauphin out. You were charged with that responsibility by his mother as I am charged with that same mission by my country. And I assure you, there are no limits to which I would not go to meet my responsibilities."

Chastised, Madame Berthoud fell silent.

"Can you find a boy who closely resembles the Dauphin?" Audubon asked.

"I will do my best," Bigot told him.

"Bring him here," Audubon said.

Bigot nodded.

"And when will all of this take place?" Audubon asked.

"The night of January nineteenth."

"Is there anything else I should know?" Audubon asked. "I do not want any surprises to come my way."

"You already know more than I ever planned on telling you," Bigot said.

Audubon smiled and with a shrug took a drink from his mug.

"Is there no other way?" Madame Berthoud asked softly.

Bigot scowled and said, "It is being done to assure your safety and—"

"We need all the time we can get," Audubon told her. "A few hours one way or the other can well mean the difference between success or failure. Bigot has done all he could possibly do."

She nodded in agreement.

And again Bigot said, "I promise you, Nicole, that no harm will come to the boy." And taking her hand, he added, "Believe me?"

"Yes," she told him, "I believe you."

Audubon glanced at Joue, and in his officer's wrinkled brow he read his own disbelief. The boy would never be allowed to leave the Temple alive, but there was no other way to buy the time he needed than by purchasing it with another life.

"We will meet here on the night of the nineteenth," Bigot said, getting to his feet.

"About ten o'clock," Audubon suggested.

"That should give you and Nicole plenty of time to get to the Temple by midnight."

Audubon nodded, and without shaking Bigot's hand or saying good-bye to Madame Berthoud, he watched them climb up the companionway to the deck. When he no longer heard their footsteps he turned to Joue and asked, "What do you think?"

Joue shrugged and said, "It is hard to know if one boy's life is worth more than another's."

"I do not know either," Audubon admitted, and sitting down, he began to drink.

"You won't find the answer in the wine, Captain," Joue told him after a while.

Audubon set the mug down, stood up, and staggering up the companionway, stepped out onto the rainswept deck. "It is a fair exchange," he said loudly. "A fair exchange!"

31

It was well past two o'clock in the morning when Robillard saw the door to the Beauharnais house open and Barras take his leave of Joséphine, who wore nothing more than a diaphanous white gown. After embracing her, Barras turned and hurried away.

A moment later Robillard went after Barras. For a heavy man he moved with surprising swiftness, and by the time Barras was at the end of the street Robillard had fallen in beside him.

Neither greeted the other, and after taking a few moments to allow his breathing to return to normal, Robillard said, "I followed Audubon earlier this evening to a barge worked by his black Joue. I managed to get aboard and hide in the stable area."

Barras said nothing.

Robillard explained that Bigot and Madame Berthoud were also aboard the barge.

"There is nothing new in the relationship of these four individuals," Barras said.

"Nonetheless," Robillard replied, "I keep thinking about it. Now if you remember, Gide introduced me to Bigot and then assigned me to follow him. I keep asking myself why?"

"Because Gide is a very suspicious man."

"I cannot deny that," Robillard said. "But so am I a very suspicious man."

"And what are your suspicions?" Barras asked, stopping for a moment to look at his companion.

"Simply," Robillard told him, "that those four—Bigot, Berthoud, Audubon, and the black—are up to something."

"My dear suspicious man," Barras laughed, clapping Robillard on the back, "everyone in Paris is up to something. A person would be out of fashion if he were not up to something."

Robillard laughed, too, and though he agreed with Barras he added, "But these four worry me. I have tried to discover something more about Bigot and cannot, except that from time to time he visits Gide. My intuition tells me that there is something between them. And as for Madame Berthoud, she is the former Marquise de St. Pierre."

"And I am the former Vicomte Paul-François-Jean-Nicholas de Barras—but does that make me suspect, too?"

"No," Robillard answered quickly, "not at all."

Barras began to walk again.

"You must understand," Robillard said, "I am only doing my job."

Barras said nothing.

"To go back to Bigot for a moment," Robillard began.

"I would much rather we did not," Barras responded wearily.

"As you wish, but I think you should hear me out. I might have stumbled onto a plot to snatch the Dauphin."

Barras stopped.

"I think it would be better if you continued to walk," Robillard said, knowing that now he had his companion's complete interest. "You see," he explained, "Bigot has a certain intimacy with Chaumette and Simon. Now that was entirely too coincidental for me, especially if it is coupled with his association with Gide. Robespierre would pay a king's ransom to have Louis Capet in his hands, so that he could make some sort of deal with the English or whoever else would be willing to ransom the bastard."

"You might be onto something," Barras admitted grudgingly.

Robillard nodded and with some zest said, "Tonight, after Bigot and his woman left the barge, Audubon remained on board with Joue."

"That could hardly be incriminating evidence," Barras quickly pointed out.

"Much later Audubon came up on deck. He was quite

drunk and shouted, 'It is a fair exchange.' "

Barras repeated Audubon's words and was silent for several minutes before he said, "I see there is no way to avoid telling you the truth." And before Robillard could speak, Barras lied, "Bigot, Audubon, and Madame Berthoud are in my employ."

Robillard sucked in his breath and an instant later noisily exhaled.

"They are indeed going to attempt to rescue the Dauphin," Barras said easily, "and they will hand him over to me, and in turn I will give him to Fouché."

Stunned, Robillard almost lost his footing. He knew that Barras was frequently called "the Snake" by friend and foe alike. Even Fouché was wary of him.

"But just to ensure that Bigot does not take it upon himself to double-cross me," Barras said, "two or three men near the barge should provide sufficient insurance."

"I will see to it," Robillard answered in a low voice.

"Well," Barras said, clapping his companion on the back again, "you have done a fine piece of work."

"Thank you."

"Once the matter is settled," Barras told him, "I will personally tell Fouché of your role."

"When will the attempt be made?" Robillard asked.

"The night of the nineteenth," Barras responded. "And by the way, lest I forget to tell you, I do not want you anywhere near the Temple or the barge. You are far too valuable a man to lose should something go wrong."

"I understand," Robillard answered.

"Remember," Barras said, "I am not asking you to keep away from the Temple and the barge on the night of the nineteenth—I am ordering you to."

"Yes, I understand that."

Barras laughed and said, "I really feel quite wonderful. . . . Would you join me for a glass of wine?"

"It would be my pleasure!"

32

Audubon pushed a large two-wheeled cart while Madame Berthoud trudged silently at his side. They wore clothes similar to those usually worn by Simon and his wife Marie-Jeance.

A heavy fog lay over the city. The air was cold and damp. The wet, slippery cobbles made it difficult for Audubon to keep the cart from sliding off to one side or the other on the uneven surface.

To Audubon they were just momentary shadows, but he saw them as they stepped back into the utter blackness of a cul-de-sac. He said nothing about them to her. When the time came he would deal with them himself. . . .

Now and then Audubon reached out and touched the sack that held the boy. He had not seen the child. The waif had been drugged and placed in the heavy burlap sack before he arrived at the barge. And when he asked where the boy had come from, Bigot had told him, "I bought him. He is sickly, and there were a great many other children in the family. His parents were happy to have the money."

Audubon wiped his brow and fought the sudden movement of the cart to the left. He swore under his breath. He was sure they were being followed. Several times he had glanced over his shoulder, and even though the fog was too thick for him to see more than a half dozen paces from where he was, he twice had caught a glimpse of someone nearby.

"Would it be easier," Madame Berthoud asked, "if I helped you push?"

"No," he answered with a shake of his head.

Another period of silence engulfed them, and then Madame Berthoud said, "We do not have to use the boy. . . . We can—"

"No," he responded sharply, "we cannot!"

"But you yourself object to—"

"I object to Bigot, too," Audubon told her, "but my objections are personal. They cannot get in the way of the mission. I object to using the boy, but that objection is personal. The boy will provide an excellent decoy. I have been in enough military actions to know that. . . ." And in a much softer voice he said, "Let us hope, madame, that the Dauphin proves himself worthy of the sacrifice."

"I will pray for it," she said.

He waved her comment aside, slowed his pace, and listened intently for the footfalls of the man who might be following them. He knew that fog always muffled sound.

"I wish there were another way," she told him softly.

Audubon understood what she meant. "As Bigot explained, we are buying one boy with another." And then he added, "It is not something that is particularly agreeable to me."

"But you were the one who suggested it," she responded accusingly.

Audubon shrugged and for some time did not answer. But when he did he reached out, and putting his hand on the mold of the boy's body in the sack, he said, "I would never have sold my son. Never!"

"God will make him worthy of the sacrifice," she said defensively after a few minutes.

And with a wave of his hand he responded, "The Dauphin will either be worthy of the sacrifice or he will not— but God will not have any hand in it either way."

Audubon did not say another word to her until they were on the rue du Temple and the ominous dark walls of the Temple materialized out of the fog. Then he said, "We will be there soon."

"Yes," she responded in a raspy voice.

"Are you frightened?"

"Yes . . . Are you?"

"Yes," he answered, still concerned about the man whose shadow he had seen.

Then to her surprise he took her hand and gave it a gentle squeeze.

"Should we be taken," he asked, "you know what you must do?"

"Prick myself with the pin Bigot gave me," she replied.

"With fortune at our side," Audubon commented, still holding her hand, "we will have an easy sail of it."

"Yes, Captain," Madame Berthoud said, "we will, as you put it, have an easy sail of it, because God is on our side."

"As you wish, madame," he answered, releasing her hand.

"Are you armed?" Madame Berthoud asked just as the dark form of the keep rose like some living thing out of the swirling fog.

"Yes."

She glanced at him.

"No more than a knife," he explained.

They came closer to the Temple.

"Well, madame," Audubon chuckled softly, "we are here!" And with a ferocious shove he sent the cart rolling quickly toward the gate.

Holding a lantern, one of the two guards came out of the gate house and barked his challenge.

And Madame Berthoud, simulating Marie-Jeance's gruffness and speech, shouted back, "It's me an' Simon, you son of a whore. . . . But Simon's had too much to drink. . . . We've come for the rest of our things."

Audubon's palms were sweaty, and his blood drummed in his ears.

"It's Simon an' his wife," the man called out to his companion.

The second guard emerged from the gate house. "Be quick about it," he growled, and unlocking the huge iron gate, he slowly swung it back. Audubon immediately bent his back to the cart and moved it through the opening.

"Off to the right," Madame Berthoud told him softly.

He maneuvered the cart toward the massive wooden door of the keep.

"The boy is on the second level," she told him. "He will be asleep. . . . I have the key to his room."

"And the door to get into the tower?"

"It has been unlocked," she answered. "Several bundles have been prepared for us. . . . They are on the first level near the table."

"Everything has been thought of," Audubon responded dryly.

She did not answer.

As soon as they reached the keep, Audubon allowed the front of the cart to rest on the stones of the courtyard while Madame Berthoud hurriedly opened the door.

"All right," she called out once she was inside.

Audubon shouldered the sack with the boy and carried it inside. A single lamp stood on the table. Its feeble glow provided just enough light for him to make out the vaulted structure of the room.

"The steps," Madame Berthoud told him, crossing the room, "are here."

"What about light?" he asked. "It would not do for me to lose my footing either going up or coming down."

"There is another lamp in the Dauphin's room," she explained. "When I open the door you will see it." And she hurried up the darkened steps.

Audubon waited. The sack on his shoulder was pathetically light. A few moments passed before he heard the door at the head of the stairs swing open, and in an instant the stairway was outlined in a faint but adequate light.

"Hurry," Madame Berthoud called out. "Hurry!"

Audubon rushed up the narrow flight.

"The Dauphin," she said, pointing to the small bed near the window, "is there."

Audubon swung the sack from his shoulder and set it down on the floor. He took a moment to glance around the room. Bird cages were everywhere, and a large metal reflector behind the lamp on the table was focused on the head of the stairs.

"We do not have much time," Madame Berthoud told him. "The guards will be changed soon."

Audubon's eyes became slits, and he asked, "How soon?"

"Fifteen minutes past the hour."

"That was a detail," Audubon said, seething with anger, "that Bigot neglected to tell me."

"Please," she told him, pointing to the sleeping child, "let us hurry!"

Audubon nodded. He would settle the matter with Bigot later. "Here," he said, "help me get this one out of the sack." And he quickly untied the leather thongs that held it closed.

Madame Berthoud knelt next to him.

"You hold the sack," he told her, "and I will pull the boy free."

"All right."

Audubon reached into the sack, and clasping the child under his arms, he withdrew the boy, stretching him out on the floor. "Now the other one," he said.

Madame Berthoud looked down at the boy and in a low voice said, "He does resemble him." And she added, "But the Dauphin would more easily pass for your son than this one."

"Now it is you who is dawdling," Audubon said sharply.

Taking hold of the sack, Madame Berthoud scrambled to her feet and went to where the drugged Dauphin slept.

"Hold the sack out in front of you," Audubon ordered. "Yes, that is right." And lifting the sleeping Dauphin, he slipped him into the sack, feet first. Then he tied it closed with the leather thongs. "Now give it here," he told her. He took the sack from her, carried it closer to the steps, and set it down on the floor. "I will put the other in his place," he said. "There," he exclaimed a few moments later, "it is done!"

"Yes," she whispered, "it is done. . . . May God be with him!"

Audubon shouldered the sack again and said, "This one weighs no more than the other."

"He has not been well of late," she commented.

Audubon started down the stairs.

Madame Berthoud remained in the Dauphin's chamber long enough to allow Audubon to descend the stairs; then she followed him.

"What about the reflector?" he asked when she joined him again.

"It will be seen to by someone else," she answered,

going to the table. "There are four sacks for us. I can manage two now."

"Take what you can," Audubon said. "I will return for the others." And opening the door, he hurried out to the cart.

"Are you just going to put him down?" Madame Berthoud asked.

"He is another sack," Audubon answered.

"But—"

"Give me the two you have," he said, taking the sacks from her, "and get the others." He placed the sacks over the Dauphin, and when Madame Berthoud returned with the other two Audubon added them to the mound.

"Are you sure he will be all right?" she asked.

"He will not be if we stand here any longer."

Madame Berthoud ran back to the door, closed it, and hurriedly rejoined Audubon. "Do not move too fast," she cautioned.

"Why?"

"Simon would not," she answered.

"Even if his life depended on it?"

She shook her head and replied, "Not even then, I think."

Audubon pushed down on the cart's handles, causing its front end to rise from the stones. "I am ready," he said, beginning to push.

Within minutes they were at the gate again, and Madame Berthoud shouted, "You mangy son of a whore, come an' open the gate for a true—"

"Stop shouting," the guard called out, leaving the gate house with a lantern in his hand.

Once more Audubon's heart began to drum, and this time his throat and lips were dry. Despite his feelings about Madame Berthoud, he had to admire her ability to shout at a time when he would be capable only of making a croaking noise.

The second guard came out and without a word went to the gate and unlocked it.

Even before there was an opening large enough to permit the cart to pass through, Audubon started for the gate—so quickly that Madame Berthoud was forced to quicken her pace to keep up with him.

"You took long enough," the guard said as they passed him. "The new guards will be posted in five minutes."

"It's the last time me an' my husband'll be 'ere," Madame Berthoud said.

Suddenly the guard with the lantern swung it closer to Audubon and questioned, "Haven't I seen you before?"

"No," Audubon answered.

"Yes, I have," the guard said, following him. "You were in La Force Prison the night Citizen Freneau took those prisoners out. . . ."

"If you want to keep your head," Audubon threatened savagely, "you will have a sudden lapse of memory."

"I'm sorry," the guard told him. "I'm truly sorry. . . . It was a mistake."

Audubon pushed past him and maneuvered the cart into the dense fog that lay over the rue du Temple.

"What was that all about?" Madame Berthoud asked, practically running beside the cart.

"Something Bigot did not plan on," Audubon answered sharply. "That guard was at the prison the night we went to free your husband."

"Oh, my God," she exclaimed, "then he has seen you twice!"

"Yes," Audubon growled.

The cart bumped and slid along over the wet cobbles even more perilously than it had before, but Audubon did not slow his pace. Sometime later the bells tolled the quarter of the hour. The actual removal of the Dauphin from the Temple had taken no more than ten minutes, but those minutes had required months to accomplish, and each minute had seemed like hours when he was inside the keep.

"The fog has worsened," Madame Berthoud commented.

"I would rather have it this way," he answered, suddenly swinging the cart off to the right.

"What are you doing?" she asked, recovering her balance and coming after him.

"This is the rue Pastorelle," he said.

"But how do you know, when you can see nothing?"

"There is no need for me to see the name," he answered. "I recognized other things that told me where I was."

"Do you think," Madame Berthoud ventured to ask after a brief silence, "that the guard would connect you to Remy?"

Audubon laughed harshly and said, "That guard is as good as dead, madame, as good as dead!"

It took the better part of an hour and a great deal of turning from one street into another for Audubon and Madame Berthoud to make their way from the Temple to the vicinity above Port Paul.

Breathing heavily, Audubon let the cart grind to a halt and said, "I want to rest for a few minutes before we go into the port area."

"But why," she asked, "when we are almost there?"

"So that we will have a better chance of arriving there altogether," he replied.

"Are you afraid?" she questioned.

"Indeed, madame," he said, exhaling deeply, "I am always afraid whenever I risk my life. . . ." He glanced over his shoulder and added, "But to put your mind at ease, I am certain that we have not been followed by anyone from the Temple."

"If we have not been followed, I do not see—"

With a wave of his hand he brushed her objections aside, and letting the front of the cart rest on the wet cobbles, Audubon let go of the two handles and stepped away from them. "I would not want to push one of those all of my life," he commented, moving his shoulders and arms to ease the tightness.

Madame Berthoud did not answer.

After a few minutes Audubon returned to the cart, and putting his weight on the handles, lifted the front of it from the cobbles. Slowly he pushed, and once more the cart began to roll.

"Thank God!" Madame Berthoud exclaimed softly.

33

Audubon heard the sound of footsteps, slowed his pace, and then stopped completely. The men he had seen earlier were there in the fog waiting for them. Intuitively, he had known they would be. . . .

"What is it?" Madame Berthoud asked.

He put his finger to his lips and whispered, "Someone is coming toward us."

Madame Berthoud moved closer to him.

"We will stay here for a few minutes," Audubon told her. "Perhaps the fog will lift a bit and we will be able to see who is out there."

"But we are almost there!" she responded.

Audubon did not answer. Though he knew they could not be very far from the barge, the fog was so thick that even the shortest distance was long enough to be fraught with danger.

"I can hear them," Madame Berthoud said in a raspy voice.

"There are at least two," Audubon commented, "and I imagine they are having the same trouble we are."

"But—"

"Quiet," he ordered. "Just listen!"

Several moments passed. Whoever was there had stopped moving, too, and the only sound Audubon could hear was the beat of his own heart. . . . The men were between them and the barge.

And then a voice drifting through the dense fog said, "I was sure I heard a cart."

"The fog plays tricks with sound," someone answered.

Audubon got a fix on the second man's position, and whispering to Madame Berthoud, he said, "That one is over on the left."

"What will we do?" she asked, clinging to his arm.

"If we stay here much longer," he answered, "they will be sure to find us."

"But they are just waiting for the sound of the cart."

"It is too risky for me to carry the boy," he whispered. "If I were caught with him, I would not be able to make a fight of it. If we get closer to the barge, I can call for Joue."

"What if he cannot reach us in time?"

Audubon shrugged and said, "That is a risk we will have to take. Now do you think you would be able to push the cart?"

"Yes," Madame Berthoud replied. "But not as vigorously as yourself."

"That will not matter," he told her. "Here, you take hold of the handles."

She slipped between him and the cart, and placing her hands on the two bars, asked, "Now what?"

"You start to push when I tell you to," he said.

"And where will you be?"

"Directly beside you," he told her. "All right, move the cart."

Madame Berthoud threw her weight against it. Very slowly the cart began to roll.

"That is fine," he whispered. "That is very good." And he added, "No matter what happens, do not stop."

Audubon sucked in his breath, and exhaling, he unsheathed his knife. He counted the number of paces from the time they began to move. By the time he reached fifteen, two figures had lurched toward them from out of the fog. "Keep moving," he whispered.

"Ho there!" one of the men said to his companion. "I didn't think no one was out except us. . . . But here we have some friends. . . . Are you friends?" He leaned toward the cart and planted himself directly in front of it.

"Avast," shouted Audubon. "Avast!"

Madame Berthoud pushed the cart straight for the man, forcing him to jump out of the way.

The second man grabbed her arm and said, "Here now, what's your hurry there, little lady? Maybe you have somethin' there that you shouldn't be carryin'."

Audubon lunged at him, and using the hilt of his knife as a hammer, he smashed it across the bridge of the man's nose.

The man yelled with pain and staggered away. His companion flew at Audubon, who dropped to the ground, letting the man sail over him.

In an instant Audubon was on his feet and running after Madame Berthoud, urging her to keep pushing; at the same time he shouted for Joue.

The two assailants lost no time in pursuing them.

Suddenly Audubon whirled around, and carving the air with the blade of his knife, slashed one of the men across his chest.

"I'm cut," the wounded man yelled. "I'm cut!"

The second man came running at Audubon, moving too quickly for Audubon to parry his blow. Audubon was thrown to the ground. In an instant the man was on top of him, and grabbing hold of his head, began to beat it against the cobblestones.

Audubon fought to tumble the man off him but could not dislodge him. He tried to gouge his assailant's eyes, but the man somehow managed to avoid his clawing fingers.

With the back of his head already bruised and bloody, Audubon was not sure he would be able to remain conscious very much longer. His strength began to wane, and his vision to blur.

Suddenly there was an explosion.

Audubon's attacker screamed, and releasing his hold on him, he started to stand. Then he toppled over.

Another explosion went off.

The second man shouted, "Oh, my God!" And then he fell close to where his companion lay.

Audubon focused his eyes and found himself looking up at Bigot. He reached up and took hold of the proffered hand. "I would not have lasted much longer," he said, stumbling to his feet, smelling the acrid stink of burned gunpowder.

"I heard you shout for Joue," Bigot said, "just as I reached the barge."

"How far is it from here?" Audubon asked.

"Not far," Bigot told him.

"Far enough," Audubon answered, "far enough . . ." And he lost consciousness.

34

Two lanterns hung from the crossbeams in the cabin, and there was one lamp on the rough wooden table close to where Madame Berthoud was tending to the bruises on the back of Audubon's head. Their shadows were so large that they bent grotesquely against the side, floor, and ceiling of the cabin.

"It is enough," Audubon said impatiently, anxious to be on deck and ready to cast off as soon as the fog lifted.

"Let me put a bandage on it?"

"There is no need," he responded, standing up. A sudden dull pain bloomed in his head, forcing him to touch the back of it with his hand.

"You will have a headache for a day or two," Madame Berthoud said.

Audubon accepted her prediction with a nod, and taking hold of the lamp, he went to the bunk where the Dauphin slept. He knelt and studied the boy. The resemblance between the sleeping child and his dead son was absolutely remarkable; he could not stop himself from commenting, "They could have been mistaken for brothers, perhaps even twins."

"He is a fine-looking boy," Madame Berthoud offered, hovering at Audubon's elbow.

He looked up at her and said, "My son was, too." Then, standing erect, he returned the lamp to the table.

"Captain," she said hesitantly, "I want to thank you."

Audubon brushed her words aside with a wave of his hand and told her, "We both did what had to be done."

"But you risked your life for me as well as for the Dauphin!"

He shrugged and said, "I am going up on deck. . . . I want to be ready—"

"Captain?" she called.

Audubon stopped and faced her. She was smiling, and in the yellow glow of the two lanterns and the lamp she looked startlingly pretty, perhaps even beautiful.

"What you so easily brushed aside," Madame Berthoud told him, "with a wave of your hand, I will remember all my life."

He nodded, turned, and hurried up the companionway to the deck.

Audubon did not understand why Madame Berthoud was so grateful to him. He had done nothing extraordinary as far as he was concerned. Now that he thought about it, she was far more deserving of praise than he, since she had been the one who had finally brought the Dauphin to the barge.

The fog was still very thick, and Audubon, having nothing better to do, paced the length of the barge while impatiently waiting for Joue and Bigot to complete the grisly task of disposing of the two bodies. Several times he stopped to peer in at the four horses in their makeshift deck stable, and once he stroked the head of one of the animals. But for the most part he found himself wondering if the boy who was sleeping in the cabin below decks was worth all the effort it had taken to rescue him, to say nothing of the lives the mission had already cost. Audubon shrugged. That was not a question he or anyone else could answer. He continued to pace and stopped only when Madame Berthoud came up on deck.

"The boy is still asleep?" he asked.

"Yes," she answered. "Bigot said that he would sleep the night through and well into tomorrow."

"It is tomorrow," Audubon commented.

She nodded.

Quite suddenly two figures materialized out of the fog and came toward the barge. Audubon stiffened, and grabbing hold of a stout piece of rope, he barked out, "Who goes there?"

"It's me," Joue replied, "Joue."

Audubon dropped the rope back on the deck.

"What good would that have done," Madame Berthoud asked, "if they had been our enemies?"

"A length of rope," Audubon said, wondering why he was even bothering to explain, "can be a formidable weapon, especially if one uses it like a whip. Besides," he added with a chuckle, "it was the only thing I could grab at the time."

Joue clambered aboard, and Bigot followed.

"Where?" Audubon asked, referring to where they had disposed of the bodies.

"Downriver from here," Bigot answered and then suggested that Audubon join him on the other side of the deck for a final discussion.

Audubon filled his pipe, and then remembering that he had nothing with which to light it, he slipped it back into his pocket.

"In the packet I gave Joue," Bigot said, "are papers for Nicole. She will be traveling as your wife, and the Dauphin as your son."

Audubon shook his head.

"There is no other way," Bigot said. "I have already told her."

"And she did not object?"

"She did at first but not after I had explained the situation to her," Bigot told him. "Then she agreed that it was the safest way. . . . But do you understand what I mean by—"

"Bigot," Audubon responded sharply, "do you have anything else of importance to tell me?"

"Robillard knows," Bigot said, "and once he gets wind of the boy in the Temple he or his agents will be after you. . . ."

"How do you know this?"

Bigot smiled and answered, "Barras told me."

"And what about Gide?"

"Gide is dead," Bigot answered. "But as soon as Robespierre knows that the Dauphin has been taken, you can be sure he will set his agents to look for him."

"Then I will be sought after?"

"You did not think, my dear Captain, that it would continue to be as easy as it has been this far?"

"I did not think that it would be one way or the other,"

Audubon commented, somewhat annoyed by the implication of Bigot's question.

"You must meet the frigate sometime between the dates specified in your orders," Bigot told him.

Audubon nodded.

"And there is a draft on the Bank of England for five thousand pounds in the packet with your orders," Bigot said. "The rest will be paid to you by Captain Ridder. . . . I believe you have already met him."

Audubon stiffened, and scowling, said, "Yes, I surrendered my ship to him at Yorktown, as you well know. How well you have managed to put your 'pieces' together, Bigot."

"Indeed I have," Bigot admitted, "and it took some doing, let me tell you. But Ridder knows you and would not be fooled by an impostor. So, if one of Fouché's men or Robespierre's agents learns of your rendezvous and attempts to substitute a boy and woman in place of the Dauphin and Nicole, he would be unable to do so. And you know Captain Ridder. . . . No one will be able to impersonate him, now, will they?"

Audubon shook his head.

"Then you see why I took the trouble to have Captain Ridder on station to meet you?"

"You have thought of everything," Audubon responded.

"It is what I am supposed to do," Bigot said, "in any mission to which I have been assigned. . . . But tell me, Audubon, what will you do?"

Audubon gave him a questioning look. It was a strange thing to ask. . . . Perhaps even insulting.

"The fog is lifting, Captain," Joue sang out.

"One last word of caution," Bigot said. "Do not ever refer to the boy by his title. Use some name or other."

"My son's," Audubon replied. "I will put the same name on the adoption papers."

Bigot nodded and held out his hand.

"Thank you for helping tonight," Audubon said, shaking Bigot's hand.

"Part of my mission," Bigot answered with a smile, "was to protect you. . . . And now I must say good-bye to Nicole. . . ." He released Audubon's hand and in a low voice said, "Do not be too hard on her, Captain. . . ."

Then he stepped away and crossed the deck to Nicole.

Audubon was so completely taken aback by Bigot's final words that he stood motionless for several moments, trying to think of an answer, and when he finally did, Bigot had already left the deck of the barge.

35

For three days Audubon and Joue worked the barge down-stream toward Meulum, a small town where they planned to beach and fire the craft before going on to Chartres by horse.

Though Audubon was in no way harsh to the Dauphin—now called John by everyone—he did nothing to encourage the friendly relationship that had rapidly sprung up between Joue and the boy.

Whenever Joue was at the tiller the boy was beside him, asking questions about the river, the barge, and anything else that came into his head.

And as for Madame Berthoud, she absolutely doted on the child. There were even times when she, the boy, and Joue would find things to laugh about.

For Audubon the Dauphin's presence served not only to reawaken memories about his own son but also to stir and bring to the surface those gray feelings of regret that he had hoped never to experience again. He had loved his son much more than he had ever dared admit to himself, and to have the boy taken from him just as he had been ready to proclaim his love by legitimizing the child's birth had been almost too much for him to bear. With the exception of his son and Joue, Audubon had never really loved any-one, and even with the boy he had always foolishly maintained a certain distance.

But as he watched the child scamper over the deck or heard him call out to Joue about every bird he saw, Au-

dubon could only purse his lips and clear his throat to ease
the tightness in it.

On the afternoon of the third day Madame Berthoud
joined Audubon at the tiller. The weather was clear but
very cold. Joue was on the towpath with the horses, and
John was asleep in the cabin below.

"Joue told me that we will leave the barge sometime
tonight," she said.

"That is right," Audubon answered.

She drew her shawl more snugly around her shoulders,
and looking at him, she asked, "Why are you so angry
with the—with John?"

"I am not in the least bit angry," Audubon told her.

"Then you do not like him?"

"On the contrary," he said, "I think he is a charming
child. . . . I would not have wanted my own son—"

"Go ahead," she urged, "say it, Captain. . . . Say what
you feel, and having said it, do not toss away what this
John would so willingly give you if you but let him. Here
and as long as he is with us, the Dauphin is nothing more
than a child. . . ."

Audubon nodded but remained silent.

"I wish," she said, suddenly standing, "that you would
change your mind."

"I have," he answered, swallowing hard, "or at least I
will try."

Madame Berthoud smiled.

36

At sundown Audubon ordered a halt to the day's progress, and when Joue returned to the barge with the horses, he tethered the four of them to willow saplings that grew some distance back from the bank of the river.

"How far above Meulum are we?" Audubon called from the barge.

"Less than a league," Joue answered, leaping easily from the bank to the deck.

"And the other barges we saw this afternoon," Audubon asked, "where are they?"

Joue sat down on the top of the stanchion around which was wrapped several turns of the heavy hawser that secured the stern of the barge to the thick trunk of an oak several paces beyond the willow saplings. He looked toward the bow, where another hawser ran out from the barge and was bent and knotted around an enormous boulder.

"How far away would the barge in front of us be?" Audubon questioned, wondering why Joue had not answered the first time.

"That's Pepe," Joue replied. "He always goes directly into Meulum and Dardis—the barge following us doesn't come past here until sometime after daybreak."

"Then we will be able to fire the barge without having to worry about snoopers."

Joue stood up, and looking forward, said in a low voice, "I got to like this old tub."

"You would not be happy on the river," Audubon told him. "You are a deep-water sailor, Joue, and sooner or later you would go back to sea."

"You're probably right, Captain," Joue laughed. "But nonetheless I got to like the river and the people on it. And I think that some of them even got to like me."

Audubon shrugged and said, "After we are done you come back here if that is what you really want."

"No," Joue responded after a few moments, "it was just somethin' that entered my head. I wouldn't be happy if I couldn't go back to the islands now and then. . . . That way I'm like you, Captain."

Audubon stood up, and putting his hand on Joue's shoulder, he said, "For us and those like us it is the sea."

Joue nodded.

By the time the horses were fed and watered it was night. The sky was very clear and filled with countless stars.

True to his word, Audubon took John on deck and pointed out Polaris, the North Star, and the constellations of Orion, the Hunter, and Cygnis, the Swan.

And the child asked, "Is that where my father and mother are, in heaven?"

It was the first time the boy had mentioned his parents, and Audubon, who did not believe in heaven or hell, quickly changed the subject.

"Later tonight," he said, "we are going to leave the barge."

"Where will we sleep?"

"You will sleep in your bunk for a while," Audubon explained, "and then we will ride the horses. . . . Can you ride?"

John nodded and asked, "Where will we ride to?"

"The city of Chartres," Audubon answered.

The boy was very still.

"It has a beautiful cathedral," Audubon told him.

Suddenly sobbing, the child clung to him.

Audubon lifted the boy in his arms and softly said, "There is no other way for us to go. It was planned that way."

"I was there with my father, mother, and sister," the child whimpered.

Audubon patted him on the back and said, "I am sorry."

The boy's sobs lessened, and Audubon set him down.

"I did not mean to cry," John apologized, "but sometimes I cannot stop it."

"That happens with everyone," Audubon said, handing the child his handkerchief. "Here, wipe your eyes and blow your nose."

"You will not tell Madame Berthoud that I was crying?" the boy asked. "If she knew she would cry, too."

Audubon assured the child that he would tell no one, and then he suggested they go below.

"You will not forget to wake me?" John asked just as they reached the companionway.

"Absolutely not," Audubon said, realizing that the child was very much afraid of being abandoned, and with good cause.

Madame Berthoud had prepared a stew on the small wood-burning stove standing off in the forward part of the cabin. And by the time Audubon and John came down the companionway she was already calling them to the table.

Audubon sniffed the air and said, "If it tastes as good as it smells, we will indeed be lucky."

And Joue added, "Anything that smells so good should be smelled and not eaten."

"I would rather eat it," John said, "than just sit here and sniff at it."

Everyone laughed, and Madame Berthoud brought the big black pot to the table. "You serve," she said to Audubon, handing him an enormous ladle.

"It has been a while," he explained, "since I have done this."

"Perhaps it is a sign," Joue commented, "that you will begin to do it again?"

"The sign, Joue," Audubon laughed as he filled a plate with the steaming stew and passed it to Madame Berthoud, "is—if it is anything—that our cook enjoys seeing me work."

John's wide, questioning eyes darted to Madame Berthoud.

And she responded with a smile, "I enjoy watching you do anything, Captain."

Audubon stopped for a moment and looked at her.

"What I meant," she hastily endeavored to explain, "was. . . ." Her words drifted off, and her cheeks filled with color.

37

The moon was up, dimming all but the brightest stars in the sky and silvering the bare limbs of the trees and the dark ribbon of the river that flowed beyond the beached barge.

The horses were saddled. Madame Berthoud and John stood far up the bank, near the oak to which the stern of the barge was fastened by the long length of hawser.

On deck Audubon and Joue poured oil over everything that would burn. When this was done Audubon set a small keg of gunpowder against the side of the craft that was still in the river and said, "The explosion will blow most of it into the river."

"And the fire'll take care of anything else," Joue commented.

"I want as little left of it as possible," Audubon told him. "Now go to the others. . . . I will be with you as soon as I start this fire going."

Joue hesitated.

"Go ahead," Audubon said. "I will take care of it."

"It's goin' to burn mighty fast," Joue observed and sniffing the air, he added, "There's enough oil to make it explode without the gunpowder. I think you'd be better off startin' the fire from the deck. All you have to do is throw a lighted lamp down the companionway an' poof!—She'll burn real quick!"

"What about the bow section?" Audubon asked.

Joue scratched his head.

"Whoever finds the hulk," Audubon explained, "must

think that everyone aboard was blown into the river by the explosion, and the horses, too, were blown into the water."

"What about the hoofprints on the bank?"

"Once the barge begins to burn," Audubon said, "we will have enough light to ford the river. I do not think anyone will think to look on the other side, and if they do, they will think that possibly the horses managed to get free and swim the river. They might even begin to look for them."

"It's a mighty cold night to come up out of the river soaking wet," Joue commented. "You an' me, we're used to bein' cold an' wet, but John an' Madame Berthoud—"

"Then what would you suggest?"

"I don't know, Captain," Joue answered.

"We must cross the river and get on the road to Chartres without having to go through Meulum and run the risk of having to explain how we got to the town without using the road—to say nothing of having to explain where we came from."

Joue said nothing.

"All right," Audubon said after a few moments of looking at the oil-drenched cabin, "I will fire it from the deck, and let us hope that it burns well enough." He took the lamp from the table and made his way up the companionway, following Joue.

Audubon filled his lungs with the clean, cold night air, and each time he exhaled, his breath smoked in the icy air. It was very cold, and he realized that neither Madame Berthoud nor the boy would be able to sustain the shock of being both cold and wet. . . .

"We will go back through the woods over there," Audubon said, pointing to where Madame Berthoud and John were standing, "to the road, and on to Meulum. . . . Hopefully everyone will be asleep when we reach it. . . . But should we be asked any questions, we must tell them we have come from Paris and are on our way to Rouen. If necessary we can change our route once we are past Meulum. Now go to the others."

Joue left the barge and hurried up the bank to join Madame Berthoud and John.

Audubon waited until he saw the three of them standing together, then, turning to the companionway, he threw the lamp into the cabin and leaped back. In an instant flames flared out of the companionway, driving Audubon against the stern of the barge.

Madame Berthoud screamed.

"Get off," Joue shouted. "Get off, Captain!" And he ran down the bank to the barge.

Audubon regained his balance. Realizing that he would never be able to reach the gangway, he leaped from the stern into the shallow water of the river and scrambled toward the shore, praying he would reach it before the keg of powder exploded. Already the flames had cast their reddish glow over the water and the nearby trees.

"Hurry, Captain!" Joue urged, coming toward him.

"Get back," Audubon shouted. "Get back!"

The crackling of the fire filled the air, and dense black smoke poured out of the companionway and from between the deck boards. Then some of the timbers cracked and the entire companionway dissolved in a great geyser of red sparks. Almost the next instant an enormous explosion blew Audubon off his feet and sent bits and pieces of the barge in all directions.

Audubon struggled to stand. The wind had been knocked out of him, and he was dazed.

Joue came running down into the water, and grabbing him by the arm, pulled him to the shore. "You all right, Captain?" he asked.

"I think so," Audubon answered. He looked back at the barge, and with a nod he said, "It is burning well."

Suddenly Madame Berthoud and John were beside him.

"You could have been killed," she wailed.

"Many times over," he answered, somewhat flippantly.

And then John flung his arms around Audubon and cried, "No . . . No . . . I do not want you killed. . . . I want you to . . . to . . . to tell me about the stars."

Audubon lifted the boy into his arms and carried him to the horses. "Come," he said to the others, "mount up. We have a long ride. . . ." And then he added, "The boy will ride with me. . . ."

38

Awakening none of the town's inhabitants other than a few dogs that noisily barked at their arrival and departure, Audubon slowly led his small band through the moon-silvered town of Meulum and across the stone bridge spanning the river.

When they were some distance from the bridge Audubon said, "We must ride as fast as we can for a while. By daybreak I want to be the better part of a league away from here." Without waiting for the others to speak, he worked his legs against the flanks of his mount. The horse bounded forward, and Audubon, with the others following close behind, rode swiftly toward Chartres.

The darkness of night gave way to the grayness of first light, and even before the sun began to show itself in the east, the sky was blue and the clouds pink. Then Audubon brought his mount to a walk, and the others followed suit. As soon as the horses had regained their wind, he again rode at a gallop, though not as fast or for as long as before.

The second time Audubon slowed down, he said, "We will stop at the first inn for something hot. And to water the horses."

"They will not last long at this pace," Joue commented.

Audubon shrugged and said, "I will buy others when we get to Chartres."

A short time later they came across a small inn, where the gray smoke from a good fire rose straight up into the blue sky until it became a plaything for the winds and the scent of freshly baked bread hung heavily in the air.

"Remember," Audubon cautioned Madame Berthoud and John, "we are a family. Use the familiar 'you' when you speak to me or each other."

"I will try hard to remember," the boy said.

The inside of the inn was clean, though roughly furnished, with several wooden tables and chairs spaced around the big room. There was a large stone fireplace in one wall and a door in the wall on the far side leading to the living quarters.

The innkeeper was a short, fat man who moved slowly and wheezed with every breath he took. He was surprised to see a family on the road so early in the morning and said so.

"We wanted to have an early start," Audubon explained.

And looking at Joue, the innkeeper asked how he had got to be so black.

Joue laughed and told him, "My mother's milk was black, and I drank too much of it."

The man gave him a peculiar look and then began to laugh, too.

Audubon drank several cups of hot chocolate, and though he did not eat much himself, he urged the others to, telling them that he did not intend to stop again until nightfall.

Within an hour they were on their way. But this time John rode his own horse.

In the late afternoon the sky began to cloud up, and because of it twilight seemed to come earlier. The wind rose, veering around to the northwest.

"There's the smell of snow in the air," Joue said.

When darkness came they reached the outskirts of Mairene, where they took lodgings for the night at the inn of the Trois Pommes.

Joue had his own room, while Audubon, Madame Berthoud, and John, since they were traveling as a family, shared another. The boy slept in a small alcove and had a bed of his own. Madame Berthoud slept in a large double bed, while Audubon made himself as comfortable as possible on one of the chairs.

He did not go up to the room directly after dinner but

spent some time drinking with Joue in order to give Madame Berthoud the opportunity to prepare for bed in privacy. Though they had spent several nights on the barge, they had always slept in their clothes, and when they did change their linen it was always done in the forward hold. But the luxury of that kind of seclusion for Madame Berthoud was no longer possible unless he willingly absented himself from the chamber.

When Audubon finally entered the room he found that Madame Berthoud had graciously left the lamp on the table near his chair turned up. He appreciated the gesture, and looking at her, smiled.

"And what is that for?" she asked.

"I thought you would be asleep by now," he said, placing two good-sized faggots across the andirons.

"I almost was, but then I heard you come in."

He apologized for disturbing her and asked how the boy was.

"His eyes were closed," she answered, "even before his head touched the pillow."

Audubon nodded, sat down, pulled off his boots, and removed his jacket. Then he slipped the pistol from his belt and laid it on the table.

"I did not know you carried a firearm," Madame Berthoud said, sitting up and pulling the blanket up around her.

Audubon shrugged and moved the chair to give him a clear field of fire from the door to the window.

"I was truly frightened when the explosion knocked you down," she told him.

"Truly," he commented with a chuckle, "no more than I."

Madame Berthoud slipped down in the bed again and said, "Good night, Captain."

"Good night, madame," he answered and turned down the lamp.

After a few minutes Madame Berthoud asked, "Do you think we will be successful?"

"I hope so," he replied.

"So far—"

"Bigot's planning has made it possible for fortune to smile on us," Audubon said. "Let us hope the smile does not turn into a frown."

"Why do you hate him so?" she asked, suddenly sitting up.

Audubon turned toward her. This time she did not hide herself behind the blanket, and the white gown she wore revealed much of her breasts, even to their erect nipples.

"Well, answer me," she demanded. "Why do you hate him so?"

"And I may ask," he responded in a low voice, "why you love him."

"That is not the same," she said, shaking her head so that her long, dark hair swirled over her bare shoulders.

"I do not hate Bigot," Audubon explained. "He is a very clever man, perhaps even brilliant. . . . And doubtless, without him we would never have been able to do what we have done."

"Then why——"

"His feelings toward me," Audubon said, "were no different from mine toward him."

"He did not trust you," she said.

"Nor I him."

"He did not trust you," she told him, "because he could not control you."

"And I did not trust him," Audubon explained, "because I knew he wanted to control me."

Suddenly she realized how much of her body was exposed, and hastily slipping under the blanket, rectified the situation.

Audubon turned away, closed his eyes, and tried not to think about Madame Berthoud.

But after a while she said, "He came to me one night, and I knew that I wanted him as much as he wanted me. But there was never any love between us. There was need."

Her confession made him uneasy. He did not want to know anything about their relationship.

"Did you love Madame Flahaut?" she asked.

"I found her physically appealing."

She gave a soft laugh and said, "Good night, Captain."

Audubon responded in kind and hoped that sleep would soon come. But Madame Berthoud was still very much in his thoughts, and this time he was the one who broke the silence. "Have you made any plans to meet Bigot afterward?" he asked.

"No," she said with a yawn. "It is over between us. Even if I had remained in Paris, I think it would have been over."

"What about his need?"

"I had fulfilled it," she answered, "the way a woman always does. . . . The way Madame Flahaut fulfilled yours, Captain."

Audubon did not answer.

"I am almost ready to believe," she commented wistfully, "that whatever else exists between men and women, love seldom does. At least not long enough to matter. . . ."

"Yes," Audubon agreed with a weary sigh, "it seems as though it is that way."

"Then all the other pleasures," she breathed, "probably belong to the Devil. . . ." The rest of what she said became incoherent as she finally drifted off to sleep.

Audubon smoked one pipe before his eyelids became too heavy for him to keep open, but in the time he remained awake he thought of all the women he had known. To his absolute amazement he came to the conclusion that he had never loved any of them—not his wife, not even Mademoiselle Rabin, who had given birth to his son. He shook his head, set his pipe down, and allowed himself to drift into a light sleep.

The following day Audubon rose before dawn. His back was stiff and his shoulders ached from sitting up all night. He turned up the lamp and first woke the boy and then Madame Berthoud. "Hurry," he told her, "we want to be on our way within the hour."

Just as they left the town of Mairene, it started to snow. Huge white flakes came swirling down from the still-black sky.

"If we push hard enough," Audubon called above the howl of the wind, "we should be in Chartres by nightfall." And he drove his mount to a gallop.

39

Just as the leaden sky was rapidly dulling to darkness, Audubon led the others into Chartres. The wind-driven snow made it impossible for them to see the cathedral until they had wended their way to the top of the high hill on which it stood. But even then, the combination of falling snow and failing light obscured all but the lower portion, which seemed more phantasmagorical than real.

As soon as the horses were stabled, Audubon took his small party to the town's inn, a two-story building whose entrance fronted on the Place de la Cathédrale. He had no difficulty obtaining accommodations as, fortunately, the inn was empty. An agreeable young clerk told him that for five sous more they could take their meals there, too.

Audubon agreed to that arrangement and asked why there were no other guests at the inn.

"The weather, citizen," the young man answered. "The weather and the times."

Audubon nodded, thanked him, and a short while later he, Madame Berthoud, and John were comfortably ensconced in what amounted to two rooms, while Joue had his own place at the end of the hall.

"I do not think I have ever been so cold," Madame Berthoud said, rubbing her hands together.

"And what about you, John?" Audubon said, turning from the hearth where he was busy building up the fire to look at the red-cheeked boy.

"I was afraid," the child admitted, "that we would never stop."

Audubon laughed and said, "I think I was beginning to be afraid, too."

"You?" John questioned in disbelief.

"Yes," Audubon responded with a nod, "even I."

"You are just telling me that to make me feel better," the boy responded.

Audubon shook his head and stood up. The fire was lively now, and he held his hands out toward it. "I think we will remain here for a night or two," he said. "We can all use the rest."

"You must be exhausted," Madame Berthoud commented.

He shrugged, and rubbing his chin, discovered it was covered with stubble.

"I wish there were some other way," she told him. "Perhaps you could stay with Joue?"

"I cannot risk that," he said quietly.

"But surely you do not think anyone has followed us?"

"I do not know," he answered, and turning away from the hearth, he surveyed the room. It was well furnished with a canopied bed, a dresser against one wall, several chairs, and a few small tables. There was even a writing desk near the window, which looked out on the Place de la Cathédrale.

He left the fire and positioned a chair to give him a clear shot at anyone who might come through the door, and then went to inspect the boy's room. It, too, had a canopied bed, but there were fewer furnishings and they were not nearly so good as those in the larger room.

"The snow is still falling," Madame Berthoud said. She was standing at the window, where the snow struck against the glass pane with a hissing sound.

"It will probably continue through the night," Audubon said, sitting down.

"I think I will rest for a while," John announced.

"An excellent idea!" Audubon exclaimed.

"You will not forget to wake me when you go down for supper?" the boy asked.

"You have my word," Audubon assured him, "that we will not make a move without you."

Satisfied, the Dauphin went into his own room.

"He is very brave," Madame Berthoud said softly, moving from the window to the hearth.

"As are you, madame," Audubon told her softly.

She looked at him in surprise.

Audubon nodded.

Madame Berthoud's cheeks suffused with color, and she practically whispered, "Thank you, Captain. I never thought that I would ever hear that from you."

"And I never thought I would say it," he replied.

They looked at each other, and suddenly they both began to laugh. But before their laughter had ceased, the door exploded open and three men charged into the room. One of them carried a pike; the other two were armed with pistols.

Madame Berthoud screamed.

Audubon leaped in front of her, and drawing the pistol from his belt, fired it at one of the men, blowing the top of the man's head off and splattering his brains on the nearby yellow wall in big blotches of gray and red. . . .

Joue came from behind the intruders and thrust his knife into the second man's back. He screamed and fell forward.

The third man charged at Audubon with the pike, thrusting it into his right shoulder. But Joue felled him with a blow on the head.

"Kill him!" Audubon ordered, breathing hard.

Joue pulled the pike out of Audubon's shoulder and drove it into the man's back.

Audubon held his hand over the wound in his shoulder and in a tight voice said, "I should have realized the inn was empty because we were expected."

But whether their plans had been discovered by Robespierre's agents or those of Fouché, Audubon could not even begin to guess. Perhaps both knew and had dispatched their men after him.

It was not a pleasant prospect to contemplate, but since it was so much a fact, Audubon realized that he would have to change his plans accordingly.

Madame Berthoud ran to John, who, wide-eyed and sobbing, cowered against a wall. She gathered the frightened child to her and looked about the room. In a matter of moments its whole aspect had changed. Not only was the sharp odor of burned powder in the air but the floor was red with blood.

"Bring the horses, Joue," Audubon told his first officer. "We must leave."

"What about the clerk?" Joue asked.

"Let him be," Audubon said. "He is probably hiding in the cellar or in some closet."

Then, turning to Madame Berthoud, he said, "There is no other way. We must get away now. The snow will cover our tracks." And then, tearing the sheet off the bed, he began to bandage his arm.

"Let me do that," Madame Berthoud said.

Audubon nodded, and beckoning to John, he put his left arm around the boy's shoulder and pressed the child to him, whispering, "We will soon be safe, my little one. . . . We will soon be safe. . . ."

A short time later they left Chartres and rode into the night. The snow and the wind seemed worse, and they moved very slowly.

Audubon's original plan had called for him to go from Chartres to Tours and then west along the Loire River to Nantes. From Nantes the village of Le Gerbetière, where he lived, was only a few leagues' distance. But now he decided to move across country, avoiding as much as possible any villages along the way. He did not discuss his plan with anyone until the following morning when the snow had stopped and they were resting in an abandoned barn.

After he and Joue had started a fire and they were all much warmer than they had been for hours, Audubon revealed his intentions.

"But what will we do for food and shelter?" Madame Berthoud asked, casting her eyes toward the boy.

"We will forage," he said. "And as for shelter," he added, gesturing at the abandoned structure around them, "there are many places such as this all over the countryside."

"And how can you be sure," she questioned, "that you will find one when you need it?"

"If not," Audubon answered, "we will be forced to risk asking a farmer for a night's shelter."

Madame Berthoud did not put forth any additional objections.

And Audubon suggested that they remain where they

were for a few hours' rest, adding that he would take the first watch.

"No," Joue said, "I will take the first watch."

"And I the second," Madame Berthoud added.

Audubon was about to object, but from the look of determination on her face he knew that any objection would be stiffly resisted and he did not have the strength to press his will.

"How is your shoulder?" Madame Berthoud asked.

"Stiff, but the bleeding has stopped."

"I could change the bandage," she offered.

Audubon shook his head and said, "In a few days we will reach my home and—" He stopped and turned away from her.

"Yes," she commented, "and Madame Audubon will see to it."

"Yes," he repeated with a deep sigh, "Madame Audubon will see to it." Then he closed his eyes and almost immediately fell into a deep sleep.

40

After Madame Berthoud had stood her watch that first morning in the barn there was never any question about her doing it again. And often during the next few days she would speak to Joue about Audubon. Sometimes their conversations took place when Audubon and John were asleep and they were sitting close to an open fire, and sometimes they would ride side by side and talk about the Captain.

If Audubon was nothing else, Madame Berthoud had reached the conclusion that he was an extremely brave man. Not nearly so dashing as some of the cavaliers she had once known at court—indeed, her husband had been a man of such elegance—but oh, what a pitiful lack of substance those gorgeously uniformed men had possessed.

One night when the waning moon had turned the snow-covered countryside into a glistening sheet of light, Madame Berthoud sat by the fire and asked Joue about Audubon's son.

"He was a boy," Joue said, pointing to the sleeping Dauphin, "much like that one there. . . . The Captain went to see him every time he went to the islands. The boy's mother, Mademoiselle Rabin, was a pretty woman, but she did not want to keep the boy. I think she was going to marry a planter. The Captain took the boy, but he gets sick, and two, maybe three days after he brings him home, the boy dies. . . . I think the Captain, he wants to die, too. . . ."

"He has become very fond of this boy, too," she commented.

Joue nodded and said, "Yes, I see that, too. . . ."

As the days passed, there was no doubt in Madame Berthoud's mind that Audubon had accepted her as a comrade in arms, though of course they had been that from the very beginning of their relationship. But even more significantly, they had become friends, and she knew intuitively that that kind of rapport was not easily obtained with the Captain.

One afternoon when she was riding close to Joue and Audubon and John were some distance in front of them, Madame Berthoud asked Joue, "How long have you been with the Captain?"

"Most of my life," Joue answered. "He came all the way upriver to fetch me."

"I thought he had bought you."

"You don't buy," Joue told her, "what is already yours."

"But—"

Joue gestured toward Audubon and said, "Ask him. . . . Perhaps he will tell you." And then, flailing the side of his horse with his legs, he trotted up to the others, leaving Madame Berthoud to ponder the implications of what he had just told her.

Audubon's reputation, even when she had first met him in New Orleans so many years before, was sufficient to make all but the most adventurous women avoid his company for any length of time. That he was a rake was countenanced by the men and whispered about by the women. Even his recent liaison with Madame Flahaut was viewed by the intimates of Gouverneur Morris's circle with the same complacent attitude as were his earlier peccadilloes by the people who had attended the ball at the Marigny house.

And though Madame Berthoud recognized that her own relationship with Bigot could be called to question, she viewed it as being substantially less reprehensible than any of Audubon's. After all, she had not made herself available to other men while she was with Bigot. In truth, her experience with men other than her husband had been so limited that she could count them on one hand. And those who had preceded Bigot had done so only briefly and had even less meaning for her.

In a melancholy mood from thinking about Bigot and the other men to whom she had given herself, Madame Berthoud rode alone for most of the afternoon.

But in the evening when Audubon found an old shepherd's hut for them to spend the night in, he rode up to her and asked, "Are you ill, madame?"

She shook her head.

"Perhaps you are too tired to take the first watch tonight?"

"No," she said, "I will take it."

They rode to the hut together, and he helped her out of the saddle.

"Captain," she asked, standing very close to him, "do you resent my having lived with Bigot?" There was an unmistakable catch in her voice, but her gaze did not falter.

Audubon shrugged and said gently, "I do not think about it."

"Never?" she questioned, brushing her hair away from her eyes.

"It is of no consequence now."

"It is to me," she insisted.

"He is an Englishman," Audubon said tightly. "I would have felt the same whether it was you or any other Frenchwoman."

Madame Berthoud closed her eyes and whispered, "Thank you, Captain. . . ." Then suddenly she felt the tips of his fingers on her cheek. She opened her eyes and looked at him, realizing with some astonishment that he was fully bearded and here and there the black hair was flecked with gray.

"I do not judge you," he told her softly. "I am wise enough to know that all of us seek desperately for happiness but life doles it out in pitifully small measure. . . ." He pointed to the inside of the hut and said, "That boy in there has already learned that hard lesson. Everything he loved was taken from him. If he were some other child, he might still enjoy the love of a mother and father. But he is willing to settle for our friendship and our love, such as it is, because it makes him happy, at least for a little while."

He lowered his hand from her face, and with the hint of a smile playing on his lips, he added, "I ask you, madame, not to judge me too harshly either." And with that he turned and went into the hut.

41

Before noon on the tenth day after they had left Chartres they crested a small hill, and pointing across the valley to much larger hill on which stood a large gray-stone house, Audubon said, "That is my home." And riding out in front of the others, he beckoned them to follow.

The sharp smell of the sea was in the air, and clouds, more gray than white, moved over the land like a vast armada. The previous night's rain had washed most of the snow from the ground. Once they were across the valley and had begun working their way up the hill they could hear the thunderous boom of surf that rose up from the not-too-distant rock-strewn beaches.

"I would dearly love a hot bath," Madame Berthoud said, coming up beside Audubon.

"And you shall have one."

"Just the thought of soaking is enough to make me gallop the rest of the way," she told him.

"I am afraid your poor horse would give out from under you," Audubon said, "if you should try."

She patted the animal's neck and commented, "I did not think she or any of the others would last the journey."

"Nor I," Audubon answered, turning onto a narrow dirt road that circled around the hill and brought them to the front of the house, still some distance above them.

But even from where they were, Madame Berthoud could see the white water of the boiling surf and beyond that the leaden sea, stretching back to where it seemed joined to an equally leaden-looking sky. And on the road above them there was a large wooden gate flanked on either side by a low wall made of the same gray stones as the house itself.

"The farm," Audubon said with a sweep of his hand, "goes from the beach back across the valley to the top of the hill from which we saw it."

"I know nothing about farms," Madame Berthoud said.

"Neither do I," Audubon laughed, "but my wife knows all there is to know. My world is out there," he told her, pointing to the sea, "and hers is all this." And again he swept his hand in front of him.

Suddenly a man began to shout, "Madame Audubon . . . Madame Audubon . . . The Captain is back. . . . He's come home again!"

"That is Michel," Audubon explained. "He lives with his wife in a cottage near the barn on the other side of the house."

A few moments later the door to the big house opened and Madame Audubon stood there looking out at them.

Even before they passed through the gate Madame Berthoud could see that the Captain's wife was tall and angular, an austere-looking woman with a long face that showed no reaction to her husband's arrival.

They dismounted, and after Audubon had greeted Michel, a short, leathery-looking man, he told him to take the horses into the stable.

"Feed them well," Audubon said. "They have served us well." Then, holding John by the hand and nodding to Madame Berthoud, he said to his wife, "Anne, this young man is John."

"I am pleased to meet you, Madame Audubon."

The woman nodded but said nothing.

"And this is Madame Berthoud," Audubon explained. "She is the boy's governess."

"It is a pleasure to meet you," Madame Berthoud said, extending her hand toward the woman.

"Is she goin' to sleep in your room?" Madame Audubon asked, looking at Audubon and ignoring the proffered hand.

"She will not," Audubon responded sharply. "She is the boy's governess."

Madame Berthoud pulled back her hand and was about to object, but Audubon spoke first. "You must excuse my wife, madame," he told her. "Her forthrightness sometimes gets in the way of her manners."

"I know what my eyes tell me," Madame Audubon said, backing into the doorway.

Audubon followed her and called to the others to enter.

"You can stay in the room on the east side of the house," Madame Audubon said to Madame Berthoud. "The boy will have the room next to you."

"Thank you," Madame Berthoud responded in a whisper.

"And as for you," Madame Audubon commented, pointing to Joue, "you can sleep in the room near the kitchen."

"We have been traveling for many days," Audubon explained, "and we would like to have hot baths and something to eat."

"You look like you've been sleeping in the fields," his wife said, "and you smell worse."

"A tub of hot water for each of us, madame, if you please."

"I'll have Michel and Lucie bring them to your rooms," she answered, stalking off to the back of the house.

"I am sorry," Audubon apologized when his wife was gone, "but her bark, as the saying goes, is worse than her bite."

"I would say," Madame Berthoud responded, "that her bite is easily equal to her bark. . . . Now if you do not mind, Captain, I would like to go to my room."

"Of course," he said. "This way . . . Come along, John, you might as well go to your room, too. . . ."

Later, when Madame Berthoud was alone, she dropped down on the bed, and burying her head in the pillow, she wept.

42

Audubon's room was splashed with the glow of a dying
sun. Enveloped in the rapidly fading reddish light, he stood
in front of the window looking across the shadowed valley
to the crest of the hill on the other side.

Anne had just entered the room, interrupting his troubled thoughts about the rendezvous he must soon make
with the British frigate. She stood with her back to the
door and said nothing.

"We will take dinner in the dining room," Audubon told
her, leaving the window for a place close to the hearth,
where a good fire was burning.

"I have a right to know what's going on," Anne said.

"In three days at the very most," he explained, "we will
be gone."

"No!" she shouted. "I won't have you going off again.
You and that black left last September. Here it is the very
beginning of February and you've come home to tell me
that you'll be off again. I do not know where you have
been these past months. . . ."

"It is not important."

". . . Or what you have been doing."

"That is not important either."

"And this time, when you leave here, where will you
go?"

"I always return, Anne," he said, moving from the fire
back to the window. The light was almost all gone now.

"And if you should not return, Jean," she scolded,
"what then?"

Audubon shrugged.

"That is not enough," Anne cried. "I am not going to stand for it this time. I want to know who those people are. The boy and that Madame Berthoud are in my house, and I have a right to——"

"No!" Audubon shouted suddenly, wheeling from the window to face his wife. "What I do, I do to protect you. You have never known what I was about and cared less, as long as you had this farm. You still have the farm, Anne."

"I will give it to you," she said, advancing toward him. "I will sign it over to you."

Audubon shrugged. It was a gesture that came twenty years too late.

"Even if I had given it to you after our marriage," she continued, "you still would have gone to sea."

"I am a sailor," he said. "I never pretended to be anything else."

"Then what difference does it make about the farm?"

"None," he told her, "except that you would have honored our marriage agreement by doing it."

"Dear God," she shouted, "you were just a boy, a twenty-year-old boy!"

"And you, madame, were ten years older and already a widow. The marriage was arranged by my father. It was to be good for each of us. It was not, Anne, good for you or for me."

"And you blame me?"

Audubon shook his head. "The responsibility is more than yours," he told her.

"I am glad you see that," Anne said. "If any woman ever tried to make her husband happy, I did, Jean."

"I would not deny that."

"But you would have me do," she told him, "what no decent woman would." Then, suddenly, she threw herself against him, and grabbing hold of his arms, she yelled, "Does that Madame Berthoud do those things for you, Jean? Does she, Jean?"

Furious, he pushed her away from him.

"Oh, I can see from the way she looks at you," Anne shouted, "that she's your whore!"

"No," Audubon shouted. "No!"

"Yes," his wife screamed. "Yes, that one is a whore if I ever saw one!"

In a rage he raised his hand.

"Go ahead," Anne challenged, "beat me. Go ahead, Jean. . . . You've done it before."

He lowered his hand, and in a raspy voice he said, "You provoke me, madame, you provoke me greatly." He went to the writing desk and turned up the lamp. Then in a low voice he said, "In all the years of our marriage I have never come home when we did not argue, did not tear at each other. I have seen wounded sharks in the seas off the islands do the same thing, Anne. We, too, are wounded and we slash at each other with words. I am sorry I raised my hand to you, very sorry." He put his arms around her and said, "Perhaps when I return we will become friends."

"I would be your wife if you'd let me," she said, looking up at him.

He let go of her and shrugged. He had not shared her bed for at least ten years, and even before he had chosen to sleep in his own room he'd seldom touched her.

"Do you want me to apologize to Madame Berthoud?" Anne asked.

"No," he answered. "There is no need for that. I think she understands."

"As you wish."

Audubon nodded and was just about to ask what was being prepared for dinner when there was a sudden hubbub of men's voices coming from the small vestibule near the front door.

Audubon, with a cocked pistol in his hand, was out of the bedroom and charging at the men who had forced their way into the house.

Primed with a cutlass, Joue, too, came running toward the men.

"Stand!" Audubon ordered. "Or I will shoot."

The tallest of the group faced him and shouted, "Captain Audubon, that is hardly a way to greet a friend, much less an old friend."

"General Charette!" Audubon exclaimed, completely surprised.

"Yes," the General said. "And some of my men . . . We have have been waiting until nightfall to come here."

"But why?" Audubon questioned.

The General laughed boisterously. "They are after you, Captain," Charette said, "and I thought it only fitting to prevent them from getting you."

Madame Berthoud had left her room and was standing short distance from the open door.

Audubon beckoned to her and said, "May I present General Charette?"

The General took her hand and kissed the back of it. "You are as brave," he gallantly said, "as you are beautiful. . . . But we do not have time for pleasantries. We have horses for you, and you must go directly to the *Oiseau*. She is anchored in a cove two leagues from here."

Suddenly the boy came out of his room.

"Your Highness!" the General exclaimed, dropping to one knee. The officers with him followed his example.

"Highness?" Madame Audubon questioned.

The boy stood very still.

"It is with great pleasure, your Grace," the General said, "that we meet with you."

Audubon looked at the General and his men. They were foolish indeed not to realize that the boy would have been more responsive to them if they had remained standing.

"I think it would be better if you and your men stood up," Audubon suggested.

General Charette growled, "His Highness will tell us when to stand, Captain."

"John," Audubon said gently, "tell the men to stand."

"Please stand," the boy whispered.

The General came to his full height, and the others also stood up. Then he said, "I have the notary from La Rochelle to attest to the legality of your actions."

Audubon nodded.

"You're going to adopt the Dauphin?" Madame Audubon asked.

"No," Audubon replied, "I am going to adopt my natural son."

"But then he will have a legal right to inherit your property," Anne objected.

"I do not think you need concern yourself over that," General Charette said.

"Then why must he be adopted?" she pressed.

"Because," the General answered, "he must travel incognito before he can be proclaimed King of France, and there are many people who would try to stop him from becoming King."

"It is all right," Audubon assured his wife, "he will never come to claim the farm."

"I only want to protect what is mine," Anne said with a shrug.

"We understand," General Charette assured her. "But now we must hurry. According to our information a certain gentleman by the name of Robillard is already on his way here from Nantes."

"And what shall I tell him," Anne questioned, "when he gets here?"

"Whatever suits your fancy, madame," Audubon said. "You may even tell him the truth. . . ."

As soon as Audubon had signed the adoption papers they were witnessed by Madame Berthoud and made legal by the notary's signature. He was a cadaverous-looking man with a tic on the left side of his face.

"Take him back," General Charette ordered, and two of the men in his party immediately escorted the notary out of the house. "Now," he said, "we must ride."

Within minutes Audubon, Joue, Madame Berthoud, and John were sitting astride sleek black horses. They moved at a walk toward the gate.

Audubon turned and saw Anne standing in the doorway. He would have called out and bidden her good-bye, but his attention was diverted by a troop of horsemen who were waiting for them beyond the wall.

"They are my guard," Charette explained with a wave of his hand. "It has come to the point," he laughed, "that I hardly know they are around me."

"There must be at least fifty of them," Audubon commented.

"I never concern myself with numbers," Charette answered. "If I did, I would never fight an engagement with the government troops, since they always come with greater numbers than I can muster."

Audubon shrugged. He did not share the General's enthusiasm for fighting with few against many, and concerned about the complement of his crew, he asked, "Is the *Oiseau* fully manned?"

"Yes," Charette replied. "But I cannot vouch for them.

They are a ragtag bunch from almost everywhere in France, though I made sure to take none from Nantes, for fear they might know you. The men were told nothing more than that they sail to the islands and that the captain, his wife, and son will be aboard. The last two of the crew signed on yesterday." The General removed an envelope from his breast pocket and handed it to Audubon. "That," he explained, "comes from your friend Bigot."

"What is it?" Audubon asked, pushing the envelope into his coat pocket.

"A letter of marque that empowers you to operate on behalf of England against the ships of the Revolutionary government," Charette explained.

"But that was never discussed," Audubon objected. The prospect of plundering other French ships was something he could never imagine himself doing.

"It was my idea," Charette admitted with pride. "And Bigot thought it a good one."

"He would," Audubon commented dryly.

"Am I to understand," Charette questioned, "that you have some reservations about it?"

"Yes," Audubon said. "Totally!"

"And if I should order you to—"

"Aboard the *Oiseau*," Audubon interrupted quickly, "I am captain, General. I am not, nor have I ever been, under your command. You engaged me for a particular mission. I am about to fulfill that mission. There is nothing between us that gives you any jurisdiction over me once the mission is completed."

"May I remind you, Captain," Charette said stiffly, "that we are at war. And that any blow struck against the revolutionaries is a blow struck on behalf of the future King?"

"I cannot take issue with you, General, on that point," Audubon answered. "But I must differ with you about the recipient of the blow, and since I am expected to deliver it I will determine who will receive it."

"And what will you tell the men on the *Oiseau?*" Charette asked.

"As little as possible," Audubon responded.

"They will expect prize money."

Audubon suddenly reined in. He was absolutely furious.

Charette halted, too, and then everyone else in the party came to a stop.

"Is that how you got the crew to sign on?" Audubon questioned.

"They needed some inducement."

"Have you ever seen a mutiny, General?" Audubon asked, his voice so angry that several of the officers in Charette's party let their gloved hands fall over the hilts of their swords.

Charette laughed and said, "Come, come, Captain Audubon, I am sure you will be able to contend with such a contingency. There are ways of taking the starch out of those men who would oppose you. Now I think we should hurry on our way." And he spurred his mount to a gallop.

Audubon followed Charette, and in a matter of moments they were all galloping along the twisting road that hugged the coast.

Joue came close to Audubon, and above the sound of pounding hoofs he shouted, "We're going to have trouble, Captain."

"Not if I scotch it before it begins," Audubon responded.

Joue grinned and dropped back to ride beside John.

They galloped until they came to the top of a small rise that looked out over the sea. Below them in a cove lay the dark form of the *Oiseau*. And up on the beach, with her stern still in the water, was a longboat. The sea beyond the cove was patched with moonlight and smooth for a winter's night.

"There are some men there, too," Charette said.

"Where?" Audubon questioned. "I do not see them."

"They were told to stay back on the beach among the rocks."

"Another question, General," Audubon said.

"Yes?"

"How is the *Oiseau* armed?"

Charette smiled and said, "Ten long twelve-pounders, two half-pound swivel guns in the stern, and a three-pounder in the bow."

"Do you happen to know, General, if any member of the crew knows how to use those guns?"

"I am told that some do," the General replied. "But since you do not intend to use them, the lack of experience should not matter."

"You are quite right," Audubon said, and suggested that they go down to the beach.

"I would prefer to take my leave here," Charette said. "I do not want to expose my men to the risk of being caught on the beach."

Audubon nodded.

Charette eased his mount around, and riding up to the Dauphin, he told the boy, "Our cause is just, your Grace, and I have vowed to see you crowned King in the cathedral of Notre Dame. We will yet see these revolutionaries brought to justice, for God is on our side. We fight for Him." Then he leaned over to the child, and embracing him, he said passionately, "God bless you, your Grace!"

A moment later Charette drew his saber, and standing in his stirrups, he saluted the boy with "Long live the King!" The officers with him were quick to perceive his intentions and added their sabers and voices to the tribute.

Then Charette turned to Madame Berthoud, and taking her hand in his, said, "All France owes you a debt of gratitude, madame, a debt that will be paid in full when the new King takes his throne."

"Thank you, General," Madame Berthoud answered.

Charette turned to Audubon and said, "I wish you well, Captain."

Audubon nodded and said, "May you win the field, General." And then he quickly added, "I would ask you not to leave until I signal from the ship."

"And why should you want me to remain?"

Audubon smiled and answered, "As a token of our mutual responsibility."

Charette frowned.

"You will wait, will you not, General?"

Charette looked questioningly at his officers.

"John," Audubon said, "Ask General Charette to wait for my signal."

"Please wait," the boy responded.

"As you wish, your Grace," Charette answered, looking balefully at Audubon.

"And now," Audubon said, "we will go down to the beach." He dismounted, helped Madame Berthoud off her horse, and then, reaching up, he lifted the boy from his mount. "Joue, take hold of John. The path is narrow and steep. Madame Berthoud, keep close behind me. . . ."

Within moments Audubon had begun to lead his small band of followers down the side of the rise toward the beach. He moved quickly, and now and then he warned those coming behind him to be wary of a large rock or an especially deep hole. In less than ten minutes he was on the beach; without pausing, he headed straight for the longboat.

44

Just as the longboat came alongside the *Oiseau* Audubon said to Joue, "Have one of the men take my wife and child to my quarters and then have all hands turn to. I want them aft."

"Aye, aye, sir," Joue responded.

The longboat was brought close to the side of the ship with a boat hook and then made fast.

Several of the crew members aided Madame Berthoud and John out of the longboat and onto the deck. Audubon followed, and Joue came last.

Most of the crew was already on deck when Audubon came aboard. It was too dark to see all their faces, but from those few he did see he gathered they were a hard-looking lot.

A short, broad-shouldered man with a scar on his right cheek stepped forward and said, "Welcome aboard, Captain. I'm Mr. Tourne, the ship's first officer."

Audubon said nothing.

Another man came forward. He was the same height as Tourne but considerably thinner. "Welcome aboard, Captain," he said. "I am Mr. Godet, the ship's second officer."

Audubon remained silent.

A third man, taller than the other two, and younger, stepped alongside them. "Welcome, Captain," he said. "I am Mr. Duplay, the ship's third officer."

Audubon looked at Joue and said, "Carry out my instructions, if you please."

Joue immediately told one of the men standing nearby

to escort the Captain's wife and son to the Captain's quarters.

The man did not move.

Joue repeated his order.

The man still did not move.

Joue nodded, turned away, and an instant later wheeled around, driving his fist into the man's stomach, doubling him over.

An angry murmur came from the rest of the crew.

"Stand fast!" Audubon roared, slipping his pistol from his belt and leveling it at the man nearest him.

Joue repeated his order.

This time the man, still holding his stomach, nodded and managed to gasp, "If it please the Captain's family to follow me?"

As soon as Madame Berthoud and John were off the main deck Joue shouted, "All hands turn to. . . . All hands turn to. . . . All hands turn to. . . ."

Audubon mounted the quarterdeck and silently cursed Charette for having brought him to this pass.

"The crew is turned to," Joue reported, coming up to the quarterdeck.

"Thank you," Audubon responded, and then, addressing the men, he said, "Come closer. . . . I do not want you to miss anything I have to say." He waited a moment until they had gathered practically below the quarterdeck. Then he leaned forward on the railing and said, "My name is Captain Jean Audubon. My first officer's name is Joue."

The crew responded with angry jeers.

"That is the way it is," Audubon told them. "Those of you who object have the opportunity to leave the ship. But those of you who stay will obey him."

"Who are your second and third officers?" Tourne asked.

"How long have you been at sea, Mr. Tourne?" Audubon questioned.

"Since I was a boy."

"And how long have you been a ship's officer?"

"Ten years."

"And you, Mr. Godet," Audubon asked. "How long have you been at sea?"

"Fifteen years."

"What about you, Mr. Duplay, how long have you been at sea?" Audubon asked.

"Seven years."

"And you were all signed on by General Charette?"

"I come first," Tourne said. "Them two come aboard two days ago."

"All right, Mr. Tourne," Audubon said, "you are the ship's second officer. And Mr. Duplay, you are third officer. As for Mr. Godet, how much do you know about guns?"

"I was aboard a thirty-two-gunner for three years."

"Then you will be in charge of the gun deck," Audubon told him. He paused for a moment and said, "Now we come to the most important thing I have to tell you. Listen carefully and make up your own minds. We will not attack French ships. If we do fight, it will not be against Frenchmen. I know what you were told, but now I am telling you what we will do. We will sail to the islands, take cargo where we can find it, and bring it back here. General Charette's men are in sore need of a great many things. But we will not raid French ships."

"But what about prize money?" one of them called out.

"If we happen upon a Spanish ship and fortune favors us," Audubon said, "we will take it. . . . But we will not kill our own."

"But the ships of the government are not our own," a sailor called.

"They are Frenchmen," Audubon shouted. "We are Frenchmen. I do not care if they kill each other on land. I will not, if I can help it, kill them at sea. Those of you who disagree have the opportunity to leave this ship. But if you stay, then you agree to sail for the profit made from carrying cargo."

"Then why do we need the guns?" Godet asked.

"First, to defend ourselves," Audubon answered. "And second, to be able to have fortune favor us, should we encounter one of Spain's treasure ships."

A ripple of laughter came from the crew, and Audubon knew that the temper of the men had changed. At least for the time being, he had gained control, and he breathed easier for having accomplished it without any bloodshed. "Joue," he said, "make the signal to General Charette."

"Aye, aye, Captain!"

45

The moment the door to the cabin swung open, Madame Berthoud left the bunk and stood waiting for Audubon.

"Is everything all right?" she asked anxiously as soon as he was inside.

"For now," he answered with a weary sigh.

Madame Berthoud pointed to a small table and said, "I saved you some stew, but it must be cold by now."

He shook his head. "I would much rather sleep than eat." Glancing at John, sleeping in a hammock, he said, "To look at him now you would never guess what the boy had seen earlier."

Madame Berthoud did not comment.

"That General Charette," Audubon said, sitting down on a chair near the table to pull off his boots, "is more boy than man."

"It was obvious you thought that when you spoke to him."

Audubon shrugged, stood up, and said, "I will sleep on the floor."

"No," she said. "You have had less sleep than any of us. Tonight, I will sleep on the floor."

"Not aboard my ship, madame," Audubon said, going to one of the closets at the side of the cabin and pulling out a heavy blanket. "We sail at first light," he told her as he stretched out on the floor and pulled the blanket over him.

Madame Berthoud turned down the lantern that hung from the crossbeam and went to her bunk. For a while she remained silent, and then she said, "I never realized how small your cabin was or even how noisy. The whole ship seems to squeak and rattle all the time."

"A ship is never still," Audubon replied. And then with a chuckle he said, "You should hear the noise during heavy weather. Sometimes it sounds as though the fiends of hell are in its hold and rigging. A good sailor can tell from the sounds how well his ship sails."

"Can you do that?" she asked, turning to look at him.

"Yes, I can."

For some moments Madame Berthoud remained silent, and then she commented, "I do not know any other man who could have done as well with the men as you have. . . ."

"Any captain worth his command would have done as well," Audubon told her with a yawn.

"Were you afraid?" she asked.

"I would have been a fool not to be."

"You are a very strange man, Captain," she said. "I do not know what to think of you. Even your politics are strange. Here you carry the future King of France and yet you will not fight his enemies. . . ." She sighed and asked, "What have you to say to that, Captain?"

Audubon said nothing. He was fast asleep, and when Madame Berthoud realized it she smiled, closed her eyes, and listened to the sounds of the ship and the Captain's slow, rhythmic breathing. . . .

46

The sky in the east began to lighten, and the water around the *Oiseau* slowly turned from black to gray. Audubon stood on the quarterdeck, his hands thrust deep in the pockets of his large pea coat and his eyes peering through the semidarkness at the main deck, where the crew was standing ready.

"All hands at stations," Joue reported from the main deck.

"And the anchor?" Audubon asked.

"Hove short, Captain."

"Take her to sea then, Joue, if you please," Audubon responded.

"Hands at the capstan," the first officer shouted, "stand by. Loose heads'ls. . . . Men aloft to the tops'ls. . . ."

The instant the anchor broke from the water Audubon ordered the helm hard over, and the *Oiseau*, with her headsails sheeted home, swung easily toward the mouth of the cove. Within minutes the ship had slipped into the open sea, and Joue ordered the mainsails set.

"Helmsman," Audubon said, "keep her close to the wind."

"Aye, aye, Captain."

"Joue," Audubon called, "send Mr. Godet aft."

After several minutes the gunnery officer came running toward the quarterdeck. "You summoned me, Captain?" he asked.

"Yes, Mr. Godet," Audubon said. "Starting immediately

I want your gun crews drilling."

The man stared at him in surprise.

"Call your men out, Mr. Godet," Audubon snapped.

"Aye, aye, Captain!"

Audubon then summoned the second and third officers and told them, "I will expect better seamanship from your men than I have seen this morning. The men at the braces were slow in bringing them around, while those at the head's sheets were too quick. I will expect a better performance the next time we change course and a better one after that until every man knows his job and exactly how to do it. Have I made myself clear?"

The two officers nodded in unison.

"We have a long voyage," Audubon said, "and this time of year the ocean is a wrathful place. And we will have to survive that wrath. To do that will take all the skill we possess."

Then Audubon dismissed the men, and calling to Joue, he said, "I want a word with you, mister."

Joue joined him on the quarterdeck.

Moving off to the taffrail, so as to be out of earshot of the helmsman, Audubon said, "We must wait the better part of a week before our rendezvous." He glanced toward the man at the wheel. "I would not risk trusting him or any of the crew with word of the rendezvous."

Joue nodded.

Audubon turned from a view of the open water to the main deck, where Godet was already drilling his gun crews. The movements of the men were ill-timed and disjointed. One gun, as it was being run out, had its muzzle jammed against the ship's side.

"They are not ready to go to sea," Audubon said with a shake of his head. "A few days of hard training will give them a great deal more skill than they have now. I want the word passed to the crew," Audubon told him, "that we will not begin to sail for the islands until I am satisfied with the crew's performance. And tell them that I intend to drive them hard!"

"Yes, Captain," Joue answered. Then he looked about and commented, "Even with a green crew, it is good to be aboard a ship again."

"Very good," Audubon answered, looking up at the

three masts of the *Oiseau*, where the sails filled with an off-shore breeze. "Very good indeed!"

All day and into the night Audubon remained on the quarterdeck, watching the performance of the gun crew or scanning the rigging to see how well the men aloft performed their tasks.

In the afternoon he allowed Madame Berthoud and John to join him on the quarterdeck, cautioning them to keep out of his way. But the boy was soon at the helm, "helping the helmsman keep the ship on course," so he claimed, much to the amusement of Audubon and Madame Berthoud.

The *Oiseau* was running under full sail, heading south with a good wind aft and a bright sun in an almost cloudless sky. Though it was cold, the air was filled with a wonderful salty tang that made Audubon comment to Madame Berthoud, "I am beginning to breathe again."

"Yes, it is exhilarating," she said with a smile. Then, looking up at the mass of white canvas she added, "And beautiful, too."

For a moment his eyes met hers, and in them he saw a certain glow. But she quickly turned away, and he was sure that it was the sun that had put the light into her eyes.

Madame Berthoud remained on the quarterdeck until the whole western sky was aflame with the setting sun. But Audubon did not leave his place until eight bells were struck and the midwatch began.

During the second and third days at sea the weather remained uncommonly good, and Audubon took advantage of every hour of it. The men were driven hard, but the results were obvious even to the most disgruntled among them.

Audubon was careful to keep clear of any other ship. Whenever the lookout shouted, "Sail ho!" the course of the *Oiseau* was immediately altered to avoid any contact. Since the *Oiseau* was rigged as a sloop of war, she carried more canvas than most vessels her size and could easily outdistance any ship that sought to examine her more closely.

Though Audubon was almost completely occupied with the task of training the crew and sailing the *Oiseau*, there were times when his thoughts strayed to Madame Berthoud and the boy. The knowledge that they would soon be departing from the *Oiseau* saddened him. Though Audubon was stern in his injunction about getting in the way, John somehow managed to be all over the ship without causing any disruption to the disciplined routine. With Joue he even went into the rigging, much to the absolute horror of Madame Berthoud. He had become a happy, laughing child, and all the crewmen seemed to enjoy having him around, if for no other reason than to hear his gay, lilting laughter and see his excitement whenever a seabird came close to the ship. The future King of France was in reality nothing more than a boy, with a boy's ways.

As for Nicole Berthoud, Audubon recognized there was a bond between them that was far stronger than any he had had with the women whose beds he had shared. And though he fought down his desire to possess her, the sight of her standing on the quarterdeck with the wind in her hair and a heightened color in her cheeks was enough to make his blood race.

That he had come to love both of them, Audubon did not doubt. That he would ever tell them, he also doubted. But he did hope that John would remember him and that Madame Berthoud would sometimes think of him. . . . He said as much to her on the third night, after he had left the quarterdeck.

"I think you misjudge us," she responded sotto voce, "if you suppose that either John or I will forget what you did for us."

Audubon, who was standing next to the transom window, looking out at the wake of the *Oiseau,* turned and faced her. The light from the overhead lantern penulated across her face, alternately splashing it with a yellow glow and casting it in shadow. Either way she was achingly beautiful to him.

He swallowed and said, "I apologize for making things difficult for you in the beginning."

She waved his words aside, and though it was obvious she wanted to speak, she was unable to.

"I will be sorry to have you leave the ship," Audubon admitted.

"We will be sorry to go," she said. "John told me this

afternoon that he would like to stay on the ship forever."

Audubon chuckled and commented, "Forever to a child is just until something else comes along."

"I would not say forever," she responded, "but I, too, have been happy here."

Audubon shrugged.

"It will soon end," Madame Berthoud said.

"Two or three days, possibly four at the very most," he answered, leaving the transom.

She nodded, reached up, and turned down the light in the lantern. . . .

Audubon slept fitfully, sometimes dreaming that he was once again aboard the British prison ship in New York Harbor. He awoke at three bells the next morning in a black mood that stayed with him throughout the day.

Toward afternoon the blue sky suddenly clouded over and the sea became the color of lead. The wind freshened from the north and then veered around to the northwest, bringing with it snow flurries that whipped across the deck for a few moments and then were gone.

Audubon ordered the sail shortened and held the *Oiseau* close to the wind.

Though the weather steadily worsened, Audubon kept the men at their gun drill throughout the day and into the night. And when he saw one of the sailors do something badly he had the man brought to him for a dressing down.

Finally the weather moderated and the wind dropped and veered to the southwest, forcing Audubon to turn the *Oiseau* to a northwest tack and hold the wind on his larboard side for the better part of two glasses before coming over on a new tack.

He left the deck with Joue in command and made his way down to the cabin. Without a word to Madame Berthoud he stretched out on the floor and fell asleep.

The morning of the fifth day the sky was still overcast and there were dark clouds far off to the north and northwest.

By Audubon's reckoning the *Oiseau* was now sailing somewhere close to the British frigate. Every few minutes he glanced up at the lookout, expecting him to sing out, "Sail ho!" He dared not tell the man to scan the horizon for a sail, lest he arouse the crew's suspicion that something strange was afoot.

Moments after five bells were sounded, the lookout shouted, "Sail ho! Broad off starb'd quarter."

"Can you make out her flag?" Audubon called out.

"Not yet."

"Keep a close watch on her!" Audubon shouted. He went to the stern and scanned the sea. For a few moments he saw nothing. Then, quite suddenly, a dark form materialized.

"She's gainin' on us," the lookout called.

"Joue," Audubon shouted, "all hands turn to. . . . Action stations."

Within moments the roll of drums and the high pitch of the pipe had brought the men to the deck on the run.

Joue reported, "All men are at their stations, Captain."

"Mr. Godet," Audubon yelled, "load and stand ready to fire with canister shot."

"Aye, aye, Captain," Godet responded.

The guns on deck were immediately rolled back and loaded while sand was strewn over the deck. Matches were lit and held ready.

"She's an Englishman!" the lookout shouted. "She's the English frigate *Dauntless.*"

"Joue," Audubon called, motioning him up to the quarterdeck, "tell them to be ready to leave."

Joue nodded and hurried to convey Audubon's message.

The British frigate was well within sight of the *Oiseau* now and was rapidly gaining on her.

Audubon eyed his own sails. They were well set, and if he ordered the topgallant sails loosed, the *Oiseau* would pick up some speed.

Joue came back to the quarterdeck and reported, "They are standing by." And then he, too, glanced up at the sails. "Shouldn't we shorten sail?" he questioned.

Audubon glared at him.

"The frigate's reaching on us," the lookout called.

Audubon looked at the *Dauntless.* She was perhaps a league away.

"She's making signal," the lookout shouted. "She's asking us to heave to."

Audubon swore under his breath.

"She's tacking across our bow."

"Prepare to come about," Audubon ordered.

Joue looked at him questioningly, and in a low voice Audubon said, "I cannot do it, Joue. . . . I cannot do it. . . . I cannot turn over a Frenchman to an Englishman."

"It will mean a fight," Joue told him.

Audubon nodded. Then, gesturing toward the gathering clouds to the west and north, he said, "Not a long one, I hope."

Joue turned to the helmsman. "Wheel down, you son of a whore. . . . Turn that wheel down. . . . Now, you men, move those heads'l sheets and bowlines. . . . Tacks and sheets . . . that's it. Now, helm alée."

The *Oiseau* swung into the wind.

"Mains'l haul!" Joue shouted. He waited a moment and then yelled, "Hard over." Another pause as he scanned the sails. Then he bellowed, "Haul off."

"Well done," Audubon said, looking with satisfaction at the frigate, which was taken by surprise by their sudden tacking.

"We're on her weather side," Joue said.

Audubon nodded and ordered, "Rig for boarding."

Joue left the quarterdeck to carry out the order.

The frigate immediately started to tack.

Audubon gave the order to wear ship, and placed the wind directly behind the *Oiseau*. . . . By now Audubon was sure that Captain Ridder must have realized that he had no intention of surrendering the Dauphin.

"Boarding nets rigged," Joue reported.

Audubon nodded.

From the lookout came word that the frigate was gaining on them.

Suddenly Madame Berthoud came up on deck, and turning to look up at Audubon, she demanded to know what was happening.

"Stay in the cabin!"

"But—"

"Stay in the cabin!"

Madame Berthoud rushed to the side and saw the British frigate. "You are mad. . . . Do you know what you are doing?"

"In the cabin!" Audubon roared just as the air was rent by two explosions and the sea on the larboard of the *Oiseau* was plowed by cannonballs.

Madame Berthoud, her eyes wide with fear, rushed back into the cabin.

Within minutes the two ships were sailing side by side and Captain Ridder was attempting to narrow the distance.

Suddenly Audubon realized his adversary was not going to risk firing a broadside that might kill the Dauphin. That gave him an unexpected advantage, and in a matter of moments he was down on the gun deck.

"Mr. Godet," Audubon shouted, "sight all guns at their masts. . . . Fire as you bear."

Within moments gun after gun went off. The deck was filled with smoke, and the air stank from burned powder. "Reload with ball and chain," Audubon ordered.

Through the smoke he could see that the first round had rent the lower portion of the frigate's sails. But no real damage had been done.

"Captain Audubon," Ridder called from across the narrow strip of water separating the two ships, "you are answerable for your actions."

"Fire!" Audubon ordered.

Again each of the five guns belched smoke and fire, but this time the snapping of spars and the shrieks of wounded men came across the water.

"Wear ship!" Audubon ordered. He was going to attempt to make a run for the storm that was coming toward them.

But Captain Ridder had anticipated his actions and was already tacking across his bow to block him off. Within moments the two ships came together, amid the sound of crashing timbers.

Instantly Captain Ridder ordered grappling hooks thrown, and the two vessels were tied together.

"Prepare to oppose boarders!" Audubon shouted. Now each man aboard the *Oiseau* was on his own, and the life and death of the ship depended upon how each of them fought, not as part of a ship's company but as individuals.

British marines were already leaping from the frigate to the deck of the *Oiseau*.

The air was filled with cries and pistol and musket shots. But most of the fighting was done with cutlasses. The men of the *Oiseau* managed to kill or wound most of the attackers in the first wave.

Audubon fought with one lobstercoat, parrying the

thrust of the man's bayonet with a cutlass until he found an opening, and thrusting home, opened the man's stomach.

The men on the *Oiseau* fought well, but they were outnumbered and slowly they were being pressed back from the railing.

Then, suddenly, the wind began to shift, and the ships ground against each other like two parts of a giant jaw.

"Strike your colors!" Captain Ridder shouted above the cries of the dying and the clash of steel on steel.

"Come and cut them down yourself," Audubon answered.

Out of the corner of his eye he saw Joue and two other members of the crew begin to ax the lines that held the grappling irons. They had sheared off four, and already the sterns of the two vessels were drifting apart.

Audubon rushed to the other lines and slashed at them with his cutlass.

Now the ships were held by two lines amidship.

Joue ran to cut them.

Suddenly Duplay shouted, "Order him to stop, Captain, or I'll kill him. Bigot guessed you couldn't be trusted. Order him to stop!"

But Joue had already severed one of the lines.

Duplay wheeled and fired. The ball smashed into Joue's chest, knocking him to the deck of the *Oiseau*.

Audubon loosed a yell of rage. Leaping from the quarterdeck, he ran at Duplay and slashed at the man, severing his right side from the neck down to his trunk.

"Fire!" Audubon shouted. "Fire, you bastards!"

The *Oiseau*'s guns roared, and the line that held the two ships snapped.

"Helm down," Audubon ordered. "Stand by to go about."

Moments later the *Oiseau* was slicing the sea, rushing toward the dark clouds as fast as she could.

The frigate turned and began to give chase.

Audubon left the quarterdeck and hurried down to where Joue lay. An ugly red wound gaped where his stomach had been. Audubon reached down and touched Joue's head.

"We win?" his first officer asked in a whisper.

"Yes."

Joue smiled, and then in a small voice he cried, "Father!"

Audubon cradled the dead man in his arms. Then, suddenly, he realized someone was standing close to him. He looked up.

"I am sorry," Madame Berthoud whispered.

He nodded and carried Joue in his arms. Snow was already beginning to fall when he stretched his dead son out on the quarterdeck.

As soon as the *Oiseau* made her escape, Audubon, standing on the quarterdeck, ordered the helmsman to hold a course that would allow him to keep steerage way. Then he summoned Mr. Tourne, and above the howl of the wind he shouted, "You are first officer now. . . . Choose your second and third from the best men in the crew. Leave Mr. Godet in charge of the guns. Weather permitting, we will bury our dead. How many did we lose?"

"Counting the first officer," Tourne answered, "twenty men."

Audubon nodded. That was one-fifth of his crew. "Have you any idea of the damage?"

"Nothin' that'll stop us," Tourne said. Then, casting his eyes about, he added, "This storm'll hurt us more than the English did."

"Yes," Audubon agreed, "it probably will. . . ." And with a sigh he asked, "Are there any wounded?"

"Not too many, from what I can see," the new first officer replied. "Most of them that's wounded have taken cuts."

"Any serious?"

"You better ask your wife, Capt'in," Tourne told him.

"Where is she?"

"The lady is down in the fo'c's'l tendin' them that's hurt right now."

"That is no place for her," Audubon said sharply.

"I told her that," Tourne said. "But she told me that

there's no better place for her to be. . . ."

Audubon's first impulse was to leave the quarterdeck and drag Madame Berthoud from the fo'c's'l. Under the best of circumstances that was not the place for a woman, and she was there under the worst possible conditions. But his concern for Madame Berthoud's sensibilities, great as it was, was of necessity far less than his responsibility to the *Oiseau* and the men aboard.

"Send the men aloft to keep the sails free of ice," Audubon said.

"Aye, aye," Tourne responded.

"And have the sail maker prepare shrouds for the dead."

"Yes, Capt'in," Tourne said.

As soon as the first officer had left the quarterdeck Audubon once more bent over Joue and whispered, "What can a father say to his dead son?" He heaved a deep sigh, and standing up, cast a weather eye up toward the snow-obscured rigging.

The storm raged for three days. The sky was dark with snow, and the *Oiseau* was tossed and battered by raging winds and surging seas. The ship screamed and groaned in agony. Lines parted and were hastily mended. The top of the mizzenmast gave way and killed another man, adding to the number of dead from the ship's encounter with the frigate.

Throughout the storm, Audubon never left the quarterdeck for more than a few minutes at a time and only when he was forced to relieve himself or soak some warmth into his perpetually cold body. Now and then the cook brought him a mug of hot soup or very strong coffee, and periodically Madame Berthoud made her way up to the quarterdeck to exchange a dry coat for the snow-encrusted one he wore. His beard and even his eyebrows were covered with snow.

Over and over again he sent men aloft to change sails, to reef or loose, according to the dictates of the wind. And with each change of sail the yards had to be braced around.

Ordinarily the work was hard, but it was made even harder by the ice in the rigging and on deck. At first the men grumbled; but when they realized that Audubon, if he did not spare them, spared himself even less, the grumbling soon became tinged with a grudging respect that manifested itself not in words—for they were incapable of expressing their feelings that way—but rather in the smartness with which they performed their tasks. Audubon saw the change and understood it.

The weather moderated somewhat by late afternoon of the second day, and each of the dead men was wrapped in his shroud and weighted with shot.

One by one they were placed on planks and covered with the fleur-de-lis, and with the whole crew standing respectfully by, Audubon read from the Bible before the plank was tilted and the body slipped into the gray waters of the storm-tossed sea.

When Joue's body was set on the plank Audubon closed the Bible. And glancing at Madame Berthoud, who with John was standing off to one side at the edge of the crew, he cleared his throat and said, "Joue was the only one of the men I knew. . . . He was a fine seaman, but more important, he was a fine man." Audubon stopped to clear his throat. "I do not think any man could have asked for a better. . . ." Again Audubon was forced to clear his throat. "I do not think that any man could have asked for a better son." And disregarding the whispers of the men, Audubon opened the Bible and read the brief passage that he had for the others. Then in a choked voice he said, "And we commit his body to the deep."

Even as the shroud-wrapped corpse began to slide, John called out, "Good-bye, Joue. Good-bye, my friend. . . . God keep you!"

"Amen!" the men exclaimed aloud, crossing themselves.

Audubon dismissed the crew, telling Tourne to send as many as possible down for a rest and some hot food. "This blow is not over yet," he said. "We might as well take advantage of what we have." Then he went to Madame Berthoud and John, and putting his hands on the child's shoulder, Audubon said in a gravelly voice, "It was a fine good-bye you gave to my son, a very fine good-bye!"

"Will you miss him very much?"

"Very much," Audubon answered, his eyes seeking Madame Berthoud's.

"We will all miss him," she said quietly.

"Thank you," Audubon said, and walking slowly away, he heard John comment, "But he is very sad."

And indeed he was very sad.

48

The *Oiseau* was off the northern coast of Spain by Audubon's reckoning when the heavy, leaden cloud cover began to break up and show lovely patches of blue sky. The wind moderated, and the wild heaving of the sea gave way to a considerably more gentle movement.

Audubon ordered Mr. Tourne to maintain a southwest course, and as he left the quarterdeck he said, "I want lookouts day and night. And if a sail is sighted, call me at once. . . . Is that understood?"

The first officer nodded, "Aye, aye, Captain."

Audubon entered the cabin and dropped wearily into the chair next to the table. "The weather has cleared," he said, looking at Madame Berthoud. She was standing near the bunk. Her brow was furrowed with a frown, and her lips were pursed.

Audubon slipped off his boots and wriggled his toes. "If you ask me why I did it," he said, "I can only say that I could not do it. I could not give a Frenchman over to an Englishman, even if that Frenchman was a boy who might someday sit on the throne of France."

"That was not what I was going to ask," she said. "I was going to tell you to sleep in the bunk."

"Madame," he said, standing to remove his heavy coat and letting it fall to the floor, "I cannot refuse such a generous offer." He staggered across the cabin and dropped into the bunk. Closing his eyes, he commented, "And thank you for not chastising me about—"

"I hardly need do that, Captain," Madame Berthoud answered. "You have paid grievously for your actions."

"Aye," he answered with a deep sigh, "that I have. And now that it is done we cannot return to France, at least not now. And probably the whole English Navy will be looking for the *Oiseau*. But she will not be easy to find. The ocean is a very big, big place."

"Tell me," Madame Berthoud asked, looking down at Audubon, "was this the way you planned it from the beginning?"

Audubon opened his eyes and smiled. "I am not Bigot," he answered with a shake of his head. "But I am not sorry that I did it."

"Even though it cost Joue's life?"

With a shrug Audubon said, "I am not wise enough to balance one life against another. I could not do it. I do not think it would have mattered who the boy was. He was French, and they were English. . . ." He propped himself up on his elbows and asked, "Can you understand that, Nicole?" Suddenly he realized he had used her given name.

"No," she said, without making any attempt to correct him, "I am not sure I do, at least not in the terms that you explain it. But I have seen you look at John, and I knew it would be difficult for you to give him up when the time came."

Audubon dropped down on the bunk and again closed his eyes. "He often brought my own son to mind," he told her in a soft voice. And he added, "This boy is brave, very brave, Nicole. . . . I think he will indeed grow into a fine man and be worthy of—"

"Those who gave their lives for him?"

"Yes."

Nicole moved to the transom and asked, "Where shall we go, Jean?"

He moved to look at her.

"Even if we sail to the islands," she said, "we will be hunted."

"Then where would you suggest?" he asked, knowing that she probably had given a great deal of thought to the question.

"America?" she suggested. "Perhaps there we would be safe?"

"They are more English there than they realize," Audubon answered.

"We could go back to New Orleans," she ventured. "I still have family there, and since it is under Spanish dominion again we would be safe for a while."

Audubon made a face and said, "I have less love for them than I do for the English. But I will think about it. The Spanish, in New Orleans at any rate, have always been willing to allow the French to be French."

"I will let you sleep," she said, and taking her wrap from one of the nearby closets, she started for the door.

"Nicole?" he called.

"Yes?" she responded, turning to look at him.

"Thank you for tending the wounded," he said.

She nodded.

"And . . ."

"And whatever else you want to say, Jean," she told him with a smile, "you had better reserve until you have had a long sleep and have thought on the matter. . . . I would not want you to regret your words."

He nodded and lay back. He heard the door open and close, followed by her footfalls on the stairway to the quarterdeck. For a few moments he listened to the sounds of the ship: the wind singing in the rigging, the whispering rush of the sea as it swished along the *Oiseau*'s sides, and all the creakings and squeaks that, like so many voices, assured him that his was a ship sound and sailing well with the wind on her larboard. Audubon closed his eyes and slept.

49

Audubon slept until the beginning of the first watch the following night and then took some time to eat, have a steaming bath, and change his clothes before going up to the quarterdeck.

The course was still southwest, though according to the log the ship had done some tacking during the time he had been asleep. The night was very clear though cold, and the sky was studded with stars.

"We will soon be in warmer waters," he said to Mr. Sante, who was now the second officer.

"Probably at the end of the week."

Audubon did not speak anymore, and leaving the quarterdeck, he inspected the rest of the ship. Except for the mizzenmast, everything appeared to be in good order. Then he went below, visiting the five men who had been wounded in the fray with the English. They were mending well, and each of them offered his thanks to the "Capt'in's wife."

Audubon returned to the quarterdeck, spent another bell's worth of time there, and saying goodnight to the officer on watch, returned to his cabin.

The overhead lantern was turned down, and Nicole was already in the bunk. He removed his boots and slipped off his coat.

"I have been waiting for you, Jean," she told him in a low voice.

Audubon smiled and without hesitation undressed. He slipped in beside her and to his delight discovered that she was naked. Without a word he took her in his arms, and pressing her warm body against his own, he kissed her long and deeply. His hands moved over her breasts, and he whispered, "I have come to tell you that I love you, Nicole."

She put her finger across his lips and said, "It is not necessary, Jean, to persuade me with sweet words. . . . It is I who have fallen in love with you."

He removed her finger from his mouth and kissed her hand. "I love you," he told her, "not because I want to cozen you with words, sweet or otherwise, but because, quite simply, Nicole, I do love you."

His mouth found hers again, enjoying the taste of her and the delightful teasing of her tongue. And even as he explored her nakedness her hands caressed him.

"I would love you in a hundred different ways," he said, playing his hand over her womanhood.

With a laugh she responded, "That would be ninety-nine too many, my darling."

Audubon kissed her breasts, relishing their warmth and jasmine scent. He buried his head in her soft stomach and then found his way between her open thighs. And when his lips and tongue found their mark, Nicole arched her body to his voluptuous kiss.

"Jean," she gasped, "oh Jean, I am melting!"

He felt her hands on him and could only answer, "I would not cast you any other way than the way you are."

"Let me kiss you," she asked, "as you kiss me."

He moved, making it possible for her to put her lips around his manhood. The moment he felt their warm circle he sighed with deep satisfaction. And when they stopped and once more lay side by side, he told her, "Most other people say we French invented that way of making love. If we did, then it is the best tribute I can think of to our appreciation of . . . of. . . ."

"I wager you cannot think of a word," she laughed.

He shrugged and with a kiss told her, "Some things are better left undefined."

"Kiss me," she asked.

"That is a request I cannot refuse," he answered, bringing his lips to hers.

"The scent of me is on you," she told him, and moving

her hand over him, she whispered, "Come into me, my darling, come into me. . . ."

Moments later they moved together, and Nicole, with her arms around Audubon's neck, told him passionately, "I wish, Jean, that there had never been anyone else."

"It does not matter," he replied, kissing her erect nipples.

"Jean . . . I love you. . . ."

"And I love you."

Nicole whimpered with delight, and her movements became more frenzied. "Oh, dear God, I love you!" Her body tensed, and with a low cry she flung herself against him, raking his back with her nails.

Almost at the same instant Audubon's own passion reached its climax, and as Nicole's body trembled against his, his seemed to burst into flame in a few exquisite moments of ecstasy. . . .

"Jean," Nicole whispered when their breathing had returned to normal, "do you love me?"

"More than those few words could possibly say," he answered, brushing her hair back.

Nicole uttered a deep, contented sigh and said, "I have never known real love before."

"Nor I," Audubon answered.

"Perhaps," she ventured, "fortune has smiled on us?"

"I would accept its smile," he said, holding her close to him, "but I would not want its laughter."

"What a strange thing to say!"

His hand found her breasts, and he said, "That is because I am a strange man."

"I cannot say whether you are strange," Nicole laughed, "but I can vouch for your being a man."

They laughed, turned again to one another, and made love. . . .

50

"If it were possible," Audubon said to Nicole one night as they lay naked in each other's arms, "Then I would marry you." Divorce for Audubon was out of the question, more because of his wife's religious persuasion than his own.

"I know you would, my love," she answered, touching his chest.

And during the long weeks they spent at sea, Audubon came to the conclusion that he would not leave Nicole, that he would make New Orleans his home.

"You mean you will never go to sea again?" she asked when he told her of his plan.

"I will not go back to France," he said, and pointing to John, he added, "I will live with my son and my wife."

"Are you sure, Jean?"

Audubon nodded.

"I wish," he said one day as they watched the sunset from the deck, "that I could give you my name, Nicole."

"You have already given me more than I ever dreamed I would have."

As for John, he followed Audubon like a puppy dog, even to pacing the quarterdeck with him. Sometimes he even allowed the boy to stand at the wheel alone, though the helmsman was always nearby should his skill be needed.

And one day, because John asked him to, Audubon took the boy high into the rigging of the mainmast while Nicole, terrified that the child would fall, shouted from be-

low, "Come down here this minute. . . . Jean, if you do
not come down here this minute, I will never speak to you
again. . . ."

Witnessing the scene, the crew laughed and joined their
voices with that of the Captain's wife. But Audubon held
fast to John and with childish delight defied them all.

"Because of you and John," he said that night at supper,
"the *Oiseau* is a happy ship, perhaps the happiest I have
ever sailed on."

Nicole agreed. "The night we came aboard, I was terrified of the men. . . . But now I would trust them with my
life."

Audubon sipped some wine and said, "They will not forget the kindness you showed to the wounded. . . . Not too
many women would have gone down into the fo'c's'l."

"I am glad I went," she answered. "I wanted to see for
myself what it was like. . . ." She hesitated, then went on,
more softly, "To touch something of your past, Jean,
something that no other woman has."

Audubon nodded, reached across the small table, and
taking hold of her hand, he said, "You have done that, Nicole."

Now and then John came to Audubon with a drawing
he had made, and one day the boy brought him a picture
of Joue and said, "This is for you so you will not miss him
too much."

Audubon was deeply touched, and sweeping the boy
into his arms, he kissed him on the forehead. Then like
any proud father he showed the drawing to Mr. Tourne,
the helmsman, and several of the other crew members who
happened to be near the quarterdeck.

"I had no idea," Audubon said to Nicole later in the afternoon when he came down to the cabin for a short rest,
"that John was so gifted." And he showed her the drawing
of Joue.

"His father," she whispered, "had some leanings in that
direction."

"I will have this framed," Audubon said, "and hang it
here in the cabin."

After that John took to sketching parts of the ship,
other members of the crew, and the birds that now and

then used the *Oiseau* as a resting place on their long flights across the open expanse of the ocean.

By the time the *Oiseau* reached the latitude of Florida, the weather was springlike and the water a wonderful blue and so clear that even Audubon sometimes stood at the side and looked at the creatures in the depths. Within days the *Oiseau* entered the Gulf of Mexico, and sailing northwest, headed for the mouth of the Mississippi River, which they reached in the late afternoon of April 15, 1794.

Audubon ordered the crew to lay off the mouth of the river until the following morning. And to assure the safety of the ship against pirates, who were often venturesome enough to strike out of their hideouts in the bayous and attack a ship, he armed and doubled the watch through all the hours of darkness.

The sky was milk-white, and the shoreline thick with dark-green vegetation. As far as the eye could see, the land was flat, heavily overgrown with vines and several different kinds of trees. And wafting out to the *Oiseau* on an offshore breeze was the perfumed scent of flowers that grew in the depths of the delta's swamps.

Audubon, Nicole, and John were on the quarterdeck. When the sun set, it turned the western sky into a blaze of red color that slowly metamorphosed into dark shades of purple and then deepened into complete darkness as the ship's bell struck five.

"We will have a fair day tomorrow," Audubon commented.

"Red sky at night," John said, "sailor's delight. Red sky in the morning, sailor take warning."

"Who taught you that?" Nicole asked laughingly.

"He did," the boy said, pointing to Audubon.

"You will make a sailor out of him yet," she said.

"I think not," Audubon said, shaking his head. "His work will be very different from mine, though if he wanted to follow my calling, I have no doubt that he would be good at it, better perhaps than I am or could ever be."

"Do I detect a melancholy note in your voice?"

Audubon shrugged but did not answer. He had always thought of himself as a practical man, but now as he stood on the deck next to Nicole he had flights of fancy that would be more fitting for a child of John's age. Had he his way, the voyage would never end.

"Will it take long to sail up to New Orleans?" John asked.

"Perhaps half a day. We will go with the tide, but even so the river's current will slow us. We will have to tack many, many times before we reach the landing. But as soon as we clear through customs, we will go to Monsieur de Marigny's house."

"Dear God," Nicole exclaimed, "it seems a lifetime ago that I was there!"

Audubon smiled and said, "It was several lifetimes ago, my dear."

Much later, after they had made love, Nicole whispered, "I shall miss the cabin. . . . I shall even miss that swinging lantern that I can see over the rise of your shoulders when we are together."

Audubon kissed the nipple of her right breast.

"The other one," she chided, "will be jealous."

"To have one jealous breast next to another would be an impossible situation," Audubon responded and immediately rectified the situation.

"Jean?" Nicole called in a whisper.

"Yes?"

"I have been meaning to ask what caused the scars on your back."

"The whip," he answered.

"You mean—"

"From the time I was a prisoner of the British," he told her.

"Oh, my love," she cried. "Oh, my love . . ." And wrapping her arms around him, she moved her hands over the scars in a hopeless effort to erase them.

"Hush!" he exclaimed gently. "I was fortunate enough to survive. There were many who did not. . . ."

"Promise me, Jean," she asked, "that you will never leave me?" And almost immediately she said, "No, say nothing, just hold me. . . . Hold me, Jean!"

Audubon clasped Nicole's trembling body to his own and told her, "Sooner or later, my darling, every voyage must come to an end."

"I know," she responded, "but I have never been so happy as I have been on the *Oiseau*. . . . Never . . . and I am afraid that I never again will be so happy. . . ."

Audubon did not answer lest he give voice to his own fears and make Nicole more melancholy than she already was.

It was slow work sailing the *Oiseau* upriver. But finally the towers of St. Louis Cathedral loomed above the cypress and willow trees, and around the bend in the river the city of New Orleans came into view.

John was so excited that he began to run up and down the deck, shouting, "That is it. . . . That is where we are going. . . . Oh, look how beautiful everything is. . . ." And he waved vigorously to the people on shore, who then waved back to him.

Audubon sailed some distance above the landing at Fort St. Louis, and then, wearing ship, he made use of the river's current to bring the *Oiseau* alongside the wharf, which was crowded with blacks, Indians, and sailors from several different countries.

It took the better part of an hour for Audubon to clear Spanish customs, and then he spent another hour tending to the ship's business with Mr. Tourne and the other two officers before he was finally able to summon a carriage for his visit to the De Marigny house.

"The *Oiseau* must be restocked with food and water," he explained to John, who asked him why it had taken him such a long time to leave the ship. "And her damaged mizzenmast must be replaced. We have been at sea a long time," he said, "and many things must be replaced or repaired. . . . And as for the crew, they must be given some time ashore."

John, imitating Audubon's shrug, commented, "I could

not possibly think of all those things. My head would explode with a *poof!*"

The carriage moved along the rue de la Levée, past the Place d'Armes in front of the cathedral, and sometime later into the long cedar-lined avenue that led directly from the levee to the house, an impressive white building with a wide gallery around it and an overhanging roofline supported by pillars.

Even before they were halfway up the driveway the door to the big house opened and several black slaves dressed in fine livery came running down the wide stairway to await the arrival of the carriage.

"Tell your master," Audubon said, "that Captain Audubon, Madame Berthoud, and John Audubon have come to pay him a visit."

"I will," the man answered. "And now, if you will follow me into the house, you can all wait in the visitors' room."

Audubon nodded, and taking Nicole's arm, escorted her up the stairs.

"I can hardly believe that I am here," she whispered as they passed through a veranda bright with flowers.

"This way, please," the slave said, directing them into a room that was directly off the enormous foyer. "I will tell the master that you are here."

Nicole paced up and down the small waiting room.

"I do not understand," she said in a low voice, "why I am so nervous."

Audubon chuckled and said, "Because you are about to meet an old friend."

A short time later they heard voices in another part of the house and then hurried footsteps. Within moments Monsieur de Marigny appeared. He was a thin, scholarly-looking man who wore a peruke and queue. The moment he saw Audubon his face became wreathed in smiles. "My dear friend," he exclaimed, extending his hand, "how very good it is to see you."

The two men shook hands.

And then De Marigny looked hard at Nicole and began to shake his head. "It is impossible," he said in a low voice. "It is utterly impossible!"

Nicole looked questioningly at Audubon, who responded with a slight shrug.

"God," De Marigny said, "must have surely had a hand in it." And advancing toward Nicole, he said, "Marquise, your husband has been my houseguest for the past two months."

Nicole blanched, uttered a weak cry of despair, and slipped in a faint to the floor.

Audubon ran to her.

De Marigny immediately began to bellow for his servants to bring water and wine.

In moments Nicole's eyelids fluttered, and she looked imploringly at Audubon.

"I will fetch the Marquis myself," De Marigny said.

"No," Nicole said. "Please wait a few minutes. . . . I must regain my composure."

Audubon held her hand but said nothing.

"How did he come here?" Nicole asked.

"An absolutely incredible story," De Marigny answered. "A rescue from the very jaws of death by two men, one of whom told him to make for New Orleans after he reached England."

"Bigot!" Audubon exclaimed in a whisper.

"Why, yes," De Marigny responded, "I do believe that was the name. But how did you know?"

"I was the other man," Audubon answered with a twisted smile.

"Then surely you want to see the Marquis?"

Audubon shook his head. "No," he answered, "I have no need to meet with him again." And then, looking at Nicole, he said, "Fortune's smile has turned to harsh laughter."

"Please, Jean . . ."

"I am hard pressed to know what to say," he told her.

Suddenly De Marigny became aware of the boy and asked, "Is that your son, Audubon? . . . He looks very much like you."

"Yes," Audubon answered, "he is my son. His mother passed away sometime ago, and the Marquise was kind enough to consent to look after him."

"How very generous of you," De Marigny said, looking at Nicole.

"Oh, do not be misled," Audubon said with a chuckle, "it was not all charity on her part."

"Jean!" she exclaimed.

Audubon turned to De Marigny and asked, "Would you allow us a few minutes alone?"

De Marigny looked at him and then at the Marquise, and with a nod he said, "Had I even guessed what your relationship was, I would never have been so gauche."

"You could not have known, old friend," Audubon said.

De Marigny nodded, made a slight bow, and left them.

"We must have time to discuss the matter," Nicole said.

"He is your husband," Audubon told her. "He has every claim on you, I have none."

"What of the boy?" she asked, looking at the child.

"John will stay with you," Audubon said. "I shall take care of all his expenses through De Marigny. . . . But I tell you this, Nicole, if I should hear that your husband is mistreating either of you, I will kill him. . . . I want you to tell him that. . . . I will kill him. . . ." He was so angry he drove the fist of his right hand into the palm of his left over and over again.

"Jean," Nicole whimpered, "how will I live?"

Audubon shrugged and did not answer. To him it seemed incredible that all the events of the past months had led inexorably to what was now happening.

Audubon closed his eyes and fought back the tears. When he was sure he would not betray his feelings to John he took the boy by the hand, and leading him off to a corner of the room, said, "I will come back to see you, John. . . . Nicole will take care of you. . . . If I could, I would take you with me. . . . But you know why I cannot do that. . . . There is nothing else that can be done. Here you will be safe. . . ."

The boy nodded.

"And you will never, ever tell anyone who you really are?"

Again the boy nodded and said, "I am John Audubon, the son of Captain Jean Audubon."

Audubon nodded and hugged the boy to him. "Someday," he said, "I will be very proud of you, John."

"When I paint beautiful pictures," the boy answered.

"Yes," Audubon replied, "when you paint beautiful pictures." Then he returned to Nicole and said, "I am not brave enough to meet him, Nicole. . . . I am going back

to the ship. . . . I will have the boy's and your belongings
sent here." And suddenly taking her in his arms, Audubon
pressed her close to him. Then, letting go of her, he turned
and hurried out of the house to the waiting carriage.

A Few Words to the Reader

Though this book is a work of fiction, many of the people who inhabit its pages are historical figures. The circumstances I have created for them can, for the most part, be authenticated.

The men and women whose roles I have depicted in this adventure are "children of their times" and have no need of an apologist. They pursued their goals with the same ruthless fanaticism with which we pursue ours. In this way we do not differ significantly from them. The causes change, the people change, but the savagery of the contest never changes.

The obvious inference at the end of the novel is that the Dauphin and John James Audubon were one and the same. I chose this possibility because it fitted my story. But I would not say categorically that Louis XVII and the renowned American painter of birds were the same person, though John James Audubon was himself very mysterious about his origins.

I am aware that there are arguments pro and con, and I imagine that such arguments will continue, with each side claiming absolute proof. The most extensive research reveals only the fact that John James Audubon, the American painter, was given to moods of illusion, or if you will, pretensions about his parentage, since he himself was the natural son of the French Captain Jean Audubon and a woman whose last name might have been Rabin or Fougère. Her identity is also shrouded in mystery. But without this mystery, which I accepted for the purpose of my story, I could not have written the novel.

Having commented on the end of the book, I would like to make a few remarks about its beginning, especially about the events that led to the rescue of the Dauphin and the people involved in those events.

Other than Renne, Gide, Joue, François, André, and several of the minor characters, all the rest were developed from people who were in Paris in 1793 to 1804.

My research has led me to the conclusion that the Dauphin was in fact rescued from the Temple and that a man like Bigot could easily have been at the center of the kind of web that is depicted in the novel. Barras would have been involved in much the way that he is in the book.

I do not doubt that the Dauphin was taken from the Temple on the night of January 19, 1794, and another child substituted for him. This child was purposely poisoned to make it seem as if the real Dauphin had died. Bigot was one of those who signed the Dauphin's death certificate.

And as for the real role of Captain Jean Audubon, I do believe that in some way he was involved in the plot to rescue the Dauphin—either in the way I have written about it, or at a later time when the Dauphin was already out of the Temple and had to be taken away from Paris. Though outwardly a fine Republican, the Captain died with the following words on his lips: "The King is dead, long live the King!"

Madame Berthoud's role was even more mysterious than Captain Audubon's. I do not know who she really was. She might have been the Marquise de St. Pierre or someone completely different.

The name Berthoud was used by many émigrés. It has been suggested that the name itself could have been a code word. But for my purposes I created her as I thought she might have been.

After the Revolution and the Reign of Terror such men as Barras, Talleyrand, Fouché, and Robillard went on to serve Napoleon Bonaparte. But others, like Simon, Chaumette, Herbert and the judges of Marie Antoinette lived briefer lives that ended with their heads falling into the basket at the foot of the guillotine.

For those readers who might be interested in some of

the sources I used, the following is a much-abbreviated list: *The Age of Louis XVI*, by Alvar Gonzales Palacois; *Audubon*, by Constance Rourke; *Audubon: An Intimate Life of an American Woodsman*, by Stanley Clisby Arthur; *Audubon the Naturalist*, by Francis Hobart Herric; *Audubon's Life*, edited by D. C. Peattie; *Daily Life in the French Revolution*, by Jean Robiquet; *Dictionnaire Historique des Rues de Paris*, by Jacques Hillairet; *Empress Josephine*, by Ernest John Knapton; *Était-ce Louis XVII Évadé du Temple*, by J. D. Saint Leger; *The Face of Paris*, by Harold P. Clumn; *Le Fils de Louis XVI: Histoire de l'Enfance du Dauphin et Sa Captivité à la Tour du Temple*, by Lille; *Fouché: The Unprincipled Patriot*, by Hubert Cole; *The French Revolution*, by Thomas Carlyle; *The French Revolution*, by Albert Goodwin; *I Who Should Command All*, by Alice Jayner Tylor (privately published); *John James Audubon*, by Alexander B. Adams; *L'Affaire Louis XVII*, by Jean Pascal Romain (unpublished manuscript); *Life in Revolutionary France*, by Gwen Lewis; *Paris Terror*, by Stanley Loomis; *The Queen of France*, by André Castelot; *The Queen's Confession*, by Victoria Holt; *La Question Louis XVII: Simple Mémento Chronologique*, by F. Delrosay; *Le Roi Louis XVII et l'Énigme du Temple*, by G. Lentore; *The Turbulent City: Paris*, by André Castelot; *We All Went to Paris*, by Stephen Longstreet; *The World of the French Revolution*, by R. R. Palmer.

I also used maps of Paris and France that were made sometime in the late eighteenth century. These were obtained from the Map Collection of the New York Public Library. And a great deal of information was obtained in Paris, where some of the streets mentioned still exist.

Irving A. Greenfield
Brooklyn, 1975

BESTSELLERS
FROM DELL

fiction

The Sleepy Town Of Tarkington Is About To Be Plunged Into A Nightmare . . .

A young man named Boyd Ritchie is fresh out of prison with a plan to take revenge on the New England town where he was framed for rape.

He has had eight years to work out his plan, and it is letter-perfect.

What he has in store for the men and women on his list makes rape look pleasant . . .

THE LONG DARK NIGHT
by Joseph Hayes
author of THE DESPERATE HOURS

"A sure bestseller . . . suspense that makes the skin crawl."—*Newsday*

4824-06 **A Dell Book $1.95**